A BL

OLD DOG NEW
TRICKS

HAILEY EDWARDS

Old Dog, New Tricks
© 2015 by Hailey Edwards
All rights reserved.

Edited by Sasha Knight

Cover by Damonza

Interior format by The Killion Group
www.thekilliongroupinc.com

THE BLACK DOG SERIES

#1: Dog with a Bone
#2: Heir of the Dog
#3: Lie Down with Dogs
#4: Old Dog, New Tricks

CHAPTER ONE

Blood clotted in my nostrils. I was scent-blind and choking on dust kicked up by my opponent's shuffling footwork. Vicious pain spiked in the center of my face, radiating from my busted nose. My swollen jaw rested on the hot ground. Spit dribbled from the right side of my mouth, tickling my cheek as it rolled back to my ear. My perspiration, blood and saliva quenched the cracked prison-yard soil.

"Do you yield?"

A slender fae man with a hooked nose bounced on the balls of his feet a yard away from my leg. The elastic band of his prison-issued pants rode high on his narrow waist. Sweat plastered a plain tee against his birdlike chest. The rich crimson bandana tied around his head dripped blood into his eyes.

My blood.

A growl pumped through my chest in response to his question.

The wet sound made the redcap's grin widen. He lunged forward inhumanly fast, swiped his kerchief under my crooked nose and then darted a safe distance away before retying it over his head.

Redcaps were a type of goblin who dyed their hats with their victims' blood. Lore said if the blood staining their hat dried, then the redcap died. Red's bandana was soaked through, which meant his powers were at their peak. I was bleeding worse and healing slower, so his magic was tampering with my ability to regenerate.

With the way my nose kept intercepting Red's fist, he was in no danger of hitting a dry spell.

"Simple question." Fresh blood smudged his fingers until he licked them clean. "Yes or no?"

A hot punch of earthy fragrance struck the humid air at the same time as a rumbling snarl raised the hairs on my nape. The pungent lure hit the redcap hard. His head whipped toward the scent. Even I could smell it, citrus undertones and all, and my aching body responded. Need coiled low in my belly.

As much as it hurt, I tilted my head back until Shaw came into view. The color had leached from his skin and hair. His bone-sharp claws hooked in the chain-link fence separating us. White voids stared back at me. He was hungry. Starving. So was I. But right now he was a distraction. A dangerous one.

I ran my tongue across my gritty lips and barked an order at him. "Stand down."

"You're hurt," he growled, lips quivering.

I braced my palms beside me. "I got this."

Please, God, let me have this.

"Is he yours?" Red's voice grated. "I might be willing to trade. You for the incubus—"

I shoved upright, the snap of vertical motion making my ears ring. Rolling forward, I got my feet under me, threw my weight into the action and slammed my shoulder into Red's gut. He grunted, thrown backward, arms windmilling for balance. Too late. He toppled, back slapping the compact dirt, momentum carrying me over him. I landed on top of him, my chest covering his groin.

Chin braced in the dimple of his navel, I threw my arms out to the sides and captured his flailing limbs. I brought them together in front of me and used a restraining Word to bind his wrists together.

"That—" I panted, balancing my weight on my palms, "—is *my* incubus. Get your own."

Linking his fingers, Red made a giant fist with his hands and socked me across the jaw.

I slid sideways, head bouncing off the ground. My split lip reopened, and he was on me in a second. He straddled my hips, tore the kerchief off his scalp and wiped the sopping-wet fabric across my mouth. He let me taste my own blood and the promise of my death if I didn't get my head in the game.

This was my third bout, third opponent, and damn it, I was tired.

"Focus, Thierry."

Bite me, Mac.

The day's activities were sponsored by my father, Macsen Sullivan. The scenic prison locale, an endless supply of hardy combatants, all his idea and sanctioned by the conclave magistrates, who fully supported his whack-a-doodle agenda to get me in prime fighting shape for our trip into Faerie.

Ours is not always a fatal gift, Mac had said. *We rule our hunger. Our desires do not control us.*

More than anything, I wanted to believe him. I wanted to be—not normal. That wasn't possible. But not a danger to those I loved. That's why I had tucked my glove into Shaw's back pocket. Why I was fighting a convicted murderer with a sadistic streak barehanded, runes firmly in the off position, and also why I was letting my ass get handed to me. Mac wanted me beaten, starving and still in control.

So far I was three for three.

That split second of inattention while my mind wandered cost me big time. Red cocked his hands back over his head, then swung them down hammer-fist style and smashed my nose. Newly healed cartilage crunched, and hot blood spilled down my cheeks over my mouth, which Red happily sopped up with his kerchief.

"Thierry," Mac bit off my name.

Anger set my teeth on edge. "I've. Got. This."

Red slapped the bandana on his head. While his hands were otherwise occupied, I drew back my arm and punched him under his left eye. He rocked back, bound hands clutching for a hold on me. He toppled backward, and I scissored my legs, twisting my hips to flip him off me. This time I clamped my hands around his ankles and spat a stronger restraining Word. Cold magic snapped them together. Anger simmered in his eyes. He tensed his abs, levering his feet in a kick that almost clipped me on the chin.

All day I had sipped and sipped and sipped when what I wanted was to let magic sink its teeth in one of these guys and rip out chunks of soul-meat to quiet the steady grumbling in my poor stomach. Snacking like this was worse than crunching rice cakes to fill the hole where a thick-cut T-bone ought to be.

Grabbing Red by the pants, I slammed his feet to the ground and crawled onto them. He popped up into a sitting position like a pissed-off jack-in-the-box, and I swung my arm hard, the ridge of my knuckles uppercutting his jaw. Red grunted. His back slapped dirt, and the air whooshed from his lungs. Panting, he peeled his lips back from his teeth, and core muscles tightened to launch another attack.

Caution forgotten, I lunged forward, pinning him under me. His heart beat steadily beneath my palm, and my magic zinged from my fingertips and sliced into his chest in search of that most precious commodity. His soul. As black and withered as it was, my inner scales had no trouble balancing. He deserved death for his crimes. Willing as I was to mete that justice, Red was not mine to punish. So instead of slurping his essence down like a tasty oyster on the half shell, I made a tight fist and reined in my power. The teeth of my control snapped at him. *Tiny bites. Tiny bites.* Nibbling. Not killing him. Not crossing the line Mac had drawn for me and not filling my cramping gut, either.

"You can't...kill me," Red wheezed.

"Probably not." I patted his cheek with my right hand. "That's kind of why you're here."

Mac had chosen fae impervious to true death. Gulp this guy's soul and it would regenerate. All he had to do was keep his bandana damp with fresh blood and his magic would revive him. Eventually.

A giant shadow fell across my face. "How close are you to finishing?"

I squinted up at the brawny correctional officer monitoring his inmate charge. The plastic name tag on his shirt read *T. Littlejohn.* "Ten minutes?"

"Make it five." He jabbed a thick finger toward the prison entrance. "It's time for shift change."

Blocking out my audience, I shrank the thrumming cord of magic wending through Red's chest until only a wispy filament of power remained. Oh so slowly, I withdrew every spark of my strength from the redcap's body. There. Done. *Somebody call time*. I shoved off him and staggered to my feet.

I had fed, sort of, and my donor was still breathing. If this had been a case assigned to me by the conclave, I could have led him to the office like this instead of dried out and rolled up under my arm. Wary of leaving Red with so much of my blood—blood he could use to work all kinds of nasty magic on me later—I squatted beside him, pinched his bandana between my fingers and held it up so I could get a good look at it. No wards stung my hand. No spell-scent flooded my nostrils. No magic vibes hit me at all. From here his lifeline seemed no different than any dirty rag due for a toss in the washing machine.

"No need to be cruel, Marshal. Give ol' Red back his do-rag." The guard lumbered over with his hand outstretched and waited for me to toss him the bandana. He caught the rag in his meaty fist then slid it onto the redcap's head. "He'll die without contact with it." He wiped his hand clean on the redcap's pants. "Not that I care, but the higher-ups do. His execution is on the books, and I'm not going to be the guy explaining to Sarge why we're short a prisoner for the chair that day. He gets cranky when things go sideways."

"The chair?" I whistled. "As in electric?"

His lips pursed while he rolled his answer around in his mouth. "Something like that."

Clicking sounds sent his gaze seeking past my shoulder. His thick brow creased at what he saw. I turned, curious at what he found so interesting. Shaw stood with one hand spread like a claw where it hooked through the fence. His other palm rested against the nearby pole. The razor nails on those fingertips *tap, tap, tapped*. The anti-violence enchantment coating the metal sparked with his intent.

"I've never seen an incubus up close. We don't keep them here. Not enough guards with natural immunity." His gaze flowed over Shaw, assessing the washed-out skin and claws, the blunt fangs set in a cutting smile. "Are they supposed to look like that? I thought they were all...sexy."

Wild laughter burst from me in a rush that left me sagging, dependent on the arm he threw out to steady me. Otherwise I might have collapsed on top of Red during my giggle fit. But Shaw had been pushed hard today, too, and that innocent touch made the air thick with tension between the two men.

Shaw's guttural claiming rumbled through the air. "*Mine.*"

I grinned, tiny bubbles bursting in my chest. What can I say? Jealousy looked good on him.

"Your hotness meter is busted," I told the guard. "He's the prettiest incubus I've ever seen."

Behind me, Shaw snarled. He probably wished I had used *deadliest* or *most dangerous* or other words I couldn't argue described facets of his personality, all attributes I admired, but *pretty* fit too, and ever since we'd kissed and made up, all I could think about was him finally being mine. *Mine.* No take backs.

Now if we could get more than five minutes alone to celebrate, preferably naked, that would be awesome.

Three days had passed after the magistrates had sequestered themselves in their chambers, and Mac had stuck to me like glue since then. He was crashing on the couch at the apartment I shared with my best friend, Mai, and he invited himself along every time I stepped out of the building, which sucked.

Behind us, the fence hissed and spat. Or maybe that was Shaw.

Between the beatings I had taken today, which he'd had a front-row seat for, rousing his protective instincts, and the *tiny* problem of my father dubbing himself my new bodyguard to replace the ones who had betrayed me, thereby limiting make-up and make-out sessions, Shaw was close to snapping.

I was too. But I couldn't fault Mac's logic. After witnessing Shaw drink me down one too many times, he'd decided to educate both of us on how not to kill each other via our feeding circuit. We both appreciated the advice. That he felt our lessons were best learned celibate? Well, that was just icing on the cake.

Guess he was trying to make up for all the years of being an absentee parent by smothering me with his fatherly wisdom and concern.

The guard unclipped the radio from his utility belt and called for a relief officer to escort Red to his cell. He refastened it, jerked his chin up and called to my guys, "You can pick her up around front."

Shaw was out of sight before the guard finished mouthing the last syllable.

Fifteen minutes or so passed while I was patted down for contraband and signed out all official-like. A female guard passed me a baby wipe to clean my face. Scrubbing off all the sweat and blood made me feel human again. Human as I ever got anyway.

A buzzer sounded, and she gestured toward the booth. "Push through the next door on your right, and you're a free woman."

I tucked the used wipe in my pocket while locating the hulking male guard. "Hey, Littlejohn, what did Red want in exchange for his cooperation?"

The prison had taken volunteers from a small pool of Mac's preapproved candidates.

"He got one last taste of fae blood—half-fae blood at least. Any blood will work. He's been living on pig's blood for about sixty years now." He rolled his shoulders. "You got your practice, and he got his last meal. Even trade."

"Yeah." I shivered. "I guess so."

I left before he filled me in on what the others had wanted. Pretty sure I was better off not knowing.

Past the guard booth and the sparse reception area, I walked through a metal detector and startled the new guard on duty with the amount of blood I was wearing. After assuring him I was fine, I shoved through the front entrance. Out on the sidewalk leading into the parking lot, Shaw waited with his hands stuffed into his pockets. The quarter hour since we parted in the yard had given him time to find a slice of calm, and he no longer resembled the whited-out feral incubus the guard had insulted.

No. This was Shaw in cucumber mode. As in *cool as a*. Faded T-shirt stretched over a wide chest. Worn jeans low on his lean hips. Scuffed boots encased his tapping foot. Okay, so *cool* might have been stretching it.

Shaw was always *hot, hot, hot* as far as I was concerned.

Rich mahogany hair curled over his ears. His eyes were molten copper when they met mine, and my gut tightened when his lips hitched in a slow smile that sent warmth spreading through my chest. Heat raced up my arm when he took my hand.

He touched my bruised cheek. "How bad is it?"

"Not bad." I squeezed his fingers. "Sore and hungry, but I can handle it."

The sound he made wasn't a happy one.

I tugged on his hand. "How are you feeling?"

With us bound together and me feeding lighter these days, that meant he was too. Our diet made for shorter tempers and general crabbiness, but when Shaw stepped into me, his arms circling me, his hands sliding into the rear of my jeans pockets to squeeze my butt, I forgot the pain and grumpiness of the past week and let him mold me against him. I had his ear between my teeth and my hand sliding down his chest when I heard rapid static zaps that lifted hairs down my arms.

My father stood three feet behind us holding a stun baton like the ones some marshals carried. It was a twenty-one-inch-long piece of telescoping black metal with a one hundred thousand volt arc running the length of the entire unit above the molded plastic handle. The *click, click, click* told me Mac had powered up in case our necking required a four milliamp intervention.

The stun wouldn't hurt Shaw, but it would make him think twice before using his mojo.

Wearing a pleased smile, Mac had dressed for our training session in crisp, dark wash denim jeans and a faded Metallica shirt he'd found in my bathroom. His arms hung at his sides, the baton's hot spot pointed downward, toward the cement.

He flexed his trigger finger again. "Six inches of personal space, please."

A soft growl pumped through my chest as I leaned my forehead against Shaw's chest. *No fair.*

Mac took a step closer. "You must not complete the circuit until you have each mastered the control required."

"Complete the circuit?" I turned my head so I stared at Mac when I said, "You mean have *sex*?"

A pained expression twisted his features, and the soft green glow emanating from his left hand caused his new toy to splutter and go quiet.

"Stop traumatizing your father." Shaw rested his chin on top of my head and clenched his hands, drawing me closer, forcing a whimper past my lips. "All this is for our own good."

"Stop sucking up to him," I muttered.

True, I had almost devoured Shaw when the circuit first snapped into place. Truer still, Shaw's control had eroded over the past year without regular feedings. Right now he functioned in feast-or-famine mode. And possibly truest, there was a real possibility that sex, which generated its own energy and sated his hunger without poaching from me, was hella dangerous until we found our balance together.

But parts of me—the portions currently pressed against him from hip to chest—were willing to gamble.

He nuzzled my cheek. "I'd rather be sucking up to—"

This time the low growl wasn't mine. Apparently, Mac wasn't a fan of dirty talk. At least not where his daughter was concerned.

Shoulders bouncing with laughter, I tilted my head back. "I'm grabbing a shower at the office."

"I should head back too." Shaw's eyes smoldered. "Got to get ready for tonight."

"Movie night," I agreed with a nod.

Mac approached us and pried the ruined baton between our chests until we separated.

"There are several showers if I recall correctly," Mac said thoughtfully.

During his first and only visit to the communal showers, he had worn a dayglow yellow panther-sized cat skin.

Diode. Crazy to miss someone who never really existed, but there you go.

"Yes," I answered cautiously. "There are six."

"Excellent. We will wash and then go to dinner together before your movie night." He patted my head like I was a good pup who had made her sire proud. "Good thinking."

Good was not the word I would have used. *Bad* worked. *Terrible* really fit the bill.

But nothing iced sexual frustration quicker than showering with your father in the next stall.

CHAPTER TWO

Midway into my lather-and-rinse routine, a wide palm flattened against my shower curtain. With a grin hooking my lips to one side, I placed my hand against Shaw's, and liquid warmth settled in my bones.

The shrill grating of curtain rings sliding over the metal shower bar next door made me flinch.

"Mac." Shaw jerked his hand away. "You're naked."

"And you're standing outside Thierry's stall. Why?"

"I—wanted to ask her something."

"Go ahead." Mac pinched the edge of thin plastic shielding my modesty and smoothed it flush against the tile. "She can hear through plastic fine."

A dejected sigh passed Shaw's lips. "It can wait."

"I thought so."

All hopes of Shaw stepping into my stall to help scrub those hard-to-reach places vanished in a puff of hot steam and fatherly disapproval.

"I'll wait for you outside," Shaw muttered.

"Thierry," Mac warned. "Finish your shower."

I stuck my tongue out where he couldn't see, because I'm that mature.

Metal rings scraped and plastic shower curtain crinkled next door as Mac reentered his stall.

To avoid any awkward getting-dressed-together moments, I stayed under the spray until I was pruney and a gust of cool air announced his exit from the room. Only then did I slink out to dress in jeans, a purple *I got your back, Pluto* T-shirt and sneakers. Afraid to leave the boys alone together, I towel dried my hair and then French braided it out of the way.

I walked very casually into the main room of the marshal's office and caught Mable's eye.

She was possibly the best perk the job offered, and her cookies were *phenomenal.*

Today she wore a coral blouse with puffy sleeves and peach-colored corduroy bellbottoms. The vest buttoned over her curvy figure was a shade of salmon, and her boots were magenta snakeskin. With her powdery white hair pulled back in a bun, her rosy cheeks and her fuchsia glasses, she could play Mrs. Claus for the local tree farm and folks would line up to inspect her shirt for reindeer hairs.

Her bow mouth drew up in amusement when she spotted me. "How are things, dear?"

I narrowed my eyes at her. "You're enjoying this way too much."

"Macsen is a good man, Thierry." She clicked her tongue. "Don't give him such a hard time."

"*Me?*" I squeaked. "You have *no* idea. None. That man—"

"—is your father," she said patiently.

"Not the point." I tugged on the collar of my shirt. "He is driving me insane."

"He loves you."

The words zinged straight to my heart. "He's got a funny way of showing it."

Just because my deadbeat dad was in the running for Father of the Year in everyone else's eyes didn't make him a contender in mine. He had never reached out to me. Not once. Nineteen years without as much as a *hello*. Let alone an *I don't regret your existence, and oh yeah, your mom's a pretty cool chick too.*

Mac claimed he had watched over me, yet he let me come into my powers ignorant. He let me go through my magical awakening alone, let me kill my best friends and didn't even offer a shoulder for me to cry on afterward. How did I forgive him for those deaths when I hadn't forgiven myself?

The best thing Mac had ever done for me was when he wrote the conclave's unlisted number for Mom on his way out the door and out of our lives. That foresight had brought me to Mable...and Shaw.

Hearing the exhaustion in my voice, I asked, "Which way did they go?"

She pointed at the front door. "They're waiting in Shaw's truck."

I had given her a jar of lemon blossom honey on my way in, so I waved. "Thanks."

"Thierry." She hesitated. "How is Shaw?"

I pulled up short. "He's good."

"He seems..." she struggled for the word she wanted, "...at peace."

Tension drained out of my shoulders. "He does?"

A knowing expression crossed her face. "You haven't noticed."

I fidgeted with the hem of my shirt. "I've been busy."

"I see."

I blushed clear to the roots of my hair. "Not *that* kind of busy."

"Mmm-hmm."

"I'm just going to go." Chin to my chest, I sidled past her with scalding cheeks. "Later."

"Enjoy your dinner," she called.

Out on the porch, I sucked in a breath of humid air and shook off the ominous feeling tightening my skin. Shaw had mentioned getting ready for tonight, but movie-night fixings were already at my apartment. We just needed to hit up a Redbox. Mac had made a going-to-dinner-together reference earlier too. With Mable making a third mention of the impending meal, I got the feeling more than food would be on the table.

Mac or Shaw or Mac *and* Shaw must want to negotiate the terms of our upcoming trip.

Well, at least I was getting a meal out of it.

The ride into town reached funeral-procession levels of somberness. Mac sat between Shaw and me on the bench seat of Shaw's truck. Mac had changed into another pair of dark wash jeans and a second band shirt of mine liberated from the laundry hamper. The tee came from my vintage rock collection. They were all guy-sized and worn thin as tissue paper long before I owned them. I used them for sleep shirts mostly. Tempted as I was to ask Mac if his dedication to wearing his daughter's clothes was some kind of scent-marking thing, I had decided days ago to believe it was because of his affinity for music of the era in which I had been conceived, and I had made Shaw swear to never ask questions either.

When Shaw pulled into the parking lot of the Golden Panda and parked, I got a very bad feeling.

Neither man made a move to exit the truck, so I fidgeted. "Did you order takeout?"

"No," Mac answered.

A cramped minute passed while we sat together, our hips touching and no one moving.

Over Mac's head, Shaw tried to get my attention by staring a hole into my left eardrum. That was when it hit me, and my simmering temper ignited.

I shifted toward my father, placing my back against my door. "You bound Shaw so he couldn't spill details about tonight."

"I did."

"Why would you do that?" I grabbed him by the upper arm. It was a nasty trick that kept Shaw from telling me what Mac didn't want me to know. "Undo it."

He exhaled, and a shiver of magic rippled over my arms.

Shaw gripped the wheel of the truck and revved the engine, but it was too late. A burnt-orange mini Cooper slid into the slot in front of ours, and the silver-haired woman behind the wheel waved. Next to her, a foot-tall ceramic garden gnome with a painted-on grin was strapped into the passenger seat.

Sven Gardener, her gnomian bodyguard, reporting for duty.

I slumped down low in the seat, my knees almost hitting the floorboard. "Get down." I fisted the collar of Mac's loaner shirt and tugged. "That's my mom," I hissed. "Hurry up before she sees you."

"We're here to meet her." Shaw tightened his grip on the wheel. "Say the word, and we're gone."

"We're meeting her?" I yanked Mac closer. "She knew you were here?"

He peeled my fingers back one by one. "I wouldn't keep something like that from your mother."

"You wouldn't—?" I choked. "In what universe are you a thoughtful ex-whatever-you-are?"

"I was your mother's lover," he said with total seriousness.

I yelped and covered my ears with my hands. "Never say that again."

My lip-reading skills sucked, but I'm pretty sure he asked me where I thought babies came from, which was an opening for a conversation I slammed shut. Any birds-and-bees talk with him was never happening.

Ever.

Shaw leaned across Mac and grasped one of my wrists, pulling until he broke the seal over my ears. He threaded our fingers and hauled me back onto the seat. "My offer still stands, Thierry. It's your call."

Knuckles rapped on the glass beside me. Mom peered in at us. "Are we too early?"

I couldn't believe what I was hearing. "You got reservations."

Mac was staring through me. "I was told it was difficult to get seating here otherwise."

I rubbed my forehead. "Who told you that?"

A slow smile spread across his face as he lifted a hand to wave at my mother. "Mable."

"Mable," I growled. That explained why she had the inside track on tonight's festivities.

He braced on the seat behind me. "She said Agnes enjoys their orange chicken."

Agnes. "Since when are you on a first-name basis with Mom?"

"Since the day we met." His hip bumped mine, urging me toward the door. "Is there a problem?"

Other than my father and mother were separated by a chunk of metal and a pane of glass, which was the closest the two of them had been since my conception as far as I knew, nah. Not a one.

Where was the shouting? The hair-pulling? The cursing? The anger? Why was my mother, who ought to be clawing Mac's eyes out for abandoning her—abandoning *us*—dressed to kill in a slinky eggplant-colored sheath with a black-sequined flower in her hair? I pressed my nose against the glass.

She was wearing *makeup*. And perfume. I smelled the vanilla and brown sugar scent from here.

"There's no problem." My fingers were numb as I worked the door handle. "No problem at all."

Once my feet hit the ground, Mom wrapped me up in a big hug peppered with the warm scent of her love for me. Excitement lent her familiar fragrance an unfamiliar tang. The rush of emotions that poured from Mom at the sight of Mac exiting the truck sent my nose into hyperdrive. Each emotion has its own distinct smell, but her mood spiked so high so fast I couldn't track how or what she felt.

All I could say for sure was the bitterness Mac must scent on me didn't cling to her skin at all.

Mom kissed my cheek then held me at arm's length. "This is so exciting, isn't it?"

"Yeah," I hedged. "Exciting."

A frown marred her brow. "Your father didn't tell you."

"Tell me what, exactly?" Old hurt simmered in my words. "That he was dragging me here tonight? That he has obviously been chatting you up behind my back? Or that you're not angry with him anymore?"

Her expression gentled. "Everything that happened—"

"No." I jerked out of her grip and backed up until I bounced off Shaw's chest, and he grabbed hold of me. "Don't finish that sentence. Don't try to brush off the past or make light of it. I *killed* people, Mom, and he could have prevented that. All my friends... They would still be alive if he had hung around." I swallowed past the lump in my throat. "It might all be in the past for you, but not for me. I see their faces when I shut my eyes at night. I still wake to their screams."

"Thierry," Mac warned.

"What did you think would happen?" Shaw challenged him. "I tried explaining it to you."

"She is our daughter," Mac growled. "This is a family discussion."

"Shaw is family." I stared down my parents and singled out my mother. "We're mated."

"Mated," she breathed, clutching Mac's arm. "Does that mean you're married?"

Behind me Shaw tensed. "Not exactly."

"I didn't ask you, Jackson." Her tone cut him off at the knees. "Why didn't you tell me?"

"Oh, I don't know." I leaned against Shaw. "Probably the same reason you didn't mention this."

"*This* is a relationship between two consenting adults," she began.

"I can't believe this." I threw up my hands. "You're back together?"

Shaw's palms landed on my shoulders and tightened. "We're causing a scene, folks. We should take this discussion someplace more private. How about we all meet at Thierry's apartment to talk?"

Mac's eyes glowed with emerald fire. "I made a reservation."

"I'm not hungry." I shoved past him and crawled back into the cab of Shaw's truck. "I want to go home." I wanted a door I could lock between the world and me. "Are you two lovebirds coming or what?"

"Yes." Mac put a hand on my door.

"Macsen," Mom murmured. "Let them go ahead. We'll eat and give her time to calm down."

He leaned into Mom, grip firm on the handle. "They can't be trusted alone."

Mom glanced between us. "Jackson, Thierry, do you really need a babysitter for an hour?"

"I give you my word," Shaw said, "we'll stick to the rules."

"There." Mom looped her arm through Mac's. "Trust has to start somewhere."

Eyes narrowed on Shaw, Mac let himself be led away while Mom chattered about whatever my parents talked about when they held their clandestine meetings. As acute as my hearing was, I could have eavesdropped. Instead, I waited while Shaw climbed in and cranked the engine, then I blared his radio.

CHAPTER THREE

Shaw killed the truck's engine and jabbed the radio's power button. "Am I in trouble here?"

I snapped out of my thoughts, shocked to find us sitting in the parking lot of my apartment building. "What?"

He stared forward, through the windshield, one hand still on the wheel. "Am I in trouble?"

I twisted in the seat so I faced him. "Did you know about them?"

"Not until today."

"Could you have told me tonight was a setup for some happy-happy family time?"

He snorted. "Definitely not."

I nudged his shoulder with my hand. "Then why would you be in trouble?"

"Your dad is keeping me apprised of his plans, then working his magic to make sure I can't share them with you." His thumb caressed the leather wheel. "It ticks me off. I figure it ticks you off too."

"Yeah." I leaned my head against the window. "We're a couple of clocks all right."

His other hand toyed with the keys dangling from the ignition, fingers ready to crank it up again if I said scram. "So that's a *yes*."

"I'm not mad at you. You can't help what Mac does any more than I can. I just don't get those two."

"Your mom looked happy," he ventured.

"I know." I thumped my head on the glass. "That's the part I don't get. She was all dolled up for him. She was smiling and touching his arm like they were—I don't know. A couple. *Something.* Not just two people who made a baby once. Like she forgave him on the spot. Like his being here now fixed the past twenty years." I leaned forward. "I don't get it. How is she okay with him?"

"She loved him," Shaw said with certainty. "She might still love him."

Needing to be grounded, I set a hand on Shaw's thigh. "What about him?"

"He listens to her." He covered my hand with his. "We're alone now because Agnes told him to let us be. I don't know what's going on in his head, but they seem like two people who worked out a lot of old issues fast. He must feel something if he broke down and went to her after just three days. Assuming he lasted that long."

"I guess."

The worst part of Mac's visit was the tiny spark of hope that thought Mac coming here would solve a lot of Mom's problems. He could take care of her. He could give her all the things I couldn't, and maybe being together now that his secrets were out in the open might heal them both. But what happened when he left us again?

Would her heart break? Had it the first time?

I'd spent so long making sure Mom only saw what I wanted her to see that until this minute I never considered she might be paying me the same favor. She might be hiding her hurt behind fear.

I didn't know, and I didn't like not knowing, and I didn't like my parents being nice-nice.

But this was about more than me. Mom had an equal stake in this.

"I have popcorn upstairs," I told Shaw. "I bought those movie-theater-sized boxes of Milk Duds, Raisinets, Junior Mints and Sno-Caps. I spaced on Redbox, but we could rent online."

It was a tiny, sugar-coated olive branch I extended but one Shaw accepted.

A smile tugged at his mouth. "Are you hungry? For real food?"

Grumpy silence ensued from my seat.

"That's what I thought." He pulled out his cell. "I'll call in an order to Marco's."

"Thanks," I said, thinking he was the only non-human outside of Mai I dared say it to.

"No problem." He opened his door. "You've got a lot on your plate."

"And life keeps dishing it out." I tugged the handle and slid out the door onto the pavement. I stared across the parking lot at the squat apartment building where I lived with Mai, and soaked up all the details. The crumbling brick first floor, the warped siding bowing off the second and third floors. Burnt toast and roast lamb teased my nose. Laughter from kids playing a game of bite or flight in the park next door under the light of the moon drifted to me. Conversation bounced between neighbors unwinding after work. Balconies held grills and patio furniture and couples making out in the deepest shadows.

"Stop looking at this place like you'll never see it again."

Shaw's voice startled so close to my ear.

I drew in the night scents and sounds and basked in the normalcy of it all. "I'm saving this memory for a rainy day."

His warm lips brushed my temple. "Come upstairs with me."

Chills peaked down my arms in a hot rush. "You promised Mac we'd behave."

"No." He chuckled softly. "I promised we'd stick to the rules."

"How much wiggle room is in those rules?" I wondered as his warm breath caressed my neck.

"I don't know. Let's find out."

Mouth scorching mine, Shaw backed me out of the elevator and down the hall. I stumbled once, and he caught me against him, savoring my taste until he blinked clear of the haze clouding his eyes. In complete control now, he lightened the kiss, grasped my wrist and spun me wide in a dance move that surprised a laugh out of me. I whirled the last steps to my door and let us inside the darkened living room. Standing on the threshold, I called, "Mai. We're back. You home?"

Silence.

I went into the kitchen and rooted in the cabinets for the popcorn. The mountain of candy piled on the counter kept my smile spreading. The note pinned to the fridge left a dent in my happiness. Its cramped handwriting announced it as Mai's before I scanned the message or spotted her signature.

I balled up the note. "Looks like the Hayashis are circling the wagons."

Shaw paused in his dialing. *"Circling the wagons?"*

"Hey." I pulled ice-cold Coke cans from the fridge. "You're old enough to appreciate that one."

"Ouch." He placed the cell over his heart. "She's a sharpshooter, folks."

I snorted. "What can I say? Mom watched a lot of Clint Eastwood when I was a kid."

He glanced around the place. "That explains a lot."

Mom had gone through what I called a Western Gothic phase that lasted many years past its expiration date. Lucky me, she had offered us a storage building full of wagon-wheel-inspired furniture and cow-skull accessories to use in our new place. Paired with Mai's family's contributions of leftover knickknacks in a cherry-blossom theme and a lumpy brocade couch, we had this circle-of-life thing happening.

I tapped a silk flower tucked into one of the matching skull planters on my way past. We both had black thumbs, so we stuck to the dust-catchers and avoided live plants, which admittedly fit the theme best. Not that we were encouraging the madness to spread. I never considered it before, but yeah. Good old Clint might be partly to blame for our décor.

"Someone must have tipped off Mr. Hayashi that conditions in Faerie are deteriorating," I said.

"The rumor mill has been churning since you won the hunt. Everyone knows Faerie is unstable, they just don't know the extent of it yet." He lifted a finger while he placed our pizza order then resumed our conversation. "All the powerful families will be making contingency plans. Mai will probably be put on lockdown with her skulk by the time we leave."

"I hope so." I popped the tab on my can. "I want to know she's safe. However it goes."

Knowing she was holed up with her family would help me push that worry from my mind. Now if I could get Mom to go to ground while we were away, I could face the trip without the possibilities running through my mind of what might happen to her if/when the Morrigan breached the temporary wards between realms Mac had spent the past few days setting.

A vile taste tickled the back of my throat, and I drank to prevent it from rising.

The Morrigan was big on vengeance. It was kind of her thing. When she crossed realms? I knew her first official social call would be paid direct to Mom to give her personal thanks for me derailing her plans for her son, Raven, the prince I murdered to save my own hide, and I had to know Mom was going to be okay. I couldn't leave her unprotected. Sure, she had Sven. Her gnomian guardian was kickass, but he was no match for a death goddess. But I wasn't out of options quite yet. I had a plan.

"You don't have to go." I rubbed my knuckle into his chest. "You could stay here."

"You're not getting rid of me that easy." He took my hand. "Besides, I don't want Rook getting any ideas when you show up to save him." He held my fist to his heart. "He's not getting you back."

"Well, he *is* my husband." I tsked at Shaw. "You're *the other man*."

"No," he disagreed softly. "You were mine first."

I gazed up at him, letting a smile bloom. "I guess I was, huh?"

"If you want to get technical..." he cradled my jaw in his palm, "...Rook was the other man."

"Ah." I kissed his palm. "Our circuit was completed first. Gotcha."

"I'm a very forgiving mate." His head lowered. "I'm willing to overlook your indiscretions."

"Aww." I tapped his nose. "You'd do that for me?"

"There isn't much I wouldn't do for you," he admitted, snatching the box of Milk Duds off the counter. "Now hurry up and join me on the couch. Tonight we are alone. Tonight your father is out of our hair. Tonight we get to pretend we're two normal people doing normal date night things like pizza, candy and a movie."

He spun on his heel and headed for the couch, ripping into the paper as he went.

"Hey, don't eat those before the pizza gets here," I called. "You'll ruin your appetite."

He tossed a few into his mouth. "You just don't want me to eat all the chocolate."

I opened my mouth to disagree but came up with, "Good point."

While he waited for the delivery guy, I popped corn and groaned when a text message pinged. I checked the screen through squinted eyes, and sure enough, it was from Mom. I hesitated a moment before swiping the screen with my thumb then winced.

We all need to talk. Wait up for us.

For Mom to cross into the fae side of town this late, she must really want to hash this out before I left, which could be any day now. But then again, Mac had to get home somehow. She was the one who invited him to stay with her, so I guess it fell to her to make sure he got home. Like a date. *Ugh.*

Eyeing the fridge, I had never wished for a higher alcohol tolerance in my life.

CHAPTER FOUR

Movie night consisted of fewer *moves* than I had anticipated. With Mom's text hanging over our heads and the possibility both my parents might catch Shaw rounding third base, we kept the evening tame. I opted to sit on the floor so I could eat at the coffee table and spread out my junk food. Behind me, Shaw sat on the couch, his thighs blocking me in on either side, providing handy armrests when I finished. Full of pizza and candy, I fell asleep two-thirds of the way through the first movie. Elbows on his legs, head tilted back into his lap, I woke hours later with dry mouth and a crick in my neck.

A wide palm was spread over my collarbone, the slight pressure keeping me upright when there was a good chance I would have face-planted in the plate of leftovers and drowned in cold tomato sauce.

I dragged the back of my hand across my drool-crusted lips. "What time is it?"

"Time for you to stop eating like you're twelve," Mom answered.

I jerked my head toward the sound and spotted her in the kitchen. "Where's Mac?"

She passed a damp towel over the countertop, not bothering to hide her dreamy smile. Now that my eyes were focusing, the whole place seemed tidier. She had obviously been here and cleaning for a while.

With her standing there, in the center of my home, I felt self-conscious about all the clutter. Not embarrassed enough to lock her in the hall while I launched into a whirlwind cleaning spree, but close.

"He's running an errand."

Seeing no room for a double entendre, I accepted her comment at face value. Though what kind of errand he was running at this hour I couldn't imagine. He was sidelined until it was time for the big vote. I placed Shaw's hand on his thigh and slipped away to join her beside the fridge.

I reached inside for a fresh Coke and spotted takeout containers. *Yum.* "How was dinner?"

She nudged me aside and passed me a bottle of water instead. "Do you really want to know?"

"I asked, didn't I?" Which wasn't an answer, but it was all I had.

"We enjoyed ourselves." A rare softness blanketed her features. "I wish you had stayed."

After twisting the cap off the water, I drank long and deep. "Well, I wish I hadn't been ambushed."

"Macsen isn't used to being around people he can trust," she said gently.

"As long as he understands trust is a two-way street and my lane is under construction."

Her chuckles made me smile. "Keeping secrets has kept him alive this long. It's going to be a tough habit for him to break. He'll never be an open book like you, but you'll work it out." She smoothed my hair. "You two have all the time in the world. Don't waste it being angry, all right?"

That sounded oddly morbid for her. "Are you okay?"

"I'm fine." She made a shooing motion. "You're using the fridge to cool the whole apartment."

"Oh." I flushed and shut the door, stirring the heady scents of honey pork and orange chicken.

Determined expression on her face, she asked, "Is there somewhere we can go to talk?"

"Sure." I glanced at Shaw, who was sleeping deeply. "We can use my room."

Mai's and my living quarters were the next best thing to cramped, so it only took a minute to cross into the hallway where the bedrooms and bathroom were located. Shoving open my door, I winced at the two laundry mounds heaped on the floor. Clean and dirty each got a pile. That was as organized as I got.

She motioned for me to sit while she shook her head and began folding my clothes. "Is there anything you want to tell me?"

My palms went damp. That question led so many places and none of them good.

I wet my lips. "Is there something you want to know?"

Instead of answering, she made a heavy statement. "I spoke with Mable yesterday."

Crap. That explained why Mac knew where to take Mom to dinner in the first place.

"Really?" I didn't have to fake my interest. "You two have been keeping up with each other?"

After years of radio silence, the two most important women in my life had gotten acquainted thanks to Mom showing up on the conclave's doorstep after Shaw rescued me from Balamohan. I hadn't expected much from their afternoon together. Figured a Thackeray family Christmas card was as far as their bonding experience would carry them. Learning they were friendly made me…nervous.

"We have." Her movements became stiff. "She knows so much more about your life than I do."

I braced for guilt or tears or some combo of each, but more than anything, she sounded sad.

"She sees me every day." I winced, hoping that didn't sound like finger-pointing. "She's the one handing out cases and monitoring our activities, so I have to keep her informed of my whereabouts."

"It's more than that." Mom went to the closet and grabbed a fistful of hangers. "She loves you."

There was nothing I could say to that. Mable was like a second mom to me. She had taken me in the day I showed up on the doorstep of her building, terrified of meeting the magistrates, so sure they would see the blood on my hands even though I had showered three times before Shaw came to pick me up and drive me over. She fed me cookies and milk and dried my tears with her apron. She made me feel normal again, like being fae was all right, like sometimes bad things happened to good kids, that I wasn't evil even if I had done wrong. She had taught me through her example to accept myself.

And yeah, I loved her too.

When I didn't respond, Mom resumed her work, keeping her back to me. "I know about the money."

I tensed so fast I almost fell off the bed. "Mable had no right—"

"She didn't tell me." With neat flips of her hand, she began folding my socks. "I already knew."

My hands fisted in the sheets. "You did?"

She glanced over her shoulder at me. "I really messed things up between us, didn't I?"

A pang tightened my chest. "Mom, no, of course you didn't."

"I knew Macsen was special from the moment I saw him. He had this calm about him, but there was an intensity in the way he looked at the world too." She smiled fondly. "The way he looked at me."

The moment felt so private I wanted to get up and leave. It was like Mac being here had opened up a floodgate of memories for her, and I was afraid of being carried away by the swiftness of them. Thinking of him made her shine. Years fell from her face, and she was, in that moment, just a woman who had been in love with a peculiar man, one she had known she couldn't keep, known she couldn't tame, but she had to have regardless or would regret the lost opportunity forever.

All that was conveyed through the girlish voice speaking to me from a younger point in her life, one she had never visited in my presence, her wide smile lit with an inner light I hadn't seen a man ignite.

"We had so little time together." Her voice turned thick. "He had to leave. I had been expecting it for weeks, but still..." She shook her head. "I found out I was pregnant with you that last night."

"I thought he left..." *because of me*, "...after he found out."

"He had already said his goodbyes." She hesitated. "Knowing I was pregnant didn't change anything. He had to go, and even before I knew what he was—*who* he was—I understood his decision was bigger than what either of us wanted."

I scrunched up my face, unsure if I was hearing her correctly. "You aren't angry at him."

She choked on her laughter. "I wouldn't go that far. I was hurt and mad and overwhelmed for a long time. But I hit a point where I was so bitter and lost I didn't recognize the person I had become, and I was so afraid of that bitterness spilling over onto you." Her lips thinned. "I had to step back and ask myself if I regretted my relationship with Macsen, and I didn't. I couldn't. How could I? He gave me you. My baby girl." Her eyes were watery when I met her gaze. "You were a perfect little angel."

A blush heated my neck. "I pooped and spat up goop like every other baby ever born."

"But you were *my* baby." She tossed a ball of socks at me. "You still are."

My heart lightened from her praise, my chest swelling with happiness. A few of the old wounds, the deep ones, between us were healing, scabs flaking to reveal the pink skin of our new relationship.

Knowing what I risked, I nudged her. "He didn't warn you at all?"

"He told me he was dangerous, that he wasn't human. The only proof he gave me was his word, but I believed him. He told me one day you might be dangerous too." She crossed to me and sat beside me, thigh to thigh, taking my hands in hers. "That's when he gave me the conclave's number. He didn't tell me who they were, only to call them for help if you ever needed it. He said they would take care of you—of us." Her fingers trembled. "You and I had so many good years, so many normal years. I let his warnings fade like his memory. I told myself you were human because it was easier."

I let the normal comment slide. I knew what she meant even if the wording stung. I wasn't normal. I didn't equate *normal* with *good*. I didn't believe being different made me bad.

Unaware of my inner debate, she pressed on like she needed the words said now, tonight. After waiting so long to hear them, I wasn't about to stop her until she was finished, until I absorbed it all.

"If I hadn't taken the easy road, if I hadn't buried his warnings, your friends would still be alive. All that guilt you carry—it's mine. Their deaths were my fault. You had no idea what you were, but I did. I knew you were your father's daughter. You look just like Macsen. I should have watched you closer. I should have told you about your father when you asked me." Her voice hitched. "But part of me was afraid if things…if you ever…that if I called that number even once, the people on the other end would come and take you away, take you where your father had gone, where I couldn't follow."

"Mom…"

"I read the contracts," she said forcefully. "I wouldn't have turned over my baby and not known what that conclave of yours had in store for you. I memorized the exact wording, I read the papers so often. They assigned me legal counsel, but he was a fae *and* a lawyer. I didn't trust what he told me."

Numbed by her confessions, I sat there and let her talk.

"I understood by signing you over to the conclave's care that I was stripping away some of your future choices, but it was the best option I had to keep you safe. I couldn't protect you the way they could. Your old school—they couldn't educate you to deal with this new life. I couldn't let you hide, but I couldn't do it all alone." She bit her lip. "When the conclave offered a stipend to help us move, to give us a new home and you a new future, knowing you had to live with my decision, I accepted."

"You did the right thing." I squeezed her hand. "The job suits me. I enjoy it. Most days."

"I'm glad." She released a tense breath. "Mable says you clock a lot of hours."

"How much is a lot?" I forced a laugh. "Not sure how I stack up against everyone else."

Marshals weren't paid overtime. We earned around twenty-five thousand dollars a year. Anyone bringing home more than that, like me, was going after bounties, but I hadn't told her about those yet.

"She also told me a large portion of your paychecks are direct deposited into my account."

The air left my lungs. *Crap*. All the Mac talk really was laying groundwork for an intervention.

"Um."

"The strange thing is the deposits were listed as coming from the Raleigh Estate."

To avoid leaving pesky paper trails leading back to the conclave, they often created benefactors, fake aunts or uncles who kicked the bucket and left behind small estates or liquidated assets to people like Mom, humans trapped in the fae justice system or living on the conclave's dime in a time when even fae paid taxes.

The Raleigh Estate passed on to Mom via her imaginary uncle Orville Mercer, may he rest in fictional peace.

I fumbled for a response and settled on, "Strange."

A wry smile twisted her lips. "Yes, well, you understand why I called Mable the first time I saw a deposit after your eighteenth birthday, since the papers I signed made it clear when support ended."

"*What?*"

All that effort to hide and sneak and trick Mom, and she knew. They both knew. All of it.

"She told me you had been taking extra cases, dangerous cases, so you could send money to my account." She traced the blood rush from my cheeks. "Seeing your face now... I can't believe I let things get this bad between us. That you felt you owed me— I'm sorry, baby. So sorry."

I dropped my head into my hands. "I can't believe this."

"I didn't know what to do, how to fix this." She stroked a hand down my spine. "I didn't want to make things worse between us by rejecting the money outright when it was obvious it meant a lot to you to care for me, and I thought you would burn out in a couple of months and then we could talk."

I slid my fingers through my hair, across my scalp and tugged. "Can*not* believe this."

The mattress shifted and a zipper sounded. "This is yours."

I didn't glance up or reach out. I couldn't process. I sat there feeling like a total idiot.

Untangling my fingers from my hair, Mom lowered my arms and placed a check into my hands.

The number registered, and my heart flip-flopped. I had never held the promise of so much money in my entire life. Mable had dug into Mom's finances for me, and she was the one to give me the figure always lurking in the back of my mind, the one that matched what her support payments had been. Once I checked that figure off my to-do list, the rest was gravy until the clock restarted at the beginning of the next month.

This was my first time seeing the big picture, and it was a *big* picture.

"I can't accept this." I slapped it back into her palm. "How are you going to support yourself?"

She leaned over and wedged the rectangle of paper between two bottles of lotion on my dresser. When she turned back to me, she was smiling. "I've been supporting myself just fine the past year."

"Oh." Yeah, I guess she had if she could afford to pay me back.

"I had a decent nest egg before things..." Her thought trailed unfinished. "I've added to it over the years. I wanted to be prepared in case the conclave relocated us again and wasn't as generous about it."

"You work part-time at the animal shelter."

"I used to." A grin tugged at her lips. "I took an administrative position a year and a half ago."

My mouth did that fish-out-of-water thing again. "You never said."

"I was waiting until you graduated marshal academy so we could celebrate together." She patted my hand. "I hadn't counted on you going straight into the field. By the time we got together, you and Jackson were on the outs. It wasn't a good time for me to share my news. Not when you were hurting so much."

The days after my final exam at the marshal academy had been spent propped up in a bed in the medical ward. I never told her about the accident that shattered my hip and broke my ankles. In fact, I had avoided her for weeks until I was back at one hundred percent. So yeah, by the time I got around to visiting her again, Shaw and I had split, and all I wanted were sundaes and hugs from my momma.

"We really suck at this communication thing." Talk about an understatement.

"Yes, we do."

I studied her. "I want to know about the important things in your life."

"I want to know yours too." She stuck out her hand. "No more secrets. Deal?"

I hesitated. "Do you mean going forward, or are we talking backdated here?"

"Thierry." She sighed my name on a pained gust of breath.

"A lot happened on my trip to Faerie." I took her hand. "Do you want the details?"

A tiny flicker of uncertainty crossed her features, but she blinked it away. "Tell me everything."

So I did. All of it. The whole truth. I left nothing out.

Mom was still digesting the story of my life post marshal academy, including her vacation to Faerie, when firm knocks at the door earned our attention. A shiver of unease rippled down my spine, and I rose onto my feet, positioning myself between her and the door. I placed a finger in front of my lips, and she nodded in understanding.

Reaching deep, I drew power into my left palm before calling, "Come in."

The door eased open, and the burnt scent of charged magic followed.

In the time it took my eyes to adjust from the overhead light to the darkened living room, a man stepped into my bedroom uninvited. Golden-skinned with pale blond hair bound at his nape, the sidhe noble took in my room, my mother and me with a single sweep of his lapis-blue eyes.

"Evander," I greeted him, not dousing the green light spilling from my fingertips.

Eyes on my wrist, he tilted his head. I got the uncomfortable feeling he was noticing the pattern of my runes, tracking their progress toward my elbow. They used to stop at my wrist. But ever since my trip to Faerie and my altercation with

Balamohan, the mystical markings were claiming new real estate on my body. I hadn't worked up the nerve to ask Mac what it meant for me, but I had my own ideas. The prevalent theory was the more powerful I became, the more my magic use branded me.

The puzzling thing was Mac only had runes on his left hand—identical to the placement of my original set. So either I had guessed wrong, or he was hiding something. I chuckled under my breath.

Yeah. Wonder which of those two possibilities was more likely.

"I knocked," he said by way of greeting. "No one answered."

"No problem." The slow burn of anger simmering under my skin was cut by an icy blast of fear. "What brings you here?"

With a knowing glint in his eyes, he announced, "We have reached a decision."

We, as in the gathering of magistrates busy determining my fate.

"Okay." I knew better than to hope he would give me a heads-up as to the verdict.

"Your father's voice was the determining factor. Recording his vote is merely a formality."

"All right." No clue what he meant there. "I'll change and meet you with Mac at the office."

"Please do."

Astringent magic scoured my nose, then he was gone. I pulled out my cell and sent a quick text.

"Thierry?"

I glanced over my shoulder at Mom. "Hmm?"

She pushed to her feet. "If they decide to send you back, how soon will you leave?"

I pocketed my phone. "Tonight. Tomorrow at the latest."

"And your father…" she swallowed, "…he's leaving too?"

My heart lurched when her eyes went blurry. "He didn't tell you?"

Mom ducked her head as a sigh shuddered from her lungs.

Please don't cry. Please don't cry.

A single, hiccupped sob escaped her before she clamped a hand over her mouth.

I decided right then if this mission didn't kill Mac, I just might have to.

CHAPTER FIVE

Mac's errand lasted long enough for me to change into a pair of mostly unwrinkled khakis, a clean white blouse, black polka dot cardigan and the black flats I snitched from Mai's closet before he arrived. I combed my hair and pulled it back in a bun then checked myself out in the mirror. Still tall. Still pale. Still Mac's mini-me with deep green eyes and inky black hair.

A quick twirl verified all my bases were covered and then I was out the door.

I bumped into Shaw, who had taken up position outside my bedroom after learning of Evander's visit. He was kind of snarly. A little mad. It was pretty hot, actually.

I walked my fingers across his collarbone. "Where are the 'rents?"

He jerked his chin toward the door across from mine. "Holed up in Mai's room."

"They're not...um..." I waffled my hand. "Wait. No. Don't tell me."

Shaw wrapped a warm palm around the back of my neck. "Agnes was loaded for bear."

Meaning Mom was pissed.

"Serves him right." I shook my head. "Mac didn't tell her he was leaving."

Wariness pinched Shaw's features. "She wants him to stay?"

"It looks that way." I shrugged. "No accounting for taste."

"We need to get moving." His hand tightened, fingers digging into my nape as he drew me closer. Shaw lowered his head, and his soft lips feathered over mine. "The magistrates are expecting us. Don't want to be late."

"Not my fault," I murmured against his mouth. "I was accosted outside my bedroom."

He nipped my bottom lip. "I don't hear any complaints."

"I'm working up to it."

"Mmm-hmm." He reared back and knocked on Mai's door. "Time to go."

The door swung open under his knuckles, and he rocked back, taking me with him as my mother darted from the room, eyes red and swollen. Mac prowled after her with a determined set to his jaw. I let her escape through the front door before I caught him by the sleeve, which wouldn't have stopped him if he hadn't let it. "You need to back off. Let Mom calm down before you go sniffing after her."

His eyes narrowed, probably at the sniffing comment. "I must speak to her."

I raised my hand. "You've had three days to tell her you were leaving."

Quiet anger crackled in his voice. "I never expected to be welcomed here again. If I had told her I was leaving, she would have shut me out. I didn't want her to be hurt. I wanted to see her...happy."

Understanding crept in and sanded the hard edges from my reprimand. "It was selfish, Mac. You wanted to see her at her best, I get that. I like seeing her happy too. But now it's over. You're going to leave her—*again*—and this time she's got nothing to show for it. She's hurting. She...loves you."

His nod was sharp. "She's my mate."

Shock buckled my knees. If Shaw hadn't caught me, I would have face-planted onto the cow-skull-shaped area rug and choked to death on the dust bunnies.

"So..." I let Shaw hold me upright. "You're saying you love her too?"

His brows sloped downward. "You have to ask?"

"Um, considering the whole abandonment thing, *yes.*"

"Life is too short not to tell the people who matter that you love them," Shaw interjected.

A spark of understanding lit Macsen's eyes. "You told him you love him."

I blinked at him. "What?"

"Your mate." Macsen stabbed the air where Shaw stood. "You tell him you love him."

"Yes." I drew out the word. "Several times a day."

What? We were still in our honeymoon period.

"I didn't know I was supposed to do that." Mac glared at us like it was somehow our fault. "She has never said she loves me. She would know that was the proper custom. Why didn't she tell me?"

"That's not how it works," Shaw answered for me. "We have to say it first."

"The male goes first?" He darted a glance at the door. "I will go say it now."

My lips parted as I reached for him, but Shaw clamped a hand over my mouth and held me still.

"Go on," he said to Macsen, holding me while I squirmed. "Make it quick, though. The magistrates are waiting."

Mac strode from the room, sparks lighting his palm.

I sank my teeth into the meat of Shaw's palm, threw my elbow into his gut and ducked under his arm. A spin on the ball of my foot had me facing him in time to catch his *whuff* of breath and a spark of white frosting his pupils.

"They're both adults," he rumbled. "Let them handle this on their own."

I growled, "He's going to hurt her again."

"She's a big girl." He rubbed his side. "She knew what to expect from him."

"He should have told her."

"He should have."

I anchored my hands at my hips. "I'm not fighting with you about this."

His lips twitched. "Could have fooled me."

"It's just that I'm leaving—*we*'re leaving—and I don't know if I'll... If you and me..." I set my jaw. "I wanted her to be in a good place when I got the call. Crying over her ex is not a good place."

He hooked his thumbs into his back pockets. "Did you tell her where we're going?"

"Yes."

"Did you tell her why we're going?"

I hesitated. "Yes."

Nodding, he lowered the hammer. "Did you tell her we might not make it back?"

I mashed my lips together until they tingled.

"You wanted to leave on a high note. So when you looked back at this goodbye, if that's what it turns out to be, you had no regrets. No memory of her fear or doubt or pain. I'm not saying what you did was wrong." He blew out a harsh breath. "I'm not saying what Mac did was right. All I'm saying is you both wanted the same thing and went about getting it the same way. Be honest with yourself."

"Fine. You made your point." My arms fell to my sides. "We'll let them sort it out on their own."

And if they couldn't, well, ten dollars would buy me a shovel and I had a Sharpie to write Mac's name on it.

After thirty minutes ticked past and neither of my parents returned to the apartment, Shaw and I made an executive decision and left for the marshal's office without them. A ball of worry tightened my gut. Not fear for Mom, exactly. I knew Mac wouldn't hurt her. But if this was it, I wouldn't get a second chance to say goodbye. The magistrates would expect Mac, Shaw and me to head out immediately.

And if things went south in Faerie, I wanted all my loose ends tied up in a bow here.

Shaw leaned forward and killed the radio in his truck. "Agnes is fine."

I toyed with my seat belt so the strap wouldn't saw off my head. "I know."

"She'll be there. She wouldn't miss her chance to send you off right." He rested a hand on my thigh. "Don't worry."

I popped his fingers when they ventured into zipper territory. "What are you, a mind reader?"

"That or you've been muttering *come on, Mom* under your breath since we left."

"Oh."

Shaw flipped on his blinker and turned the wheel. The orange lights illuminated his face and his tight expression. The truck bounced hard once then the tires dug in and spun loose gravel. Careful of potholes, he navigated the familiar road leading to the charmingly dilapidated farmhouse the marshal program called home. Behind it hundreds of acres of dried cornstalks bent and swayed in the breeze.

Moonlight spilled over the pitched tin roof, glinting off the sparse patches where rust hadn't eaten through the metal. The structure stood two stories tall with white clapboard siding sliding down the walls and teal shutters hanging on by the determination of corroded hinges. Busted slats gave them gap-toothed grins that smiled at us in welcome. The stairs leading up to the front porch were missing boards, and the dentil molding could use a good flossing to clean out the abandoned birds' nests blackening the gaps.

The truck rolled to a stop, and Shaw killed the engine. We sat there in the silent cab, gazing up at the heavy moon as tension built between us. Every step we took tonight held an unsettling finality to it, whether real or imagined. The thought of never seeing this place again, never sitting here again…

But the thought of the Morrigan enslaving Faerie was worse. The possibility she might bring her war to this realm, to humans who had no hope of surviving a magical attack, was the absolute worst. Regardless of how unresolved I left things with Mom, everything I sacrificed was to keep her safe.

That was enough. It had to be.

"Do you want to go inside?" Shaw's voice sliced through the quiet.

"Sure." I unfastened my seat belt and hefted our messenger bags from the floorboard, passing his to him and opening my door. "We can wait on Mac in my office." I eased out, feet crunching on loose gravel. "That should buy us a few minutes before the powers that be get twitchy and come looking."

Not to mention a breather before we had to face the roomful of scheming magistrates.

Careful to watch my step crossing the rotting porch, I grasped the front doorknob and spoke the Word keyed to the lock. All around me, the glamour concealing the farmhouse slid down the walls to pool on the ground. The flaking wrought-iron doorknob became smooth brushed steel in my hand. A ripple of magic revealed the modern brick building protected from human sight. Other buildings that were a part of the compound appeared to flicker into existence where before dried acreage sprawled.

"Thierry, dearest, there you are." Wearing magenta glasses, a persimmon blouse and white hobo skirt, Mable greeted us at the door. Her white hair hung in a single braid down her back, her red cheeks glowing flush with excitement. "I thought I heard someone. Get inside. Come on."

"Hey, Mable." I hustled inside. "What's with the rush?"

"So much has happened." She gestured Shaw to hurry. "The magistrates have made a decision."

"We heard." I lowered my voice. "They can't make it official until Mac gets here."

"Macsen has been upstairs for half an hour." She linked her fingers. "I thought you knew."

"He's slippery," I told her. "Like an eel. Wonder if he has one of those skins."

Things with Mom must not have ended well if he beat us here on foot. Two legs or four. Demanding she fess up and admit she loved him? Huh. Who would have thought that could ever possibly go wrong?

Parents.

Shaking my head, I pushed those worries aside. "Where do you want us?"

Mable twirled a finger. "Why don't you two wait in your office?"

"All right." I dug in my messenger bag. "That we can do."

Her eyes followed the motion. "I'll fetch you as soon as they're ready."

From the depths of my bag I pulled a jar of pine honey I'd had imported from Turkey for a special occasion. Tonight was shaping up to be one, so I felt it required a commemorative token. That and if I didn't make it back, I wanted her last gift from me to be the very best I had squirreled away for her.

With a flourish, I presented the delicate brown glass jar to her. "This is for you."

She clapped with delight. "What is it?"

"Pine honey." I winked at her. "The only jar in Wink."

Maybe even the state of Texas. I had pulled strings to get a conclave outpost in Turkey to ship it here.

"Pine honey," she repeated. "I've never heard of it before."

I shooed Mable toward her desk where she kept her dainty tasting spoons. She walked in a daze with the jar held up to the light, studying its contents, and I laughed. "Let me know what you think of it, all right?"

"I'll do that." She sat in her task chair and placed the jar on her desk. "You didn't have to—"

"I know." I smiled. "We'll see you in a bit."

I reached behind me and grabbed Shaw by the wrist, hauling him up a short flight of stairs to my office where I shut the door and locked it behind us.

"This is moving too fast." I pressed a hand into my gut. "How did Mac beat us here? And where the heck is Mom?"

"Breathe." Shaw gripped my upper arms. "She's probably blowing off steam. Don't get yourself worked up. We knew this day was coming."

I puffed out my cheeks. "They're upstairs deciding our fate right now."

His eyebrows lifted a fraction. "They've been doing that for days."

"But now Mac is up there with them. They could flap their gums all they wanted, but the motion couldn't pass without him being present and giving his formal vote, and he's been with us, so I knew they were just blowing hot air. Politics, right? But if he's up there, then it's real. This is happening."

Shaw led me across the office toward the task chair where I seated visitors, and shoved down on my shoulder until I sat. Then he kept shoving until I bent forward and my head was between my knees.

"Just breathe." His wide palm stroked down my back. "Everything is going to be okay."

Tears gathered in my eyes. "I wanted to see Mom before we left."

"There's still time," he soothed.

I turned my head and caught him playing with his cell. A few days ago I would have snapped a nasty comment about booking hookers, but we were past that. Or trying hard to get that way. I didn't want to be the girlfriend who kept dredging up the past to poison the present, but it was hard. The old pain was sharp, and fear made it so much worse. Times like these I wanted to still be a little girl. I wanted Mom to pull me onto her lap and rock me and tell me everything was going to be okay, but I was an adult now. I was a marshal. I used to be a princess, and here I was about to reclaim my throne. A freaking crown I never wanted. A title I couldn't care less about. But it was what it was.

The doorknob wiggling made me jerk vertical, and blood rushed in my ears. I clutched at Shaw's arm and stared at the door as though the frame was an archaic gateway into a future that terrified me.

"Hel-to the-lo," Mai sang. "I brought coffee and donuts."

I was on my feet with the door open and Mai in my arms in a heartbeat. "You got my message."

She lifted a finger. "Daddy only thinks he knows all the places a girl can hide her cellphone."

I burst out laughing, which almost covered the pained noise Shaw was making.

"Um." Her fair skin flushed red hot as she escaped me. "That didn't come out how I meant it."

On her way past I plucked a cup of coffee from the paper tray she carried. "You're the best."

"No argument here." She passed Shaw a cup before setting the tray and donut box on my desk.

While perusing the assorted pastries, I asked, "So the Hayashis are going on lockdown?"

"No," she grumbled. "The Hayashis *are* on lockdown. I was the last holdout."

I picked up a chocolate-covered candidate. "It sucks, but it will be the safest place for you."

"I'll pretend you didn't say that." She pointed a finger between Shaw and me. "If this doesn't work out, let me know. With that mentality, you and Dad could be a match made in heaven."

I snorted. "Heaven is exactly where we would end up too, if your mom caught wind of our torrid love affair."

"Good point." She made a grouchy face. "Though I have to admit I'm a little disturbed you took it that far."

I shrugged. "It's what I do."

Her gaze slid to a point behind me, and her eyes narrowed. "Why is your closet glowing like that?"

"Glowing?" I turned around and froze. "Oh crap. It's not supposed to do that."

Sultry red light pulsated in the crack between the door and the floor, flashed between the hinges and snaked through the wood grain to make eerie patterns that throbbed with an unsettling intensity.

"I have some herbs in my bag." Shaw eased forward, placing himself between the closet and me like it was a bomb waiting to explode. "I can cast a divining spell. See if someone tampered with the closet."

I stepped up beside him. "As in divine who caused the whatever-is-in-there to start glowing?"

"Or divine what it does." He grabbed my arm. "We don't want to open the door and have it go boom."

"See, that's the thing." I laced my fingers. "I know what the closet does—*did*—and the door doesn't open."

"What it does?" He turned me to face him. "Since when does your closet do anything?"

"The Morrigan gave me a present, and I didn't know what it was until she had done it." I stuck a hand down the front of my T-shirt and pulled out the battered silver pendant marked with a triskele.

Each marshal since the start of the program was gifted a medallion that would summon the Morrigan to accept tithes. Though I wasn't sure what it entailed for other marshals, for me it meant when a case went bad and I exercised my right to use lethal force, the Morrigan collected the body once I had consumed the soul. Meat and bones were paid as a tithe to her in thanks for erasing our messes.

After Balamohan, I was second-guessing what she gained from helping the conclave conceal the existence of fae from humanity. A free meal, yeah, but there had to be more to it. Obviously, she had no issues revealing fae to the human race seeing as how she planned to come out of the closet—no pun intended—in a genocidal way.

Death magics were complex. Far more complex than I had realized, which was worrisome given that was the root of my power. The more I learned and the more Mac taught me, the more worried I got.

When a fae or half-blood died, where did their magic go? Did it vanish in a puff of smoke? Was it absorbed into the ground or air and made clean by the earth? Or was it, as I was coming to believe, locked in the tissues of the fae themselves? Meaning each meal was a power snack in a literal sense.

The worst scenario imaginable was the magics stayed in the body and the Morrigan gained strength each time she ate fae flesh. Given its world-ending consequences, I was betting that was the case.

"You know how these handy-dandy pendants used to summon the Morrigan? For tithe collection and all that?" I rolled my hand. "You know, before she went totally bonkers and took over Faerie?"

"Yes," he said slowly. "I think I can remember as far back as three days ago."

"Okay, well, mine also acts as an anchor for a portal." I pointed toward the closet. "To there."

Muscle leapt in his jaw. "Portals are illegal."

Shame wormed through my gut. "I know."

He drew us back several steps from the door. "Do the magistrates know about it?"

"No." My shoulders slumped. "I didn't tell anyone."

Admitting moral weakness to Shaw hurt. It meant offering proof of my corruption by not giving up the pendant in the first place. I'd intended to collect the contents and turn the whole mess over to the magistrates. But I hadn't. Something kept me holding on to the pendant, the secret, even after I was rescued and sent home to recover. For the first time in my life, I had Mac's wealth of knowledge at my fingertips, and I hadn't said a word to him or to Shaw or to Mai or to Mable. Not a single peep.

Studying the pulsating glow, Shaw advanced. "What are you keeping in there?"

"My skins." I closed my hand over the pendant, my thumb sliding through the familiar groove in its center. "I needed a safe place to keep them after Faerie, and she knew that. I guess Rook mentioned it. Then I called her for pickup, and she did something to my necklace. She had already been here, anchored the portal in the closet and I just... I'm an idiot."

"This is serious." A snarl entered his voice. "This is an anchor of power for the Morrigan in the heart of the marshal's building, right below the magistrates' office. This is dangerous for us—and for them. Did you consider you might not be the only one with access to it? To what you store inside of it? Or that the portal might not end here?"

The blood rushed from my face, and I swayed on my feet. "We have to tell them."

Red light strobed under the door and exploded through the wood in an electric blast.

Thrown against the wall, I collided head first with the baseboards, and the room went dark.

CHAPTER SIX

Slashing pain woke me as fire burned my palm. Steel fingers clamped my wrist, and my left arm popped, yanked out of its socket. I gasped through the hurt, forcing my heavy eyes open on chaos.

The closet door was gone. Inside what used to be a three-foot-square area, magic churned in red waves like a choppy sea after a storm. Shadows moved through the smoky light. Sharp teeth. Claws.

My knee slammed into a bookshelf, and I yelped. The constant pressure on my arm lessened.

A slim line of blood trickled down my right arm. Mine?

"It is alive." A grunt sounded unhappy about that. "The Morrigan wants a word with it."

I tilted my head back. A bulky troll was dragging me across the floor toward the closet—toward a freaking portal straight into Hell for all I knew. Movement to my right made me squint. Wide gold eyes blinked at me from between two filing cabinets. *Mai.* Thank God. Oh no. Shaw. Where was...?

Two more trolls hunched over a mass in the corner. Boots. It wore black boots. *No, no, no.*

"It will break," one murmured.

"It might," the other agreed. "It's tough. Not good eats."

A sour taste rose up the back of my throat. I swallowed it down and forced myself to soak in the damage caused by a portal mouth opening inside the closet and transporting a troll mini strike force.

All my fault. This is all me. I can't blame my magic this time. This is all my doing.

"The other thing," the one holding my arm said. "Find it. Furry thing. Might make good eats."

The other two grunted agreement.

Mai. They were discussing her as a menu item. She must have been scared furry after the blast.

How long had I been out? Not that long if they hadn't caught her yet. Hadn't dragged me through the portal. Long enough for Shaw to get hurt. He must have fought them. Stupid, stupid, brave incubus protecting his idiot mate from herself. If he was... I would kill them. All of them.

My magic, always balanced on the sharp edge of hunger, driven to the brink of starvation by my exercises in control, shot from my left palm, through my glove, a powerful blast that bowed my spine.

The troll holding on to me bellowed in agony. No stopping it. No saving him. He was toast.

Magic slid underneath his skin, scalpel-sharp, cleaving flesh from muscle. Sliding deeper, into his chest, through his heart, a fist of magic grabbed the organ and squeezed it to pulp. Reaching wider, the fingers of power stabbed into the nugget of soul and ripped it free, devouring his essence before I gained control of myself. His body crumpled, landing in a heap beside my head. His skin landed in a fragile sheet half on top of me. When I breathed in, I inhaled flakes of skin and burnt hair.

"What did it do?" one of the corner trolls yelled. "*What did it do?*"

"It killed him," the other barked. "It killed him with a touch of its hand. I saw it."

"I'll kill it with my hand." The first troll made a fist. "See how it likes that."

"It's going to die," the second troll sneered.

Pushing upright, I twisted into lotus position. That was as far as I made it before they charged.

The second troll palmed my entire head. I clamped a hand on to his thick wrist and used the fresh energy coursing through me to rip his soul through his chest with magic fingers. More in control this time, I reeled my power in like a lasso and flung it at the third troll as he landed a kick to my side. Gripping his ankle, I shoved more energy into him. His essence leaked from his heel to puddle underneath me like black sludge.

When I released him, his body, balanced on one foot, teetered, hitting the floor and bouncing. The second troll loomed over me, dead fingers spearing my hair, until impact jostled him and he toppled, landing on top of the third one with a thud. Both were hard as the stone they became in daylight.

Jaws stretched in primal screams. Eyes peeled open wide and blank. Their last breaths reeked of terror.

Left hand raised high like a beacon, spilling light into the room, I scanned for more trolls.

"Mai," I called. She bounded to me, fur standing on end, thick tail swishing. "Where is Mac?"

She pointed her nose toward the ceiling.

"He's still in the magistrates' office? Are they hurt or—?"

The fox leapt from my lap, hunkered down on the floor and covered her ears with her paws.

"They're hiding?"

A growl.

I took that as a negative. "They can't hear us?"

A yip.

As I stood, it hit me. "They activated a privacy spell so they wouldn't be disturbed."

Mai nodded, the gesture looking too human on a fox.

Leaving her where she sat, I crossed to Shaw and fell to my knees at his side. "Oh, Jackson."

He groaned at the sound of his name and turned his head toward me. His face was ruined. Blood covered him from scalp to collarbone, and when he parted his lips, I counted missing teeth. Potent anger ignited in my gut. All that remained of my glove was a charred scrap of fabric that I tore away.

Clasping hands with him, I trusted Mai to watch my back while I gently pushed a portion of the energy I had consumed into him. Healing worked best with several slow transfusions of magic. That was a luxury we didn't have, but I couldn't pump him full of juice. Not when he had been eating light for days. Instead I fed him a trickle until some of the swelling left his cheeks and the skin crept over exposed bone, reknitting the split halves of his face together. Lids regenerated over his eyes, which cracked open a fraction to stare up at me.

"I need to get my father," I said softly. "I'm going to leave Mai here with you."

Slight pressure on my fingers told me he heard and understood.

Shoving to my feet, I whirled on Mai. "Bark if anything moves. I'll be back as fast as I can."

I took the stairs three at a time, reached the door of the magistrates' office and pounded on the gleaming silver wood panels with my fists. "Hey," I called. "Open up. There's a situation out here."

No one answered. No one flung open the doors. No one ran to my rescue.

A sick, sick feeling curdled my stomach.

How long had I been out? What else had strolled through the portal? Where was my father? Had the magistrates been captured? Killed? *Mable*. Oh, God. What if she had been hurt? What if Mom…

No. Shut down the fear. Twenty questions had to wait. This wasn't a drill. This was real.

Faerie had brought the war here. And I had helped.

Exhaling slowly between my lips, I shoved the memory of Shaw's battered face out of my mind and grasped the fraying sense of calm Mac had struggled to teach me. From there I summoned magic into my runes and flattened my palm against the door. Through that link, I sensed a heavy enchantment as thick as cotton batting shrouding the room. I couldn't hear a peep through it, and I bet they couldn't either. Great. On the upside, this meant the threshold remained unbroken. That was a good sign.

If the fighting downstairs hadn't punctured the spell, how was I going to manage the job?

My bag of supplies was in my office, probably, unless the trolls had taken it. But this was out of my league. I didn't have Shaw's experience or knack for cracking enchantments. Dragging him here for this wasn't an option. Not unless I spent more time healing him first. By then it might be too late.

Sizzling noises drew my gaze to where red liquid popped and bubbled on the floor.

A thin cut severed my palm, and blood dripped from my hand. Weird. Had I been bleeding all this time? I flexed my fingers, waiting for the wound to knit closed, but it didn't. It kept weeping in a slow but steady drip. Kneeling by the hissing blood splotches, I wiped my finger through them, and a pulse of magic raced up my arm. Again I called magic into my hand, hotter and faster this time. I let it build, pressed my runes and the sore against the door simultaneously, and a *pop* unblocked my ears.

I smacked the wood with my open hands. "Can anyone hear me? *Hello?*"

Inside, I heard the legs of a chair scooting backward. Footsteps. A *click* as the knob turned.

I don't know what Evander saw in me right then, but he shouted quick orders in his native tongue, and the others leapt to their feet. Even Kerwin, the Unseelie magistrate, and not my biggest fan showed concern. Each dipped a hand into the air and withdrew their weapons from the pockets of ether where they stored them, and as one they all turned their eyes toward Mac.

Emerald light burst in his hand, darkening until a viscous black magic swirled around his feet.

He lifted his head, and his nostrils flared. "Trolls."

"I killed three of them," I said, voice trembling, "but Shaw's hurt."

Mac's gaze swept over me and left me cold and miserable. "Take us to him."

I sprinted down to my office, Mac hot on my heels, squinting against the strobing light painting the hallway red. The portal was growing. I swept inside my office and pulled up short.

Shaw was gone.

No body. No blood. No tracks. No scent.

Vanished without a trace.

"He was right there." The sharp edge of panic cut into my voice. "Mai?"

Small as she was in fox form, she might have hidden. She might have…

I jumped when a hand buzzing with power landed on my shoulder. Heart pounding, I jerked away from the touch, gulping hard at Mac's grim expression. The icy coldness in his green-black aura clung to my chilled skin. He stalked toward me and snarled in my face. "What happened?"

I eased back a step. "Shaw—"

He dug his fingers into my upper arms. "This is bigger than Shaw."

"He's hurt." Panic narrowed my focus to a fine point. "He was right there. *Where is he?*"

Green eyes blazing, Mac homed in on the pendant I hadn't tucked back into my shirt, and his lip curled. "Why do you still wear that?" He uttered a feral growl. "Remove it and give it to me."

My hand closed over the skin-warmed pendant. I meant to lift it over my head, I did, but my elbow locked. I stood there clutching the Morrigan's coin, frantic for Shaw and desperate to find Mai, my pulse sprinting like my life depended on this moment, frozen in the face of Macsen's anger.

A strange expression settled over his features, and his fury dissolved. "It's a compulsion."

"No, it's not." I tossed my head until my brain rattled. "I would know if it was."

"Give me the necklace," he demanded.

Fingers cinched, I extended the hand holding the pendant toward him, but I couldn't loosen them, couldn't take off the necklace, couldn't remember if it tied or clasped or what. The idea of removing it was insane. What would I do without its comforting weight around my neck? Where would I keep my skins? *My skins.* My gaze broke from Mac and skittered to the closet and its whirling red vortex.

All my skins.

Lost.

The puca. The hound. The selkie.

All gone.

Confused tears welled in my eyes.

"It will be all right," Mac said gently.

Faster than my eyes could track, he fisted the chain and jerked. It snapped at my nape with a bite of pain. His arm completed its downward arc, yanking me forward when my hand refused to unclasp and let him take the coin from me. His hand clamped over mine, and he pried loose my fingers one by one.

Once he alone held the coin, a flare of magic burst from his palm and engulfed his clothing. Red magic lashed him like a tongue of unquenchable flames while a piercing cry made the room tremble.

Throat burning, I understood the scream came from me. I curled onto my side on the floor and rocked back and forth, stomach roiling, skin too tight, feeling wrong, like a T-shirt turned inside out.

Face lined with concentration, Mac rubbed his hands together until ash rained from his fingertips.

The chain, the pendant, all of it, reduced to silver-black dust.

With a bone-weary sigh, Mac settled his attention back on me, and an emotion dangerously close to disappointment shrouded his features. Power thrummed in his voice when he ordered me, "Sleep."

My eyes rolled back in my head.

Consciousness burst through me like the first gasp of breath after spending too long under water, a shock to my system that jolted me the way a hit of espresso can and jangled my nerves in a sudden fright.

I bolted upright, magic pooling in my palm, and froze when I saw I wasn't alone.

A man wearing a long black cloak stood with his back facing me as he studied an odd collection of archaic implements pinned onto a velvet backing on the table in front of him. A quick downward glance confirmed my worst fears. I sat on another such table, velvet crushed under my sweaty palms.

My frantic mind supplied me with the mental image of me pinned to the cloth like a butterfly, as part of this freak's collection. Memories hammered at my sanity. I had been part of a collection once.

Balamohan laved his sticky-sharp tongue over my skin while he feasted on my death.

I had to clamp my lips shut to choke the dry heaving. "Where am I?"

"It doesn't matter." The black-clad figure turned. "We're leaving."

"Mac?" He was dressed in black leather armor similar to what I had worn during the Coronation Hunt.

"The outpost in Wink has been warded. The marshal's office has been blood warded. By me."

In Wink sounded like we weren't there anymore, but we had to be, right?

The bitter sweat from an adrenaline dump soaked through my shirt. A burst of ripe panic pushed me to my feet. Jittery as a spider on caffeine, I was all twitchy legs and a frantic heart.

"Where is Shaw?" Fear dried my tongue. "I have to finish healing him."

Mac rapped his knuckles on the wall in front of him, and a door swung open behind me.

I turned in time to watch Mai enter wearing baggy sweatpants rolled up at the ankles, socks and a T-shirt she could have worn as a dress with the right belt. Her hair was damp and her face bruised.

My throat squeezed tight. "Mai…"

She stopped several feet away from me and asked Mac, "Is she clean?"

Clean? I recoiled from her harsh tone, the cold phrasing.

"I examined her again before I let her wake," my father answered just as cryptically.

I leaned against the table for support. "What's going on?"

Cool and assessing, Mai studied me for signs of…foaming at the mouth? Dilated pupils? I don't know what she expected to see.

"The Morrigan rolled you." Mai cocked her hip and crossed her arms over her chest. "When she one-upped your 'gift', she took the liberty of coating it with one hella nasty compulsion." Fingers tapping her upper arms, she added, "All so you wouldn't remove the pendant, wouldn't want it removed, and would give whoever tried to force you holy hell for the attempt. She needed to make sure it stuck to you so you wouldn't squeal on her closet renovations until she was ready for the big reveal." She eased closer. "You were lucky, Tee. If Mac hadn't been there to absorb the kickback when he broke the chain, you would be dead."

"Is that...?" I wrapped my arms around my middle. "Is that why you're angry with me?"

"She isn't angry," Mac said without turning. "This is the third time I have woken you."

"The third time?" I rubbed my forehead. "The last thing I remember was..."

"It's okay." Mai stepped forward again. "Some of your memory is missing."

I spluttered before my brain got traction. *"How is that okay?"*

"You lost four point three seconds," Mac said. "You won't miss them."

"How did—?" I pointed at his back and asked Mai, "Did he—?" I swayed on my feet. "I think I need to sit down for a minute." My knees buckled, and my butt hit the floor. "Was anyone hurt?" A gut-wrenching flash of Shaw's pulped face in my mind kept me swallowing to keep my throat clear.

No Shaw. No body. *There had been no body.*

"Oh God, Shaw." My nails scraped over the tile. "Where is he? What happened? Is he all right?"

Mac turned at last, and his color was ashen. "He was taken."

"Taken," I parroted.

"There was a fourth troll," Mai said quietly. "He must have been the lookout on the opposite side of the portal. When the others didn't return, he popped in, saw what happened and grabbed Shaw." Her head dropped, chin bumping her chest. "I fought them. I tried—" Her voice broke. "I was too scared to shift back. I got stuck. *Stuck.* I couldn't cry for help." She sniffled. "I should have followed them."

Numbness drifted into my thoughts, cloaking me like fog from the truth of it all.

Shaw was gone.

The trolls had taken him.

The Morrigan...she would demand a report, and they would use him as their scapegoat.

The weight of Mai's stare pressed down on me until I forced out, "You did the right thing."

"A kitsune is no match for a troll," Mac soothed.

This shed new light on Mai's anger. She wasn't pissed at me over the compulsion. She was mad at herself for letting fear stop her from acting. Or worse, what she thought *I* would see as cowardice.

"He's right." I placed a hand over my heart to reassure myself it was still beating. "They would have..." I held my tongue. "Trolls don't play nice. You did the right thing by keeping yourself safe."

Mai's lips pinched into a flat line, but she didn't argue with me.

"The Morrigan won't kill him," Mac rumbled with certainty.

A sour grin puckered my mouth. "I notice you didn't say she wouldn't let him die."

Enough pain made you long for death. Starvation was an ugly way to go.

Feet planted wide, he gave me what he could. "Shaw is too valuable as a hostage."

As much as I hated the thought of Shaw being used as leverage, I had to believe Mac was right.

Lock it down. Stow away the fear. Strangle the panic. Shaw needed me at my best.

"Why today?" I lowered my hand when Mac noticed its placement. "What did they want?"

"The timing," Mai said, "was too perfect. You aren't at the office every day, and the Morrigan is smart enough not to leave a freaking portal into Faerie humming until you showed up. She knew the decision was being announced today. She knew she had to act. It's the only thing that makes sense."

Gut dropping, I said, "There's a mole in the office."

"Fifteen people knew the vote was coming," Mac said.

Ten were magistrates, so five pairs, one Seelie and one Unseelie, from each of the five conclave divisions across the

United States. Shaw made eleven, Mai twelve, Mac thirteen, Mable fourteen and I was fifteen.

"Families going to ground, like mine," Mai added, "are heeding rumors straight from Faerie."

I nodded, understanding what she left unsaid. She had known, and she hadn't told her skulk. She trusted that her father's connections would get word out to her family without compromising herself.

"Each of us was summoned personally by Evander. For the Morrigan to know, someone reached out to her after he visited them." Mac returned his attention to the table. "For the portal to have been active when you arrived, she needed time to prepare. That means one of the first informed her."

"Or that he informed her first." I considered the likelihood of a Seelie setting aside millennia of hatred for the Unseelie. Even if richly compensated, it was a tossup. "There's also the possibility Kerwin snitched to the Morrigan while Evander's back was turned."

Mac was right. The trap had already been set, and we walked right into it. The only reason Mai was involved at all was because she came with Shaw to rescue me from Balamohan. Evander had no reason to tell her about the vote. I had done that, because I selfishly wanted to see her before we left.

Shaw and I were the last ones rounded up, and thanks to my folks' spat, we arrived at the office well after the charm had been activated upstairs, promising the trolls and the portal plenty of privacy.

Speaking of the parental units... "Where is Mom?" Calm as Mac was, I knew she must be fine. "Did she make it to the office? She's okay, right?"

Grimness settled into the lines around Mac's mouth. "She is at home under Sven's guardianship."

Sour as his expression turned, I wasn't about to ask how his declaration went. Instead I let it slide and tipped my head back. Sven was a good guy. He would protect her with his life. "What was the point of the attack?"

"The trolls came armed with never blades."

Never heard of them. "What are those?"

"If the blade pierces your skin, you won't stop bleeding without magical intervention." Mac hesitated. "Sometimes even that isn't enough."

I glanced at my right hand where the cut had been but wasn't now. "You healed me."

"No." He shook his head. "It's beyond my abilities to heal. I stopped the bleeding, for now. The wound is concealed beneath a layer of glamour so that no one who doesn't expect your injury will see it."

I flexed my hand. "It doesn't hurt."

Had it hurt before? I couldn't remember.

"It's all part of the enchantment folded into the blades. Victims are slower to panic if they don't feel pain. By the time most notice they've been cut, they're weak and easy prey to what hunts them."

I gulped hard. "Can it be cured?"

"Once we're in Faerie," Mac said solemnly, "I know a place we can go."

Mai came closer, extending her arm down to where I sat, and I hesitated. I was right-handed, but I shied away from putting pressure on the binding and offered an awkward left-handed grip instead.

A grunt of effort later, she tugged me onto my feet beside her.

"I'm not *that* heavy," I grumbled.

"It really is you." She laughed. "I wasn't sure."

Still woozy, I leaned my hip against hers for balance. "How bad was it?"

"The Morrigan had her hooks in deep. She was talking through you. Screaming through you was more like it. Mac called it a suggestive echo from keeping the pendant against your skin for so long."

Considering what had happened to Shaw, I felt selfish for asking, "What about my skins?"

"I retrieved them before I warded the portal." Mac turned. "You can have them back when you master creating your own *aer póca*. Until that time, I'll store them with my things. Sound fair?"

"I don't sense I have much say in the matter, so sure." I rolled a shoulder. "I'm guessing the *aer* thing is the pocket of air sidhe use to hide weapons? I saw the magistrates use them. Rook does too."

Mac was right to want me able to protect what was mine without borrowing from higher powers.

I had learned my lesson the hard way today.

"By right of creation, I am sidhe and their powers are mine to use as I will." He considered me a moment. "As my child, their magics are yours as well."

Meaning their language, which had always fascinated me, was mine to learn as well.

Interesting.

But not interesting enough to distract me. "How common are never blades?"

"They aren't." With his finger, Mac traced a design on the table by his hip. "The cost of kindling one is so great few can afford them. They require a sacrifice. A life for each blade awakened." He let me think on that. "They aren't carried by trolls for longer than it takes one to complete its mission. Then the blades are returned to their masters."

Their mission was obvious, but saying it out loud gave me the willies. "They came for me."

Mac faced me fully, grim lines aging his flawless skin to match the weary strain in his eyes.

"The Morrigan needs my blood to erase the threshold. If she has you—your blood—she may not barter with me until she knows if yours is as potent. Even knowing it might not work, even if it takes every drop…" his voice lowered to a thick rasp, "…the Morrigan won't stop until you bleed for her."

I stared at my glamour-encased hand. "It was a test."

Quiet anger thrummed through him. "I think so, yes."

"She had me cut, fixed it so the trolls used a blade that would short out my healing abilities and then told them to drag me bleeding through the portal." I pieced it together. "The Morrigan planned to sit back and watch what happened. If I smudged the threshold on my way across or shorted it out…"

"It would prove your blood could erase the ward," Mac finished.

I rocked back on my heels, glancing between them. "So where does this leave us?"

"The magistrates are tucked away in pairs in remote locations across the country." Mai tucked a lock of hair behind her ear. "Mable, of course, will stay put at the marshal's office. She's monitoring the portal and relaying information as it develops between us, the marshals, the magistrates and their respective outposts." Her attempt at a smile waned. "Basically just another day at the office for her."

My throat tightened, and the room became veiled by unshed tears I blinked rapidly to dispel.

I would *not* lose someone else I loved to this war and my own foolishness.

Mac widened his stance. "She has options if the main floors have to be evacuated."

I almost laughed. "How many options can a bean-tighe have with her house under attack?"

"More than you might think," he answered. "Her kind is heartier than you know."

"Fine." I caved. "What about us?"

"We go to Faerie," he said, "and we sever the tethers—"

"Just like that?" I had expected the answer, but it stuck in my craw. "We let the Morrigan win?"

"Shush." Mai rested her hand on my arm. "Let the man talk."

With a polite nod to Mai, Mac continued, "We will go to Faerie and sever the tethers, cutting off the Morrigan's escape routes. When she can't slide into the mortal realm through existing pathways, she will realize she has to forge her own, and she can't without my blood to anchor a new tether."

"Then we go after her," I clarified.

"We won't have to." His smile showed teeth. "She will come after us."

"Wait." I rewound the conversation. "So the magistrates made the call? They voted yes?"

"Thierry," Mai said, "if you don't do this, there won't be a conclave to come home to."

"If we go vigilante now, who reins us in next time? Thinking we know what's best, that our way is more valid than someone else's, is a slippery slope. One good push and we're all wallowing in the mud with hands just as dirty as the Morrigan's." I pegged Mac with a stare. "I'm ready to fight, but I want orders. I want to know what we're about to do is viewed by our ruling body as the right thing."

Hard to explain where the hesitance came from when it hadn't been there earlier. Maybe it was a way to check myself, to know this course of action was honorable in the eyes of people I trusted and not a sliver of the Morrigan's influence still corrupting me. And, if I were being honest with myself, I wanted permission to savor my revenge, an iron-clad absolution of guilt for my actions after I found Shaw, because once he was safe, I would show the Morrigan how much of a daddy's girl I really was.

The internal scales I inherited from Mac were swaying like a seesaw inside my head. Knowing I had fallen under the Morrigan's spell, I lost touch with the part of me always certain my actions were just. Until I shook off the bitterness, if I ever got that far, I would rely on others' internal compasses.

As though he expected things to swing this way, Mac picked up a scroll from the table behind him. It unfurled, the weight of quality parchment and the thick, familiar wax seal drawing it downward. His arm extended, and from his shoulder height, where he held the top lip, it stretched down to his navel.

I didn't have to see the fine print to recognize the signatures scrawled along the bottom edge.

"The vote wasn't formalized before the Morrigan attacked," he said. "We held a special session in a conference room at the airport to gather signatures before the magistrates were sent into hiding."

A burden fell from my shoulders. "Okay." I glanced between them. "Let's do this."

Mai worried her bottom lip between her teeth. "First you'll need to change."

Bending low, Mai retrieved a long box from under the table where I woke and pressed it into my arms. It had already been opened. When I lifted the lid, I recognized the outfit. Black leather armor like Mac wore. My fingers traced deep furrows in one wristlet. Teeth marks. This was the exact suit Rook had given me. The one he had tricked me into wearing as part of his elaborate scheme to claim me as his wife. I hadn't wanted to wear his gift then, and I sure didn't want to now, but it seemed I had no choice.

Again.

"I hope you had it dry-cleaned," I muttered.

I hauled out the topmost piece, the wristlet, and froze. Rubbing a thumb across the oval-shaped enamel emblem, I studied it. Instead of the inverted House Unseelie coat of arms I expected, this was an emerald shield inlayed with a black stylized hound clamping a single rose between its sharp teeth.

I held up the emblem. "What's this?"

"Shaw commissioned the design." Mai looked everywhere but at me. "He was having the armor restored for next year, just in case, but there was no time to finish the job. He asked me to hide it for him until tonight." She gulped air then pushed out the rest. "The design is called *Queen of Thorns*."

The breath I took rattled in my chest, a sob stuck between my gut and throat.

I locked the pain down before a single whimper escaped.

"It's beautiful." The words were torn from my soul.

Mac took a step forward, like he was afraid I would shatter and wanted to catch the pieces.

"I should change." There. That sounded normal. "Where should I...?"

Mac gestured behind me, and it hit me then his armor carried no crest. I shouldn't have expected to see one. He couldn't be loyal to himself and to me. No one's interests dovetailed every time, even if he and I were of a like mind on this occasion. Shaw's crest was the final nail in my coffin, a visual representation of how far I had fallen. Mac was a true neutral, and I...was not.

CHAPTER SEVEN

I ended up changing clothes in a nearby supply closet. Quarters were tight, but I made it work. I wriggled into the underclothes and leather suit then tightened the scuffed armor pads. Mai had brought my favorite pair of boots from our apartment. Black to match the outfit. Even better, they molded to my feet after months of wear. No blisters for this girl.

This kind of forethought was what defined a best friend.

Banging my elbows on the metal racks filled with tear-inducing disinfectant and individually wrapped toilet paper rolls, I finger combed my hair and French braided the unwieldy mass without mangling it too badly. Maybe. I had no mirror to check, but all I needed was the flyaways pulled back from my eyes.

Patting my hair as though appearance mattered, I let the absurdity of caring catch up to me, and I choked on the sob that had been lodged in my throat since learning Shaw had been taken. Palms up in supplication, I surrendered to grief, let it swamp me, thick and fast and so heavy I sagged under the weight of my loss. Tears burned my eyes and scalded trails down my cheeks. I sank to my knees when they quivered and planted my hands on the floor to keep from collapsing as loss hollowed me out. Once I was empty, I slapped a lid on all that pain and sealed it tight. Face hot and itchy from saltwater tracks drying on my skin, I sniffled once then got back on my feet.

Hiding in a closet didn't get me one step closer to finding Shaw. Crying accomplished nothing. I had given in to my guilt, to my fear, and I had purged. Time to woman up and bring him home.

After a deep breath, I stepped out and bounced off a hulking man's rock-solid chest.

Power surged into my palm a split second before I recognized him. "Oh. Hey. Officer Littlejohn, right?"

His startled expression soured in a blink upon noticing my no-doubt-splotchy face. Whatever he read in my red-rimmed eyes persuaded him against asking me what was wrong.

Smart man.

I shook the magic from my fingertips. "What are you doing here?"

He canted his head. "I work here."

My back hit the closet door. *"We're inside the prison?"*

He wiped the amusement from his mouth with a wide palm. "Where did you think you were?"

"An underground bunker? A basement?" I didn't know and hadn't asked. I indicated the door I had stepped out of, adjacent to the wannabe break room where we stood. "What's with that room?"

"It's an all-purpose room. Sometimes we use it for visitation when the chow hall overflows." He shrugged. "Right now it's set up with tables and chairs for a lecture. One of the continuing education classes the prison holds to keep up our certification without trucking us all the way back to Lebanon. I haven't been called yet, but I heard it's a history of shanks, shivs and other homemade weapons."

"I just came from in there." And a weird room it was too. "What's with all the velvet?"

"Some folks take their collections seriously. All weapons found on the premises are supposed to be turned in to the brass, but some pocket the good pieces like souvenirs." Littlejohn rolled his massive shoulders. "Gives 'em a prop to spice up their prison tall tales. Don't know why some take this place home with them. I don't bring nothing that comes from here into my house or near family if I can help it."

"I don't blame you." I hesitated. "Mac said the marshal's office is on lockdown."

"The whole complex is." His radio squawked a garbled update. "Mr. Sullivan evacuated the civilians, but we have nowhere secure to go. These inmates..." he shook his head, "...they have to stay right where they are, right where their evil put them. We can't risk the likes of them escaping."

"You're a good man for staying behind," I said, and I meant it.

A tight nod stretched his neck. "This is what I signed up for, Marshal. Same as you."

Except times like these drove decent men to desertion. Honoring a commitment, that was commendable.

The guard resumed his rounds, and I eased back in the room to find Mac waiting for me.

A grim smile curved his lips, and I read into it his eagerness for us to get moving.

I adjusted my belt to give my hands something to occupy them. "When do we leave?"

"At dawn." He left no room for argument. "Regardless of what else the Morrigan may be, she is Unseelie first. She is at her most potent during the night. We need the sunlight advantage."

Biting my tongue about how that still left us to deal with pissed-off Seelie, I bobbed my head.

"You guys need every advantage you can get." Glancing around, Mai added, "We do too."

I flung my arm around her and rested my chin on her shoulder. "You're going to be okay."

"I'm not so sure." She leaned into me. "The magistrates got lucky, Tee. Like hit the jackpot."

I straightened so our gazes were level. "What do you mean?"

"I read the transcripts."

A pained groan dragged past my lips. "I'm not going to ask how you got those."

Though if the complex had been evacuated, there was no one to chastise a snooping kitsune.

Sly fox is sly.

"Every person in that room views this realm as their private sandbox. They don't care what happens to the fae—or the humans—here. They just don't want the powers that be in Faerie to sweep in and steal their toys." Her lips pursed. "It's different for fae born here. My parents and grandparents are all Earth-born. We're loyal to this realm…if not always to its native people. It's different for you and other half-bloods. You're more invested in the big picture, because this is your world and these are your people, but this one time, I think we'll all end up on the same page. Cutting the ties between realms is no one's salvation." Her chin dipped. "It will only prolong the inevitable."

The burden of doubt pressed on my shoulders. "You think we're making a mistake."

"The Morrigan struck before the magistrates finalized the vote to sever the tethers." Voice light, she mocked, "History will remember her attack and their swift response to it. Not the transcripts. Fae here put down roots and start families. For their families' sakes, they will bow to magistrate law and call them saviors because of this moment, because of what you're about to do, even without the support of Faerie. I worry what you're doing won't save this realm so much as enable a new regime to rise within it."

Without thought, my gaze sought out Mac, who had turned his back on us.

I worried the emblem on my armor. "The scales balance or Mac wouldn't—*couldn't*—endorse this."

"Severing the tethers is for the greater good. For now." Mai studied my father too. "The reprieve might last a week or a month or, if we get lucky, a few years, but we're going to find ourselves here again, and next time the fight won't be in Faerie. Next time the mortal realm will be the battleground, and humanity will pay the price."

"You're right. *We* will be here again. That's how I know all this will turn out okay." I drummed my fingers on her arm. "Even if no one outside the conclave knows the truth, we do. We'll keep them honest."

She snorted.

"Okay, so honest is a stretch," I conceded. "We'll keep them balanced. How's that sound?"

Her grumbled non-answer struck a doubtful note. Close enough.

"The sun is rising," Mac said softly. "Gather your things."

All I had was a chair full of rumpled clothes. Hardly worth asking the guards to locker them for me.

"Here." Mac reached behind a partition and dropped my messenger bag and a backpack on the table. He passed me a long knife sheathed in a thigh holster.

Mai chimed in, "You've got MREs, iodine tablets, a first-aid kit, a thermal blanket and other considerations."

Figuring *other considerations* must be code for girly products, I nodded.

The knife got strapped on first. Shrugging into the pack, I clicked a thick strap under my breasts to secure it and looped my bag over my head. Weighted down and heart pounding, I was ready. Time to catch the Faerie Express.

Dawn was a hazy promise written in wispy lavender and blush clouds across the distant horizon when Littlejohn entered the conference room. The starched collar of his pale blue uniform shirt bent under the weight of wet blood soaking the fabric. Marks slashed across his throat. Not deep. Hairline scratches really. As though he had been swiped by the claws of death itself and lived to face the inconvenience of washing out the stains.

"Inmates are getting restless." He touched his throat when he caught me looking. "They smell blood on the wind."

Wasn't that a comforting thought?

"We should go." Mac clasped the guard's shoulder. "We appreciate all your help."

He gave Mac a respectful nod. "Whatever I can do, sir."

Mai shifted her weight, ducking her head when Littlejohn's gaze lit on her.

The guard turned on his heel and waved us after him. "Follow me."

We got the grand tour of the prison by accident. Whole sections were shut down and the inmates herded into the center of the institution for safety, meaning we took the long way around the block to skirt the locked down portions. The door Littlejohn led us through this time emptied out into the field. I spotted the windmill, the physical tether between this realm and Faerie, rising stark in the distance.

"Use these." He reached into his pocket and brought out two button-sized discs. "They snap on your collar. Activate when the metal receptors touch. We use them to see through glamour on the back forty where the earth fae in the work-release groups tend their gardens." When my brows crept upward, his voice went gruff. "We don't kill 'em till the paperwork says so. Until their expiration date comes due, they get all they need to survive. Dirt, air, blood or water, provided within the letter of the law."

Meaning they were given just enough to survive incarceration. Like Red and his pig-blood diet.

Until Rook smuggled me to the tether, I had never touched a toe to this section of the property. I didn't have the clearance for it. I visited the marshal's office every few days, so that was a non-event. The office where Mai interned was open to the fae public, as were the three other buildings surrounding the prison, but this was all new. My second visit to the prison in as many days and now this. Unrestricted access to what few Earth-born conclave employees ever saw and never without the proper documentation and a guide.

Mac and I each took a disc from Littlejohn, working the small pin backs through the collars of our underclothes before we fastened them. Metal clicked, and the burnt scent of an activated charm fragranced the air. Magical light flared behind my eyes, temporarily blinding me, and I hissed out a breath. "A warning would have been nice." Blinking away the negative image of the field with its bent cornstalks seared onto my retina, I parsed out the landscape beneath the glamour and took an unconscious step back.

Too afraid to point, I jerked my chin toward a winding path. "Those are…"

"Gargoyles," he supplied. "Flew in from the Washington National Cathedral in D.C. a few hours ago. They're settling in for the day. Long as you don't go poking at them you should be fine."

I counted six, all gray-skinned and menacing, each as tall as the guard and most twice as thick. The bulkiest resembled a ram, to his right stood a fish-like creature, and a very horror movie-esque rabbit sat on his left. Between them lurked a stout-jawed bulldog I felt zero kinship with, and behind it, nearest the windmill, a snub-nosed bat paced while biting into an apple. But sitting on the ground so close to us I could reach out and touch it with my toe was a humanoid...thing. It was nude and winged, but I didn't see it and think *demon*. Noticing my stare, it glanced up from a handful of playing cards. It sniffed the air once in my direction then went back to arranging its hand, but it was watching me too.

"Look all you like." Its voice scraped like boulders grinding. "But touching costs extra."

Mai blushed prettily, proving us both guilty of ogling, and the thing grinned at her with delight.

Littlejohn popped it on the back of its head. *His*, I should say. After all, he was very naked and sat very close and had no modesty at all. Let's just say whoever had carved his junk wanted to make sure his sex was never questioned by tourists passing underneath whatever arch or ledge he usually occupied.

The move would have broken my hand, but the guard didn't flinch. "Watch your mouth."

The gargoyle grunted and went back to its game, which I realized Littlejohn had been playing too when he withdrew a thin stack of cards from his back pocket, shuffled them around and slapped a few down on the cinderblock they were using as a table.

Mac eased around the guard and startled Mai with a brief embrace. "Be well."

"I will." Stiffly she patted his back. "Take care of our girl, all right?"

His gaze strayed to me and warmed. "You can count on it."

With the glamour removed, a stone-lined path became visible, leading from the rear door of the prison straight to the tether. The coming morning muted its subtle glow, but magic throbbed in the air above the rocks.

Mac set off down the illuminated path, and Mai snickered when I didn't immediately follow him. Too late she slung an arm across my shoulders and turned me on my heel. A hot flush of embarrassment scalded my nape when the seated gargoyle caught me ogling his crotch—*again*. But he was packing a granite cucumber, and it was just...*there*.

Mai led me several steps away from Littlejohn and the gargoyle. "Roll your tongue up, girlie."

"It's not like that—" I started to protest.

She shushed me. "Sizing up some gargoyle's stone salami isn't being unfaithful."

"Shaw is missing." I sobered. "I'm not going to find him dangling between a 'goyle's legs."

Mai's grip gentled. "He's going to be okay, Tee."

I nodded because it was easier to agree with her.

"I mean it," she said, missing nothing. "The Morrigan needs him to control you."

Steps lightening, I grumbled, "That's a happy thought."

With a lopsided smile, Mai flung her arms around me and squeezed until my lungs deflated.

"Watch yourself over there, okay?" Mai sniffled. "Best friends don't come along every day."

"I will." I hugged her back. "Hey, if something happens, tell Mom to cut you a check for the money she owes me. There's one made out to me on the dresser. Just tear it up or something. Use the cash to pay our rent through the rest of the year and to cover my half of the utilities."

She withdrew, brow puckered. "Money *your* mom owes *you*?"

"Long story." I shook my head. "Just do that for me, okay?"

"I'm not taking your damn money." Her delicate jaw set. "You're coming back and paying your own damn rent, damn it." She settled her hands on her hips. "Rent's due in two weeks. Remember that."

Two weeks was a blip of time, but I bobbed my head like I was agreeing. Across the way, Mac cleared his throat, signaling it was time to go. I wiggled limp fingers at Mai and stepped onto the path.

Nervous about walking the gargoyle-lined gauntlet stretching between the tether and me, I spent the next several minutes staring at the tops of my shiny boots as I kept to the exact center of the stone-marked trail. The other gargoyles appeared more animal than human, and I didn't want to know if their maker had overcompensated there too or if the mischievous, human-like 'goyle had gotten the long end of the...

Never mind.

Eager for a distraction, I inhaled the scents of the waking world and categorized them.

A pungent tang hit the back of my throat, and I slowed to identify the source. The walkway was packing heat. Far more than a standard glow spell required. I wondered if, like the gargoyle imports, the glowing path was a new addition. Or if Rook, with his glamour-shredding magical pipe, had guided me to the windmill down this exact way with such care I didn't stumble or bump any of the stones out of line?

Rook.

The closer I got to the tether, the harder Branwen's plea to save her brother tugged at my heart. She had kept me sane while we were trapped in Balamohan's caves, and I owed her for her kindness. For all the trouble Rook caused me, for what he did to my mother alone, he deserved what the Morrigan had done to him. But he wasn't evil, just self-serving and egotistical, and I wondered if Branwen could redeem him.

Ahead of me, Mac stood beneath the towering windmill.

"Almost ready." He flipped open a narrow panel fused onto one of the legs, and his fingers tapped out a complex sequence on a series of flat keys etched with glowing green runes similar to ours. It was almost, but not quite, what Rook had done. Mac's initiation sequence required more time, which was odd considering the tethers were his own work. I had figured he could speed dial them or something.

"All right." He waved me forward absently. "Stand inside the circle."

He checked to make sure I was where he wanted me then jabbed a final button before slamming the panel shut, stepping inside and tilting his head back to gaze up through the guts of the windmill.

A gust of air stirred a warm breeze that raised chill bumps of anticipation.

I wrapped my arms around my stomach and whispered a prayer.

Mac kept to himself, his knees loose and braced for impact, a smile twitching his lips.

Happy, I thought, to be going home.

CHAPTER EIGHT

I tumbled from everywhere and nowhere, consciousness scattering like dried leaves on the wind, blowing away thoughts before they formed. Twisting, swirling through a vortex of whirling reds and oranges and greens, I smelled crisp fall days and warm apple cider. The trip lasted forever and only a second before the ground rushed up to meet me, and my back smacked damp soil.

Air whooshed from my lungs, and when I inhaled, I breathed in Faerie's magic-rich atmosphere. I exhaled as the lush fragrances soaked into my bones, welcoming me back with breezy kisses from a stiff northerly wind and the warm embrace of the sun on my cheeks as though I belonged to this place.

Autumn, I thought. *We're in Autumn.*

Gnarled branches stretched skyward as if the trees were rousing for the day. Foliage rustled and songbirds trilled *good morning*. Of course, Faerie being Faerie, I spotted fanged slugs gliding up tree trunks, trailing glistening slime. A pair of green mantis chittered in conversation as they sprang from leaf to leaf decked out in teeny silk vests, balancing thimble-sized teacups so as not to slosh while conducting their acrobatic tea party. Not to mention the tiny clusters of squidgy mushrooms farting hallucinogenic spores into the air, because Faerie wasn't weird enough already.

Still, Autumn wasn't where I'd expected us to enter. We came and went through Spring last time.

Mac kept a den near here, though. This was where I first met him—as the saber-toothed cat, Diode—and where my odds of staying alive had doubled by winning him to my side. Except, being my father, he had been on my side all along. More or less.

I groaned. Thinking about Mac/Diode made my head hurt. Worse.

"There you are."

Speak of the devil.

I waved a hand. "Here I am."

"That's what I said." Mac approached from the south, stopping when he loomed over me. "How do you feel?"

"Like I rode the Tilt-A-Whirl after eating a fully loaded sausage dog with a funnel-cake chaser."

He cocked his head. "Was that in English?"

"I'm dizzy," I managed. "I have an upset stomach and might puke." *Puke*. Hearing the word clenched my stomach muscles. "How are you?"

Mac's expression, which seemed to say, *Fine, why wouldn't I be?* was answer enough.

Raising my head sloshed my brain around my skull and threatened to spill it out of my ears.

"Walking will help shake the effects." Mac reached down and clasped my forearm, lifting me onto my feet slowly. From a pocket, he produced a thin, reddish roll the length and thickness of my pinky finger and extended the fragrant stick to me. "Until then, chew this. It will dispel the disorientation."

Thinking it looked familiar, I accepted and scratched it with my thumbnail. "Is this tree bark?"

He nodded. "Cinnamon bark."

I rubbed it between my fingers, heating the wood and warming the oils inside until its fragrance burned my sinus passages. Huh. Guess my tolerance was increasing. My first trip left me head-blind, unable to smell or process what my oversaturated senses were telling me. This was an improvement.

While I chewed, Mac drew a penny-sized charm out of another pocket, dropped it and crushed it under his heel. Ears popping, I winced as all ambient noise vanished, leaving us in deafening silence.

"Forgive the precaution. The woods are full of spies." His gaze slid past my shoulder and back. "The Morrigan will have Unseelie patrolling the grounds near my den and guarding the door, I'm sure, but the grounds are warded and no other magical defenses can be set." He drew in a scenting breath. "Dangerous as it is, we must take the den."

I expected as much. "We need access to the Hall of Many Doors, right? That's your plan?"

"The Hall of Many Doors," he said, lips twitching with amusement, "is our only hope of finishing the job we came to do before madness takes your mate." He gripped my shoulder. "I know this is difficult, but I trust you to think with your head, not your heart."

I clamped my lips shut and nodded. I had a job to do. I would do it. And then I was going to find Shaw. The sooner we cut the Morrigan off from the mortal realm, the more pissed she would get and the easier it would be locating her feathery ass. Five minutes. That's all I wanted. Five minutes alone with her to…negotiate.

Hall of Many Doors, here we come. I had suspected each door operated its own tether, and Mac had all but confirmed it. Diode once told me they only worked for Mac and me, so the doors were useless to everyone but us. Using them, we could finish severing the tethers in a few days, I hoped, in plenty of time to find Shaw before hunger turned him feral.

Otherwise it would take days—if not weeks—to trek to each location and disable each tether.

Then again, maybe *useless* wasn't accurate. Just because the Morrigan couldn't operate them didn't mean she couldn't use them against us. Blocking our access to those doors would cripple our efforts.

"Wait—what about the tether we just used?" Behind us, a sagging bridge spanned a crevice that might have once been a dry creek. We'd landed near where its rotten planks began. "Should we start here?"

"Yes." A grin twisted Mac's lips. "You should."

"*Me?*"

"This is one of the skills you must learn. One of many I hope to teach you before…" Mac's jaw bunched, emotion hot behind his eyes. "If we are separated, it is imperative the work be continued."

Wiping my hands on my pants, I stepped forward. "Okay, how do I do this?"

Mac reached for me, and a strange comfort rippled up my arm when our fingertips brushed. His skin was warm against mine, rough where I slid my hand into his larger one. His palms were thickly calloused, reminding me of paw pads on the hound he once was and sometimes still pretended to be.

Leading me onto the bridge, he stopped when we stood balanced on the first rickety plank, and a spark of bone-cold energy froze my palm. His runes ignited against my bare skin, feeding me power.

"Tell me." He turned his head toward me. "What do you sense?"

With him ramping up my power, there was only one thing to feel. "Magic."

"Faerie *is* magic." A hint of a smile. "What else?"

I let my free hand hover over the splintered railing, and waves of subtle power caressed the underside of my palm. "There's a complex enchantment on the bridge." I squinted. "It's like a bluish-green net rolled into a tube. This end of the tunnel is wide open, and it's almost as tall as we are. The far end—and this might be part optical illusion because of our perspective—looks like it's six inches around."

His grip sparked brighter. "Anything else?"

"There's also a faint compulsion inlayed into the wood to help camouflage the bridge's magic." My gaze cut left each time I focused. It made distinguishing between what my eyes saw versus what my magical oversight perceived that much harder. "To deter the wannabe tether jumpers, I assume."

"Go deeper," he coaxed. "You're almost there."

Shutting my eyes, I blocked out everything except the pulse of energy flowing through the tether into us. "I see a flare of some kind. It's bright blue with pinpricks of white." I opened my eyes, and I knew. "Two planks up on the right, at the base of the railing, there's a compartment." I pointed it out like Mac was the blind one though it was his magic coursing through me. "The control panel, right?"

Seeming pleased, he nodded. "One step more."

I scrunched up my face. "The symbols...I see them in my head. I can *read* them." Shock pinged through me. "I see the coordinates for where we are and where we came from. It recorded our trip."

"You did well." He squeezed my hand once before releasing it. "Now, try it again."

The magic Mac lent me vanished the way it had come, leaving me off balance with a slight headache.

"It's gone." I sagged, almost too weak to move my lips. "All of it."

"You have seen the path," he said. "Remember it. Take it."

Blowing out a frustrated breath, I did as he asked. I shut my eyes and opened myself as fully as I knew how, so that each wisp of magic brushing my skin left its own faint impression. Even knowing where to search didn't make it easier. I turned my attention to the magical net cast over the bridge. The imprint was faint now, transparent, instead of the shining beacon it had been while I drew from Mac. Once the tunneled structure coalesced, I latched on to the tether's magical signature and followed the steady flow of energy through the complex enchantment to where it pooled above the second plank.

"I see the board, the switch." Eyes squeezed tight, I strained for more. "I see..." I growled under my breath, but the intricate runes failed to appear even as I trembled. "That's it. That's all I've got."

Knuckles rapped against the side of my head.

"Ouch." My eyes sprung open. "What did you do that for?"

"Think," Mac admonished. "Pull the knowledge from your memory."

Keeping my eyes open and on him this time, I reached inside my thoughts, to the place Mac's power had kindled. Specks of green flared in my memory. Delicate runes matching my hand—our hands—danced before my eyes in translucent waves over the bridge. Slowly, slowly, their meaning returned.

"Got it," I breathed. "How is this possible?"

"The mantle of the Black Dog is knowledge." Mac gazed out at the tether with me. "In an instant I was lifted up, transformed, reborn as the man you see before you. All that I knew was ripped from me as the collective knowledge of the sidhe nobles responsible for my gift wedged all that they were into me." His brow puckered. "My mind and body were broken to pieces before they were reforged."

I flinched. "That sounds painful."

A wry twist of his lips was his answer.

I studied him from the corner of my eye in the dappled sunlight, comparing our features and our magic, awed by him despite myself, waiting for the old anger to resurface, but it was slow to rise and easily shoved aside when it did.

Yes, he had hurt my mother. He was hurting her even now. But I was raised as a human, and it wasn't fair to hold Mac to human standards. Not when he obviously loved my mother, and not when his responsibilities in Faerie had been greater than any love he had for her...or for me.

I tilted my head. "Do you remember what it was like...before?"

"I do." A melancholy sigh escaped him. "I miss the simplicity of that life."

Another question came to my lips, but he hushed me as he would a child.

"Later, you and I will talk, and I will answer any questions you have." He drew himself up taller and rolled his narrow shoulders. "For now, we must focus on the task ahead. Time is running short."

Seven days—six and a half after our slow start—until hunger turned Shaw rabid. Bonded as we were, even raging in his incubus form, I was his only food source. The circuit he burnt into himself during sex with me meant he could be faithful. Had to be, actually. He was now dependent on me to keep him alive, a job I would normally relish, but finding him starved meant he might kill me.

"We've stood exposed too long." Mac scowled. "We need to sever this one and get moving."

I blew out a breath. "What next?"

"We find out if the Morrigan's fear is justified." He held out his hand. "You have to bleed."

Slapping my right palm into his, I grimaced. "I thought you might say that."

Metal rasped as he drew a dagger the length of my forearm from his thigh holster. "Look away."

He sounded exactly like Mom when I was about to get a finger pricked at the doctor's office.

"I can handle it." Swallowing, I uncurled my fingers and braced myself. "I'm a big girl." Sharp as his blade was, I still winced as faint pressure sliced open my index finger. "Freaking monkeys."

Blood rose along the seam of the cut, but none fell. The cut crusted over as I began healing.

"I was afraid of this." Mac sheathed his blade. "You heal almost as fast as I do."

"How do you control your bleeding for spellwork?" I wondered.

A chuckle slipped from him. "I keep a never blade I confiscated in a cabinet in my office."

Removing my left hand from his, I flexed the right, which was marked by my own never blade wound, and wished there was another way. I really didn't want to bleed out. "Can you remove the enchantment?"

"I can." He took my hand, palm up. "It's an original spell of mine crafted for the same reason."

"So you willingly cut yourself with a never blade often enough you had to figure this out, huh?" I watched as pink spilled onto his cheeks. "Yet you still can't heal the wound. Isn't that dangerous?"

"Unless another source of magic is introduced into our blood, interrupting our own, our gift mends us too quickly." Mac's expression turned pensive. "There are a few fae who have natural immunity to us. It was their blood used to spell the first never blades. It's a necessary failsafe that must be broken once in a while in order for us to do any good with the gifts we have been given, but as in all things, we pay a price."

Thinking back on the past year, I got an inkling. "Hobgoblins are immune, aren't they?"

"Yes."

"Redcaps too."

"Yes." His head lifted, eyes softening. "They are."

I was about to ask why he would let me go a few rounds with one of the rare fae who could hurt me, not to mention leaving him with plenty of my blood he could use as a focus object for dangerous spellwork later, but Mac pressed his palm to mine, and a pulse of searing pain dropped me to one knee.

Forget ripping off a bandage. This ripped off the top layer of my freaking skin, and I screamed.

Mac slapped a hand over my mouth until I could clamp my jaw shut and get it under control.

"The original spell grafts skin." His voice thickened. "The counter spell removes it."

So I was right about the reverse tearing off skin. Yay?

With a jerk of my chin, I signaled I could handle it. *Please, let me be able to handle this.*

Blood trickled from the neat cut, pooling in my palm until Mac fished a wad of cotton gauze out of his pack and pressed down hard. A flash of panic spiked my pulse. No matter how long he held it, the bleeding wouldn't stop, which was kind of the point. And yet...*gulp.*

"Now what?" I took over for him, applying steady pressure like it mattered. "The control box?"

"Whether you jump a tether to the mortal realm or ride it to another location in Faerie, all tethers are anchored by a physical object to keep them stationary. Otherwise, they would drift. This location is pinned by the bridge. The control box is an amenity I added so that others could adjust their coordinates and travel more easily, but that is the limit of their power. To sever a tether, you must locate its anchor, and then you must counteract the spell I laid on the object. To do that, you use your magical sight to locate the threshold of the entrance. Once that is done, smear your blood across it and use the Word unique to its location." Mac gestured before folding his arms across his chest. "Go on. You're bleeding too much."

Huffing, I did as instructed. I stared at the bridge, letting my sight go unfocused. As the shimmering net superimposed itself over the bridge, I focused on the thin weave forming a tunnel and followed the rim of the circular entrance down to the ground, where the magic hit earth and rippled.

I crept forward, wary of the energies lapping against its mooring. Once on my knees, I pocketed the gauze and let my blood drip in a line from one side to the other, then I smeared my hand over it to even out the drops and create an unbroken threshold. Nothing flickered. Nothing surged. Disappointment had me balling my fist, but when I twisted to glance at Mac over my shoulder, he gave me a pleased nod.

"Say the Word," Mac said patiently.

I scowled at him. "You didn't give it to me."

He jerked his chin toward the tether. "I shouldn't have to."

Great. He was testing me. Again.

Figuring the answer must be right in front of my face, I studied the net and then the control box, but nothing jumped out at me. All I saw were the coordinates. Mac wouldn't use those... Would he?

"Numbers aren't technically words," I muttered.

The snatch of laughter I caught told me I had guessed right. With my hand planted on the blood smear, I spoke the coordinates under my breath. Waiting until my leg muscles quivered, I shoved to my feet, faced Mac and threw out my arms. "I guess this means the Morrigan will have to eat crow."

All her scheming, all the people she had hurt, all for nothing.

My blood wasn't counteracting his. My counter spell hadn't kindled.

Shoulders slumping, I had to find a new bargaining chip if I wanted to get Shaw back.

His gaze strayed past me. "I wouldn't be so sure."

Wood groaned behind me, and I spun around in time to watch as the supports buckled. Mac and I leapt backward as the bridge collapsed on itself. Old as it was, magic was all that had been holding it together. When I cut the tether, the magic spilled into the ground and the ancient structure toppled.

"I did it."

I severed a tether.

"You did indeed." He sounded pleased. "Now, let's tend your hand so we can get moving."

Still reeling from what I had done, I drifted to Mac in a daze of possibility, and he clasped hands with me, pressing his runes against the hairline cut on my right palm. A whiff of burnt skin rose, and I growled viciously through the pain. He inspected the temporarily cauterized wound before humming low in his throat, seeming satisfied.

"There." He sounded apologetic. "That ought to hold."

I curled my numb hand into a fist. "How many are left?"

"There is one tether in Winter and one in Summer. Autumn and Spring each have two."

"So we have five to go."

And then it was time to find the Morrigan.

CHAPTER NINE

Mac drifted as silent as a wraith through the tittering forest, his boots picking familiar paths with confident strides that left me panting in his wake, trying to keep up with him. Leaves crinkled under my heels despite my attempts to muffle the noise. Prickling on my nape confirmed we were being watched, but I scented no one. Mac walked on, unconcerned, so I mimicked his body language, using false confidence as my shield.

Five tethers remained. One more here in Autumn. But first we had to secure Mac's den. Success meant we could make a quick trip to sever the tether and be done with this portion of Faerie. Failure meant we needed the tether active as a means of escape. In fact, I liked the idea of saving it for last for that very reason.

Figuring we were safe until reaching the den, I took in the sights. I hadn't had time before to admire the impossible collection of trees. Bald cypress, sugar maple and black tupelo trees brushed limbs in greeting while aspen, sourwood and sassafras stood alone. Sweetgum trees dropped tiny balls on the ground for us to roll our ankles on while towering longleaf pines provided spots of green amid all the reds, oranges and golds. As an added bonus, the trees produced pinecones the length of my forearm.

A burst of mischief hit me, and I punted one such pinecone at Mac. He glided to his right, and my kick went wide. The cone bounced twice before smashing into an aspen instead of his backside.

The impact startled a *caw* from overhead, and my blood ran cold. The urge to search the sky was a twitch in my neck. But I took Mac's lead and kept my eyes glued straight ahead and my head level.

Keep calm and carry on.

Ahead of us, a familiar giant redwood rose from the ground. It stood well over three hundred feet tall. Its reddish-brown bark had peeled in a few places. Handfuls of its spiked green needles had shed. Hard to tell if the damage had occurred when I led the hunt on a chase through Mac's living room or if the damage was recent. I hadn't seen the den after accidentally riding a tether via one of his doors.

Unfazed, Mac led on while gooseflesh peaked my skin, though his pace slowed until I caught up easily. He planted his feet as the wind changed, and the scent of wet feathers and musk hit my nose.

An eager gleam lit his eyes, and black-green power sparked in his palm. Together we tilted back our heads. Black bodies perched on the limbs above us, humanoid but covered in silky feathers.

"Aves," Mac growled.

Curious what the heck an Aves was, I glanced at him in question. Eyes tightening at the corners, he shoved me behind him. Or he tried to. I tripped on an exposed root and fell onto my hands and knees, spitting mad, ready to break him off a piece of my mind.

Then I saw them.

Aves.

Swarming.

"Oh crap."

Pain radiated through my shoulder. My face smacked into the dirt, and I spat moldy leaves. Talons pierced my back, wings brushed my cheek and hot breath blasted my nape. The dull scrape of a beak followed. A flash of bird-boy snapping my neck flickered in my head.

Not today.

Torquing my upper body, I threw all my strength behind my elbow, slamming it into his ribs. It squawked and flapped its wings, achieving liftoff and lightening the load on my back.

Bracing palms on the earth, I shoved up and yanked my feet under me. Bird-boy toppled with a grunt when I stood.

Static crackled over my skin, and I yelped when green light flashed by my foot, blasting clods of dirt into the air. I half-expected smoke to curl up from my boots. None did, thank God. My assailant, however, wasn't as lucky. He had been reduced to a heap of charred bones and vaporized feathers.

The almost magnetic pull of Mac's emerald gaze drew mine to him, and I gulped. "Mac?"

Intricate runes mapped every visible inch of his face and neck, including his scalp under his closely cropped hair. Symbols covered his lips. His eyelids, when he blinked, were also marked. This was the real Macsen Sullivan, the one fae whispered about behind their hands and feared crossing in the dead of night. This was the face of Faerie justice. Even in this, he maintained balance, the patterns symmetrical, carrying equal weight in proportion to the area of his body they emblazoned.

All this time I had been seeing him through a layer of glamour.

I stared into my possible future, terrified of so much magic owning real estate on my body.

"Thierry."

His voice snapped me to attention, and I cut him a sharp nod.

After turning a slow circle, I spotted three more scorched-earth marks left from where Mac had ended lives with a flick of his rune-stained wrist. Standing there stunned, I whooshed out a surprised breath when another bird-thing leapt onto my back. I spun toward the nearest tree and rammed my spine against the trunk until the creature's grip slacked, and I scraped it off me using the rough bark.

Staggering forward, I scanned the forest and then the limbs over my head. Both were clear.

"Are you all right?" Mac's voice rose behind me.

"Fine." I rubbed my shoulder. "What were those?"

"Aves—half man and half bird." He came to my side. "The Morrigan bred them herself."

Eww. I wasn't going to ask how that was possible.

"I counted seven bodies," he said. "Females mate with two males. That means two escaped."

"What about him?" I pointed to the one I had knocked unconscious. "Do we leave him?"

"We might as well." Mac dusted his hands. "The others flew straight to the Morrigan, I'm sure."

"Great." The giant redwood caught my eye. "She knows where we are and what we've done."

What *I* had done.

Confirmation from her spies ought to buy Shaw more time. Silver lining, right?

Mac walked to my side and stared out at his home. "We should get inside."

I grabbed his arm when he rocked forward. "How do we know it's not booby-trapped?"

"The den is more heavily warded than the grounds." A twinkle lit his eyes. "Why do you think she sent Aves?"

"They kept to the trees." I considered it. "That's why they attacked us physically."

"Aves possess no magic, but even if they had been armed with spells, they are useless here."

I fell into line behind him, watching our backs. I lifted my chin and drew a long breath in to fill my lungs. Burnt feathers and cooked meat stuffed my nose. A troll could be right behind us, and I wouldn't smell him. Given their diet, that was saying something. Generally, when a person had corpse stuck between their teeth, you smelled them long before they got close enough for a chat.

Rubbing my hands down my arms, I asked, "Do you think she'll try to stop us?"

"Not yet." He sounded resigned. "She'll want to see what you're capable of herself."

Great. Lucky me I wasn't one to suffer performance anxiety.

The Morrigan's ability to shapeshift into a crow meant she had a bird's-eye view for everything Mac taught me. Well, I hoped she enjoyed the show. My one-woman act would be coming to a tether near her soon. As an Unseelie, she must have set up camp in the Halls of Winter. Mac said there was a tether there, and she would be guarding it I was sure. The denizens of Summer were no less lethal, but after Balamohan, I was nursing a healthy...not fear...but respect for the Morrigan's ruthlessness.

The short walk from the Aves slaughter to Mac's den took no time. I kept an eye out for Aves or other fae loyal to the Morrigan, but it seemed we were alone. As Diode, the lock on the massive door had given Mac trouble. Thanks to the power of opposable thumbs, Mac worked his lock in seconds. I scooted aside as a three-foot section of the trunk swung open, and smoothed my fingers over the shaggy bark, tracing claw and teeth marks left from the hounds who had hunted me. With a shiver, I dusted my hands and sidestepped Mac. Entering his circular living room, I gave him space to heft a bar into place behind us.

While he fidgeted with the lock, I stood on a ratty woven mat and breathed. Tobacco smoke and parchment tickled my nose with a pleasing familiarity. His floor-to-ceiling shelves held tomes with gnawed spines, and broken knickknacks littered the floor. Chewed shoes and shredded paper huddled in corners, and the stink of urine near Mac's bedroom door made my lip curl.

I thought the hounds had followed me straight from here after I killed Prince Raven. Apparently, they hung around long enough to destroy everything they could get their teeth and paws on. Mac was lucky he left his other doors shut, or he might have lost everything. As it was, the place was wrecked.

"Forgive the mess." He nudged a broken ceramic owl with his toe. "I had no time to clean."

"You're forgiven." I chuckled. "Considering you were busy saving my life at the time, I'm glad you didn't stop to straighten up. It's not like you've been here since that day to do anything about it."

"Still—" he bent to straighten a fallen chair, "—there are rules of hospitality."

I snorted. "Have you ever seen my bedroom?"

He raised his head. "You have a point."

Debating whether I ought to be insulted by his swift capitulation, I rolled my shoulders. "Hey, I wash clothes. It's

the hanging-up-and-folding part I don't get around to. That's
half the battle, right?"

He hummed low in his throat. Not a disagreement, but an
acknowledgment.

A bumping sound froze us mid-conversation. Mac's head
swung left, toward his bedroom. Light sparked in his palm,
green-black and menacing. Power leapt into my runes, and we
stalked forward together. A quick hand signal indicated I
should open the door, and he would rush in the room to clear it.

Rolling my eyes at his mile-wide protective streak, I got in
place. Then again, if something had broken his wards and
gained entry, it must be nasty. Or really stupid. The hounds had
battered down the door, sure, but they were relatives of ours.
Magic was fluid, and—like me with the tethers—often a
familial tie was enough to break a ward or a spell if you had
finesse, were willing to spill your own blood and had enough
juice to power a counter spell. Maybe Mac's bum-rush idea
was smart after all.

Hand on the knob, I caught Mac's eye, flung open the door
and jumped back. The glow of his magic lit up the room, and I
glimpsed a shadow dart across the foot of the bed. With a
curse, Mac extinguished his energy and shook out the residual
sparks. He turned to me and sighed.

His hand flung out to gesture at a dark smudge on the floor.
"I believe this belongs to you."

Creeping forward, I let my eyes adjust to the darkness and
realized the smudge was a body. Not just any body, either.
Crap on toast. I crossed to him and knelt, gripping his chin and
lifting his face.

"Hey, Rook." Runes lit, I held them close to his face. "I
heard you were dead."

"I'm harder to kill..." he sucked in a shuddering breath,
"...than I look."

Most cockroaches are.

Sucking on my teeth, I caved. "What are you doing here?"

His answer was to roll his eyes up in his head and slump
forward, all but falling into my lap.

Great. Just great. This was all I needed. My soon-to-be ex-
husband passed out, drool sliding from the corner of his mouth,

bleeding from dozens of nasty scratches crossing his pale face and neck.

Really, was it too much to ask to be a widow?

Mac and I stood shoulder-to-shoulder at the foot of his bed, watching Rook flip and flop on the mattress. Sleep hit him hard once I cleaned him up and Mac scrounged together a meal for him. The hounds had eaten most of Mac's stores since his compact kitchen sat off to one side of the living room.

My foot jiggled. "How did he make it past the wards?"

"I invited him to cross my threshold, remember?" Mac sighed. "What's done is done."

With the hounds at our heels, Mac—Diode—whoever—had to act fast. He had allowed Rook in so that I wouldn't argue and waste precious time. Now it seemed I had compromised his den. *Go me.*

Hopeful as I was that was the only reason the wards reacted favorably to Rook's presence, I had to put it out there. "I was afraid it was the blood thing. You know—him being my husband and all."

"It was my first thought too." Strain registered on Mac's face. "But he used no magic to enter."

A chill whispered over my skin. "You don't think the Morrigan can use that bond too?"

He turned his head so our eyes met. "It's a possibility."

Fear crackled like ice over my heart. "Through that bond, her blood could null my magic?"

"I'm not sure," he admitted. "Our magics have similar roots. We are all death-bringers."

A low groan drew my gaze to Rook. "Do you think he'll die?"

Mac laughed. "No such luck."

Pressing my lips together, I wasn't sure if the answer pleased me or not. I could make Branwen happy by returning her brother to her, but should I set Rook loose in the mortal realm? I wasn't sure.

A firm hand dropped onto my shoulder, and I glanced at Mac.

"You must get this marriage annulled before we face the Morrigan."

Eager to be free of Rook, I gripped Mac's hand. "How does that work?"

Rook had tricked me into performing a barely legal marriage ceremony by dining with him on food he served me, wearing clothing he bought for me bearing his crest, and by changing in his bedroom. Part of me wondered if it could be that easy to break the bond. Say I cook for him, give him back his armor and...I don't know how to reverse the last bit. You can't un-flash a room where you've changed.

"You must go before the High Court and plead your case."

I groaned. "Are you serious?"

"They acknowledged the union, and they must be willing to dissolve it."

"No way is Daibhidh going to vote for freeing me from a union with an Unseelie. That was half their claim to the throne." My fingers curled into my palms. "Liosliath might agree to it just to piss him off, though."

Mac was nodding. "You need a majority, not a unanimous vote."

Hope sparked in my chest. "You're the tie-breaker."

"I am."

I grinned at him. "Can I assume you're going to vote for the annulment?"

"I would have annulled the marriage with a swipe of my claws had you let me."

I leaned my head against his shoulder, smiling when he stiffened. "I appreciate the sentiment."

Before Mac figured out where his hands went to make a hug work, I chickened out and shifted my weight, straightening before he got an arm around me. Awkward as heck, but it had felt right for a second, until we each had a chance to think about what we were doing instead of going with it.

Ignoring his hurt expression, I mentally added this newest item to my to-do list.

Sever the tethers. Annul my marriage to Rook. *Rescue Shaw. Get the heck back home.*

An odd feeling bubbled up in me. Relief maybe. Shaw and I had been willing to ignore my wayward husband and move on with our lives. The fact Shaw had claimed me first meant, to us, that Rook's marriage scheme was just that—verbal acrobatics—and he stuck one hell of a tricky landing.

At the time, yeah, I was grateful. I wanted to live, and playing along with Rook meant I not only lived, but I got to go *home*. Now our circumstances had changed. I wasn't the Unseelie princess, and I wouldn't become queen, either. I was of no value to Rook, and he of no value to the Morrigan.

We were square as far as I was concerned, pending the dissolution of our marriage.

I retreated to the living room, and Mac did the same, pulling the door almost shut behind him.

Feeling my internal clock ticking, I pressed, "Why do you think he's here?"

Mac shrugged. "Either he's a spy, or he had nowhere else to go."

"With the Morrigan ruling Winter, he may not be able to return home." It begged the question... "How long do you think he's been hiding out here? His wounds look recent, but they don't smell fresh."

"I would guess no more than a day or so for him to be half-starved and not acted on it yet."

I set my hands on my hips. "You're thinking he got himself trapped in here."

Thanks to the hounds, the cupboards were bare. He might not have expected that.

Mac nodded. "The Aves would have told the Morrigan he was here, if she didn't already know."

"And if he has fallen out of favor with her—and was injured—he made an easy target."

"I doubt even they would have been brave enough to peck her son to death." He shifted his weight. "But I understand if he wasn't brave enough to risk the woods in his condition to learn if that was the case."

I snickered at the thinly veiled insult. Very thin. Like tissue paper.

"Once he regains consciousness," Mac soothed, "we will find out what he knows."

My foot started tapping. "It will take a while for Sleeping Beauty to catch forty winks."

Mac started toward the Hall of Many Doors, grasped the handle, and a soft pulse of magic lit the room. Holding the door open for me, he smiled. "I have an idea of what we can do in the meantime."

A burst of adrenaline sent me scooting under his arm. "Where are we headed?"

"To Spring."

I rubbed my hands together. "I was hoping you'd say that."

CHAPTER TEN

Three hours later, I slumped in a wingback chair in Mac's office with my right leg propped on a matching floral footstool and a light-as-air cushion spelled with ice magic balanced on my kneecap. Cold muted the pain and the sip of brandy Mac offered took the edge off, allowing me to sit and rest.

Spring had kicked my butt. That season's primary tether was deactivated, but it had cost me torn ligaments.

Head tilted back, I stared up at Mac through blurry eyes. "So that's where you got the fur."

We had been ambushed by four saber-toothed cats the second our feet touched the ground.

Mac could hop right back into the tether and ride it to his den. Me? Not so much. The first time I used a tether in the Hall of Many Doors by accident, I found myself standing alone in Spring with no clue as to how I got there or how to go back. The doorway I had walked through vanished, and there was no door back. Without a physical object anchoring the tether, I was stuck unless Mac guided me.

And stuck had almost gotten me killed when the tigers decided we smelled tasty.

"Yes." He paused in his search for a charm of some kind. "Saber-toothed tigers in Faerie behave more like lions than tigers. The pride denning in Spring prefers the swampy area around the tether for raising their young. One of the older males became too weak to hunt for himself, and the younger males prevented the females from providing for him. Out of desperation, he snatched someone out of the tether and ate them. I was sent to put him down. He was such a beautiful animal, I kept his pelt."

I clapped my hands. "And thus the legend of Diode was born."

A dark flush rising in his cheeks, he cleared his throat. "How is the pain?"

"Fine." I gave my knee a test wiggle. "Another hour and I ought to be able to walk on it."

He bobbed his head, half-listening while searching drawers in the bureau by the door.

"Ah," he said at last. "Here we are."

He walked the tarnished amulet to me and placed the silver disc on my open palm. Flat and cool, it hung from a matching chain that coiled in my lap. I ran my thumb across the pale blue stone set in the center. Lilac veins flashed like lightning across the strange gem. I had never seen anything like it.

It also reeked of magic...and Mac.

I turned it over to examine the back. "What does it do?"

"It's a homing beacon I designed for myself when I was first learning to create and navigate the tethers. It requires a drop of blood to attune the spell to you, but it's better than a compass for getting you where you want to go." He leaned over me and adjusted my grip so my fingers eased into grooves on the sides of the circular amulet. "Grip it like this and speak the name of the place you want to go."

The ability to operate the tethers without knowing individual coordinates would help big time.

He stuck out his hand, ready to invoke the charm now. I tucked my fingers under my armpits and wiggled back in the chair. "Do me a favor. Wait until we tackle the next tether to attune the amulet?"

Laughing under his breath, he changed course and slid one hand under the back of my knees.

"Hey," I yelped. "What are you doing?"

"I hear my guest bumping around." He cocked an eyebrow at me. "I thought you would want to speak with him as soon as possible." He snaked his other arm behind my shoulders and lifted me. "If you would stop squirming, I could get you into the living room. Or do you want to wait in here until you're healed enough to manage the walk on your own? We both know this is no time for risks."

"Fine," I grumbled, snagging the icy cushion before it fell.

Being carried like a small child in Mac's arms blackened my mood. He was right. I wanted to speak to Rook—the faster the better—and couldn't afford to reinjure myself. By the time I put the screws to Rook, maybe we would have our first lead in finding and taking down the Morrigan.

After settling me on a wooden chair in need of a cushion and elevating my leg by propping it on a low bookshelf, Mac went in search of his guest. Sniffing the air, he skirted the bedroom and hit the kitchen. Murmured conversation drifted to me, too low to hear, and then they entered together.

Gone was Rook's hip-length hair. Chunks of it were shaved to the scalp and others were missing altogether. His usually grayish complexion—healthy for an Unseelie—had turned bone white. Thick, pink scars marred his handsome face. During the hunt, he recovered from a broken arm within hours. Those raised marks should have healed smoothly. Whoever had done this had marked him on purpose so he would not soon forget his punishment. This cruelty smacked of his Mommy Dearest, and I shivered.

My parents had issues, yeah, but this? His mother was whack-a-doodle.

I crossed my hands over my middle. "Sleep well?"

Rook ran a hand over his scalp, and clumps of hair came away in his fingers.

"I apologize for trespassing." His head lowered. "I had nowhere else to go."

"Were you expecting us?" As in, had his mother sent him to spy on us?

"No." He shook his head. "Last I heard, Macsen was still missing. That's why I thought I would be safe here. Thierry..." he shoved his hands in his pockets, "...I never thought I would see you again."

Unwilling to let myself soften, I snarled, "The Morrigan took Shaw."

"I know." Rook's head hung lower. "I saw him."

My heart beat hard once, and I wet my lips. "Where?"

"In my home," he admitted. "She kicked me out and put Bháin in charge of him."

A fraction of the tension left my shoulders. "That's a good thing."

"Thierry..." he began, eyes finding mine. "Bháin is a servant of Winter."

I rolled my hand to encourage an explanation.

"His people are only as kind as our current ruler demands they be." A frown twisted down his lips. "It makes them unpredictable and impossible to control. That's why Unseelie employ them—as a badge of honor—like breaking a wild horse and then riding it through the streets for all to admire."

The vise around my heart clamped tight. "He was good to Mom."

"King Moran was a good man," he admitted with a hint of reluctance. "My mother..."

"You *broke* Bháin. You're here, comparing him to an animal. Of course he's going to buck the system given half a chance." Fear lent me strength. "Will he hurt Shaw? Why does your mother want him? Leverage? Give me *something*."

"Bháin will do whatever my mother asks him to without qualm." Rook broke eye contact. "I doubt she'll have anything permanent done to Shaw, not until she has a chance to speak with you, to bargain with you."

"Permanent." I shoved onto my feet, wincing when my weight hit my tender knee. "If Bháin touches him, I will kill him. We've come too far for this—"

Mac skirted Rook, got between us and pushed until I toppled backward into the chair.

"Sit," he ordered. "If you blow out your knee again, that's another hour wasted."

Snarling under my breath, I shifted to get comfortable.

"No one survives Faerie without making contingency plans. The front door to his home isn't the only way inside." Mac angled himself to keep an eye on Rook. "There are others. He didn't use them because he knows his servant would kill him. Servants of Winter are proud people. Given the chance, broken or not, he could best a half-blood." Rook stiffened until Mac added, "That is not a slur, but a fact."

This explained a lot. Bháin was kind to my mother and polite to me, but he clearly hated Rook.

I understand completely.

"Is he right?" I pressed. "Can you get us into your home?"

After a short hesitation, Rook answered, "Yes."

Unconvinced, I rubbed my shin. "Will Bháin be a problem?"

"Once I'm back inside," Rook promised darkly, "Bháin will fall in line."

"Good." I gave Mac a weighted look then turned to Rook. "You hungry? Thirsty? Need to pee?"

The last option pinked his pale cheeks. *"No."*

"Grab what you need to entertain yourself and get back in bed." I flicked my hand. "Go on."

Moving stiffly, Rook gathered three of the gnawed-on books from the floor and twisted them to show Mac the titles, asking permission to read them. Once Mac gave the okay, Rook scuffled his way back into Mac's bedroom. He pulled the door flush, but didn't close it, so Mac did it for him.

Mac quirked his eyebrows. "Don't trust him?"

I scoffed. "About as much as I would trust one of those tigers with a baby púca."

Sudden pressure built in my ears, popping them. He had invoked another charm.

He scooped up and pocketed the broken remains. "This will give us some privacy."

I dropped my head into my hands. "This is too easy, too convenient, isn't it?"

"I had the same thought."

I peeked through my fingers at him. "No one is stopping us from severing the tethers. The Aves gave us a hard time, but the Morrigan could have sent worse. The tigers, well, you said yourself they often den near the tether because they like the swamp. We've been hassled, but not hurt. Not really."

Mac leaned a shoulder against the wall, his gaze tagging the door to his bedroom.

"Yeah, then there's that. He shows up on your doorstep of all places within a day of our arrival? He was tossed out on his can, but he happens to know where Shaw is and who is in charge of him? It doesn't ring true to me. Plus the fact he's the only one who can get us in? No. I don't like this at all."

A thoughtful expression crossed his face. "We must observe him and see what he does."

"He claimed Branwen was the reason he played nice with his mother. Do you think telling him I found her would win him to our side? Or—" this was more probable, "—do you think he was lying?"

"His involvement might have started as a means of finding a beloved sister, but he's moved past such innocent beginnings now. A taste of power leaves one hungry for more, and Rook is starving. A half-blood surviving in fae society for as long as he has is unheard of. Faerie shreds their humanity."

The hard edge in his voice woke my curiosity. "Is that why you didn't bring me here?"

"Yes." His tone gentled. "I wanted you raised among humans, and your mother wanted you raised without my interference, limited though any visitation with me could have been. She and I struck a fitting compromise. I hoped you would soak up humanity's kindness and wonder, their compassion. I wanted you to be true to yourself, to learn who you are and what you value, not conform to what this place would have made of you."

Compromise? The old me would have pointed out Mom didn't care what Mac wanted. He had left us, and even though she had forgiven him, she had done what she herself thought best for me. But he was kind of growing on me, and it was sort of cute he thought his opinion on my upbringing carried weight with Mom where I was concerned. We might have had our differences, but she was one hundred percent ferocious momma bear when it came to her offspring. Love affair aside, Mac wasn't her baby. *I* was.

Still, I womaned up and admitted, "I do wish I had gotten to know you sooner."

Mac's eyes shone, and he sat up straighter. "That means a lot coming from you."

"Yeah, well, don't let it go to your head," I groused. "I'm still a momma's girl at heart."

"As long as you have room in there for me," he said softly.

Heat creeping into my cheeks, I changed the subject before it got too touchy-feely in here.

"Rook must know what we're doing." I removed the icy cushion. "He hasn't tried to stop us."

Mac caught the cushion when I tossed it to him. "We haven't given him the opportunity."

Testing my knee, I found it held my weight with barely a twinge. With one last glance at Mac's bedroom door, I headed for the Hall of Many Doors, ready to go again. "Let's make sure we don't."

Mac and I didn't give Rook a heads-up before we ditched him, slipping back into Spring before night fell to finish the job of disconnecting its secondary tether. The lack of tigers was welcome. So was the lack of, well, everything else. The second tether was the one Rook had used to bring me here the first time, and I felt a twinge when the ornate arbor collapsed without its magical supports. But it had to go. With that done, we were left with three working tethers…and no sign yet of the Morrigan.

A burst of inspiration led us to make a pit stop at the remaining Autumn tether where Mac warded the ground to prevent anyone from using it until we returned. Once fae started catching on to our demolition streak, they would start checking each tether until they found an active one. Most couldn't operate them, and Mac would know instantly if anyone tried, but why take chances? Better to lock them away from the escape hatch than risk having to hunt them down in the mortal realm later.

Back at Mac's den, we tucked into a hearty meal Rook had prepared with supplies Mac had brought into the kitchen before we left. Rare as company was for Mac, he didn't own a dining table or chairs, so we made ourselves comfortable in the open living room while the chef fumed at being left behind and gnashed his teeth when Mac performed a spell to check the food for poisons and drugging herbs.

I found it hilarious. What did he expect? That Mac and I would trust him? Where Rook and food were concerned, I had zero faith in any good intentions. I would have refused the meal altogether if I weren't already hitched to the feather duster and reasonably sure that he wasn't after Mac for a triad.

Shudder.

"You never said why you're here," Rook said around a piece of meat.

No clue what it was, and yeah, no intentions of asking either.

"You didn't ask," I demurred.

He lowered his fork. "I just did."

I stabbed a hunk of chickenlike meat. "Can't a girl want to visit her father?"

"I thought you hated your father." His gaze zinged to Mac. "No offense."

Mac chewed thoughtfully on a potato in answer.

Enjoying needling him, I shrugged. "We have issues, but who doesn't?"

"Last I heard no one knew where you were." Rook studied Mac. "Are you back?"

"I seem to be." Mac stood with a smirk and carried his empty plate to the kitchen.

Conversation *over*.

"I heard you talking about tigers earlier." Watching Mac leave, Rook balanced his plate on his knee and reached for a cup of water on the floor. "Where is yours? I haven't seen Diode since you arrived. Shouldn't he be with you?" He sipped and smiled at me. "Or has he left now that Macsen is back?"

I took another bite to buy me a minute to decide what to tell him. "We left Diode behind."

Folded in a box in my closet after Mac wisely decided to retire the skin.

"We?" he echoed. "Behind where?"

"Thanks for dinner." I stood and gathered my dishes. "It was nice."

"You didn't answer my questions."

I paused beside him and patted his cheek. "I know."

His low growl amused the heck out of me. Growling in the den of the Black Dog? Precious.

I found Mac standing at a rustic basin functioning as his sink. *Indoor plumbing for the win!* Suds covered his hands from the dishes he was washing, and a smile spread across his face when he spotted me.

"Enjoying yourself?"

I held my thumb and finger as far apart as I could. "A little."

"Come here." He scooted over to make room. "I want to show you something."

"You want help with the dishes?" I puzzled. "All you had to do was ask."

He squirted a dime-sized amount of an opaque liquid into his palms and worked up a lather.

"No." He added a few drops of water. "It's time for your next lesson."

I darted a glance over my shoulder, but Rook sat right where I'd left him. "Should we do this now?"

"What I have to say, he already knows." Mac kept his fingertips and thumbs together, but spread the backside of his hand so a thin sheen of soap made a bubble covering the gap by his pinkies. "It's time you learned how to create your own *aer póca*. If you had access to your skins earlier, you could have shifted into a bird and flown away to avoid confronting tigers. This is a skill you must master."

"For one thing, I don't have a bird skin. For another, I don't want to die in some feathersplosion when I fail to master properly shaking my tail feathers and end up splattering my birdy brains on the pavement. I have the amulet now." It suited me just fine. "I could just *poof* myself back here if I get in trouble."

"You could," he agreed too readily, "but you're not a coward."

"Hey," I spluttered. "Knowing when to stand and fight and when to retreat isn't cowardice."

"No, it isn't." He blew air through the gap his thumbs made, and a bubble formed on the back of his hands. "But willful ignorance is." It burst, and he added more soap and water. "Don't be afraid."

"Easy for you to say," I groused. "The shape-shifting thing... I'm not sure I need it."

"Is your hesitation a morality issue? Or something else?" He tried again to hold a bubble in his hand and failed. "You have only to reflect on your recent history to see the value in mastering such a skill. It has already saved your life more times than it has cost someone theirs. I fail to see the issue."

"The skins remind me of where they came from," I admitted. "I can accept my actions cost lives to save others." I added softer, "And to keep me alive." I sighed, having trouble voicing the problem. "I worry it's getting too easy to hurt people. Wearing the skins, I feel the remnants of the fae born to them, and some of them aren't all bad. Or they didn't used to be. They made bad decisions, and their lives ended—by *my* hand—because of them." Shame washed over me. "It's like taking trophies, like I'm proud of what I've done and want a reminder, when it's not like that at all. Even the princes..." I took a shuddering breath. "I'm glad I'm alive, but I'm not glad they had to die to keep me that way."

Mac's damp hand landed on my shoulder. "You have nothing to worry about."

I scoffed. "If I start slipping, who is going to rein me in? Tell me no?"

"Shaw? Your mother?" He waited a beat and added, "Me?"

The grim reality that I would go right back to being fatherless when this mission ended slapped me in the face. A handful of days was all I got? Really? How was that fair? Just when I got to see the real Mac, he was taken away from me? No wonder Mom had left in a huff. I was starting to understand, I was starting to...I don't know...more than like Mac? *Crap.* We were bonding. How had that happened?

The bottom line was Faerie was his home. This was his life. He had chosen it over us once before, and with the realm in turmoil, I believed he would again. Even if he wanted to be with us—with Mom—this was bigger than one man's wants. It always had been.

"I guess," I managed through a tight throat. "So...you were blowing bubbles?"

His eyebrows slanted in a way that said *this conversation isn't over*. But he let me have my way.

Dampening his hands, he bolstered his lather and made another bubble cradled in his palms.

"*Aer pócas*," he began, "are fragile. They are magical constructs whose size is only limited by the power and imagination of their creator. Think of it as a closet that follows you wherever you go."

A memory of the red balloon Mom bought me at the zoo when I was five popped into my head. Probably the only reason I remembered it as well as I did was its tragic end. After spending all day at the annual carnival, eating funnel cake and playing games, I bumped into a clown and started screaming my head off. I'm not scared of much, but clowns? *Shudder*. To shut me up, he cranked up his helium tank and inflated a balloon for me, red to match my dress. All was right with my world until we left. At the car, a gust of wind teased the balloon out of the backseat, and Mom slammed the door shut on it. It burst, and wailing commenced. From then until I hit my teens, she would say *don't make this into a red balloon* every time I pitched a hissy.

I had almost forgotten about that fateful zoo trip. Mom's favorite scold had slipped away into memory like so much else after my magic kindled.

Sensing Mac's eyes on me, I cleared my throat. "It's not a portal?"

"No," he answered thoughtfully. "It doesn't lead to another place so much as it is another place."

"If it's basically a traveling air pocket, how are its contents invisible?" Or better yet, "How is it accessed?"

"Think of it like a soap bubble." He lifted his damp hands to get my attention. "Pócas are hollow spheres shaped by magic." He flexed his thumbs to show the seam. Cupped between his palms was empty space. Behind them was the wall of soapy liquid. A quick twist of his hands set the bubble floating into the air. Light hit the iridescent sides, reflecting a shiny green. "Easy does it."

The tip of his finger pressed into the flimsy side of the drifting bubble, and I braced for a *pop*.

"Huh." While I looked on, his finger pierced the film without bursting it, and I admitted, "I didn't expect that."

"This is how fae children are taught to make their first construct. Soap isn't required. It's purely a visual aid." He curled his finger and rocked the sphere onto his thumb, which he spread to show he could make a hole without rupturing the bubble. He gestured behind me at the sink. "Choose a cup."

I picked one he had set upside down to drain on a cloth. "How about this one?"

"It's fine," he answered distractedly. "Now—" he spread his fingers, "—set it inside."

Hesitant, I waited until the mouth of the bubble grew large enough for me to wedge the cup past his hand. It landed on its side, rolling back and forth, but the walls held, and I breathed out a, "Cool."

"Grab a knife," he instructed.

I removed the one strapped to my thigh. "Now what?"

He closed his fingers and got them out of my way. "Test it."

Jabbing the circle got me nowhere. The knife slid off like the tip was greased. "Very cool." I pursed my lips. "What if I want my cup back? Do I reach in and grab it like you did?"

"You can only access another person's *aer póca* when they themselves open it for you. No verbal permission will grant you entry. They are impenetrable except by their creator. That's what makes them the preferred storage method for fae."

With the construct between his hands, Mac returned to the sink and held it under running water. He turned back to me, seeming to hold nothing more than his cup. His arms extended in an invitation to touch, and I reached for the handle. My fingers bumped against nothing, and I smoothed a hand over the hardened sphere with a silly grin in place. It was a neat trick. One I wasn't sure I could replicate.

"What about making it invisible?" I rocked back. "And once it is invisible, how do you see it?"

"You overlay a modified enchantment similar to the ones your guards used." His voice went flat and cold near the end, probably remembering how Daire and Odhran had betrayed me to Balamohan. "See the faint glow? The spell was kindled with my magic. I can sense that, so locating it is simple."

Made sense. All magic bore the mark of the one who kindled it, like a fingerprint.

"How do you place it—or whatever?" I tilted my head. "You don't carry them around, right?"

"They're thrice charmed." He murmured a word and blew across his hand. The bubble lifted off and drifted in the air between us at his shoulder height. "Part of the spell buffers the sphere. Prevents it from bumping into me or other people and objects nearby." He raised his arm high, and the bubble drifted toward me. Again, he reached, this time with his hand, and it remained still. "Otherwise, we would knock our heads into them all the time. Most fae keep clusters for serving different purposes."

"I can believe it." Fae were always pulling things out of thin air.

Gesturing toward the sink, Mac stepped aside. "Are you ready to try?"

Anxious to hit the next tether but knowing it was smarter to wait until dawn, I accepted this was a wise use of my time. Pacing the halls wouldn't make morning come any faster. This distracted me from worrying about Shaw, mostly, which was a good thing, and these were skills I needed to survive not just Faerie, but when I got home. *If I got home...* So I said, "Yes."

I set my knife on the counter, dipped my hands into the water to wet them and then waited while Mac placed a dollop of soap in my palm. After working up a lather, I presented my bubble for his inspection. He braced one hip against the counter and let me get a feel for cradling the construct.

He gave me a nod. "The Word to solidify the air bubble yet keep it elastic is *buille*."

"Buille." The exterior walls of the bubble expanded until it filled the inside of my cupped hands. Maybe I was projecting because of where my thoughts had gone earlier, but the pocket felt like latex, like I was holding a balloon. It gave when I pressed down. Solid, but flexible. "Should it be this smooshy?"

Mac grinned. "I told you the charm keeps it elastic."

I squished it again. "Yours was solid."

"To you," he agreed. "Only the caster can manipulate the bubble."

"It's solid to everyone else?"

"And everything else." He tapped the domed top. "Objects placed inside can't pierce its skin."

"Good to know." I held it up to eye level, letting suds drip down my arm. "Pass me a spoon?"

"Live dangerously." Mac lifted my knife off the counter and extended it. "You won't break it."

Doing as he had done, I spread my fingers until there was space to slide my knife inside the bubble. It seesawed across the bottom until coming to rest. "Hey." I shook it. "I just realized I don't hear it."

"No." He chuckled. "You don't."

"This is wild," I marveled.

"Are you ready for the next step?"

"Sure." I balanced the bubble in one palm. "Hit me."

"The second Word is *eitilt.*"

I puffed up my cheeks, murmured the Word on my exhale, and watched the bubble drift upward.

"Very good." Mac cleared his throat. "You don't have to blow on it for the charm to activate."

My cheeks burned. "Oh."

Stifling a laugh, he reached toward the sphere to send it rolling. "Can you sense it?"

Again, the balloon analogy worked for me. A slender thread of energy had attached itself to my aura, and my skin prickled when I focused on the sensation. "It feels like someone is watching me."

Mac's gaze slid past my shoulder, and his jaw clenched. "That's because someone is."

I caught the sphere before it rolled out of reach and narrowed my eyes on Rook.

"I didn't mean to interrupt." Rook studied my work. "I came to put my dishes away."

A grunt slipped past Mac's lips. "I'll take those." He accepted Rook's plate, cup and utensils. "I will handle cleanup tonight since you were gracious enough to cook for us. We appreciate the meal."

Hearing Mac's dismissal, Rook exhaled and shuffled his boots as he walked back into the living room where I figured he had been eavesdropping. Not that I blamed him. Guy must be getting bored.

"The third and final charm is one I must caution you to use with discretion." He took his bubble in hand. "Invisibility charms have questionable legality in the eyes of the conclave, and I must agree there are more abuses for it than justifiable applications. The one commonly used for this works only on inanimate objects. Invisibility charms that work on living creatures require special permissions."

I mulled that over. It made sense. Hiding a precious object was a simple matter of security. Hiding a person? Well, that one was harder to justify. It was a recipe for mischief, as I had learned firsthand.

Mac waited for my nod of understanding then breathed, *"Imíonn."*

The cup vanished.

"Whoa," I whispered, reaching for his not-empty hand and touching a hard dome.

Dusting his palms, he rolled the sphere into the air and set it loose. I waved my hand between us and over our heads, but my fingers didn't find it again. I smiled at Mac when I caught him watching.

He gestured toward my sphere. "Your turn."

Pushing out a long breath, I spoke the Word. *"Imíonn."*

The knife disappeared while the drying, bubbly sheen of soap on my air pocket remained.

A smile lit his eyes. "Perfect."

I flushed, caught off-guard by the urge to hug him twice in twenty-four hours.

He cast me an indulgent look. "Would you like to transfer your skins?"

I rolled onto the balls of my feet. "You're sure they'll all fit in my pocket?"

Pocket, because the whole *aer póca* thing sounded way too pretentious for a magic bubble.

"Trust me." Amusement wrinkled his cheeks. "They will."

With wide eyes, I watched him pull the silky black pelt of my hound from his own pocket. Even knowing the trick, it was still impressive. He handed the fur to me, and I pierced the bubble with my fingertips, spreading the opening as wide as I could. It wasn't enough, and I growled under my breath until Mac set a hand on my shoulder and motioned for me to start pushing the skin through it.

"It won't hurt the pelt," he assured me.

Trusting him, I did as he asked and began feeding the fur through the hand-sized hole. Once the tip made it inside, a slight suction began, supporting the weight of the skin as it slowly and carefully devoured it. Unlike last time, there was no comforting window to see through. The pelt had vanished before my eyes, which was both exciting and worrisome. "Shoot. I forgot to remove the knife."

Mac turned it into a teaching opportunity. "Reach inside and think of the object you want."

When nothing happened, I clenched my fist. "Hey—Rook always snaps his fingers. Should I do that?"

"Theatrics." Mac shook his head. "You don't need to develop a crutch."

Crutch or not, it made for a cool effect the first time I saw him do it. *Okay. Focus. I got this.*

Sticking my hand in the pocket, I expected soft pelt but got cold air. I bit my lip, thinking of the trouble the pelt cost me. The memory of how it was acquired popped in my head, and fur pricked my fingertips. I caught myself before letting it ease out to slink down my arm and focused on my weapon instead. A slow blink later it pricked my palm. Twisting my wrist, I snagged the handle and removed the blade with a hum of satisfaction.

"Excellent." Mac removed another of my skins from his bubble. "Now try it again."

Easing the knife back through the hole, I called it to me and then returned it, practicing until Mac announced his satisfaction.

Moving my skins boosted me with a sense of triumph, and the hard work of learning a new skill meant I was exhausted when Mac showed me to a tidy guestroom I wasn't entirely sure had existed when we first arrived. Otherwise, wouldn't Rook have taken that bed instead of Mac's? Given how much living space he had already crammed into the trunk of his tree house, I wasn't about to complain about him conjuring one more room, especially not when it came complete with its own private bath.

Maybe Mai was onto something. There were perks to being a daddy's girl.

CHAPTER ELEVEN

Morning smelled like sizzling bacon, and I lay in bed listening to the clatter of pans and utensils in the kitchen. Eyes screwed tight, I let myself pretend the bed I was in belonged to Shaw, that I was at his place, that it was him—not Rook— humming in the kitchen while he fried breakfast for three.

But it wasn't Shaw. This mattress lacked the dip in his that made it hard to climb out of bed. Not that I ever wanted to when he was around. I inhaled again, scenting bacon when I wished it was the scent of bergamot and patchouli making my mouth water. A tear leaked from the corner of my eye, wet on my cheek. I wiped my face dry with the corner of my sheet. *Pity party, table for one.*

Shaw would kick my ass if he caught me curled up in bed, knees tight against my chest, fighting off sobs. Forcing my legs straight, I swung them over the edge of the mattress and let them dangle. I rubbed my shoulder where my bra strap had left jagged red lines. It couldn't be helped. My undies were all I had for sleeping. With Rook two doors down, commando snoozing wasn't happening.

Bare feet hitting the cool floor, I stood and stretched before snagging my bag where I'd hung it on the doorknob. While I dug through the contents for a stick of deodorant and toothpaste, I fought off a shiver. Tingles down my arms told me my air pocket floated nearby. Smiling, I relaxed my shoulders.

Brush. Spit. Rinse. Ready.

After climbing back into my armor, I strolled into the living room, murmuring my thanks when Rook noticed my entrance and carried a plate heaped with pinkish eggs, rolls and yellow-orange bacon to me.

I swallowed. "Um."

He handed me a cup filled with sweet-smelling purple juice. "Is something the matter?"

I balanced the plate on my knee and poked the contents with a fork. "This is safe to eat, right?"

"Of course." Rook crossed his arms. "It's only—"

"Nope." I waved my fork around. "I don't want to know."

Mac smiled between bites, showing me the food wouldn't hurt me without saying it outright. He seemed to tolerate Rook better now that the guy was cooking and cleaning for him. If Rook couldn't go home, he might have a future in domestic work. Strap an apron on him, and let the bidding begin.

A guy who cooked, cleaned and looked good while doing it? *Cha-ching.*

Unaware of my musings, Rook cleared his throat, half-daring me to try some of his eggs.

Hungry as I was, as little as I had fed, I didn't hesitate again before shoveling down the meal. Summer was on the docket for today, and I doubted very much they would be happy to see either Mac or me.

Reclaiming his chair from last night, Rook smiled. "Where are you two heading so early?"

I smiled right back. "Touring Faerie one season at a time."

His lips pinched. "You can tell me the truth."

"You speak it so rarely, I doubt you know how it sounds," Mac said.

Red splotched Rook's cheeks. "I am not a spy."

I bit into a crisp strip of...*not going to ask.* "No one said you were."

"I sensed the privacy charm you used last night." He accused, "You don't trust me."

"No, I don't." I leveled a glare at him. "You haven't given me a single reason why I should."

"I saved your life," he said in a quiet voice.

"You endangered it in the first place," Mac growled, slamming down his plate. "You have done nothing but lie since the moment you entered her life. Nothing but cause her pain. It is what I expect from ones such as you, but Thierry was an innocent. You dragged her into this world." His jaw bulged. "*You* wed *my* only daughter against her will, allowed her to run in the hunt in my stead to further your and your mother's ambitions. Why should she trust you? She is too smart to play the fool for you."

Blinking at Mac, I swore he was more pissed about the marriage than the near-death experience.

"You're right." Rook hunched over his plate and began picking at his meal.

A twinge of pity rose in me, evaporated by the reminder he was here and Shaw was not.

I glanced at Mac's cracked plate and the fork on the floor. "I'm ready to go when you are."

His decisive nod sliced through Rook's protest.

We rose, and Mac took my dishes with him into the kitchen. Alone with Rook, I tried to be nice.

"Mac has unspoiled books in his office," I said. "I can bring some out to you before we leave."

He pushed food around on his plate. "I could help you."

"As Mai would say, puppy eyes don't work on me. You don't know what I'm doing."

He glanced up at me. "Then tell me."

"Were you listening just now?" I hooked a thumb over my shoulder. "That whole speech?"

His gaze slid behind me. "I'm tired of being stuck here while you two pop all over Faerie."

I bit the inside of my cheek. I hadn't told him about the Hall of Many Doors, and I doubted Mac had, but Rook wasn't stupid. Me limping in dripping mud and feeling sweary didn't lend itself to supporting the theory we were holed up in Mac's office all day.

"You have no idea what we're doing." I tapped the end of his nose. "Let's keep it that way."

He caught my wrist, his eyes going sharp. "You need my help."

"Not yet I don't." Come time to infiltrate his home, sure. "Sit tight a little longer."

"I'm tired of sitting tight," he grumbled.

I broke his grip with a quick upward tug that shot past his thumb. "Then try standing."

Expression churlish, Rook settled into his chair as Mac rejoined us and raised a questioning brow.

I wiggled my fingers at Rook. "Tootles."

His lip curled. Bet he would be thrilled with an annulment right about now too.

Boots thumping on the floor, I headed for the Hall of Many Doors and zapped the doorknob with a pulse of magic. I held it open for Mac, earning me a wry grin as he slid past me, heading for a door we had yet to use. He let me do the honors, and we stepped out of cool darkness into the hot Summer sun atop a grassy knoll overlooking a round pond rimmed by cattails with thorns the length of my pinky finger.

My thigh muscles quivered, primed to run, and I fell back a step before forcing myself to hold steady.

"The Halls of Summer?" I squeaked. "The tether is out here?"

"No." Mac started walking. "It's *in* there."

I snagged his forearm, nails scratching his armor. "The Seelie aren't just going to let us stroll in."

"We aren't taking the front door." He angled away from the Halls and lengthened his strides. "It won't take the Seelie long to sense us, assuming the Morrigan's spies don't trip the alarm first." He glanced behind me, where a copse of sapling maples swayed, despite the absence of wind. "Aves."

Sure enough, black dots marred the newly green treetops like cancer, bowing the graceful trunks under the sentries' weight. Excited chirrups drifted to us, muted by the distance, but none took flight.

"Great." I had a bad feeling about this. "I guess there's no door number three?"

"This is it." Mac turned his back on them and walked on. "The others are too well guarded."

I fell into step with him, curious about the back door. The front entrance to the Halls of Summer led visitors through the pond into a round foyer with halls extending outward like spokes on a wheel.

Focused as I was on the Aves and tracking our location, I bumped into Mac when he stopped.

He caught my arm to balance me. "Here we are."

"I don't see—wait." I kicked a tuft of grass aside. "That's a hole."

"No." He reached over his head. "That is a tunnel."

I inhaled deeply and pulled the scent of fur and rabbit urine into my lungs. "Púcas?"

"Yes." He spread his fingers, and his hand vanished into an air pocket from the wrist down.

Summoning a rabbit skin, no doubt. "Those boogers get around, don't they?"

He hummed, distracted, and I used my magical sight to locate my own pocket. Once I got my hand inside, I thought about Rook dropping the poor, dead bunny at my feet and telling me to skin it, and its silky weight hit my palm. I withdrew it carefully, exhaling with relief that it was undamaged. The pelt was a faded baby pink shade like no natural bunny I had ever seen. I found it morbidly beautiful.

Mac examined the black pelt in his hand. "Do you know how to speak while wearing a skin?"

"Yes." I exhaled my jitters. "The púcas taught me."

His eyebrows climbed. "That's good. They're experts at it."

"Well, I'm not." I shrugged. "I managed it before, but I'm out of practice."

"Practice makes perfect." He placed the skin on top of his head, snugging it down until his eyes lined up with the dried slits where the rabbit's eyes once were. Black as the fur was, his might have been an actual púca pelt. My bunny skin was native Faerie stock, but not a sentient fae like a púca.

"Mac?" Aware I might never get another chance as good as this one to ask him, I rushed before the magic transformed him into a sleek rabbit. "Does it bother you wearing the skin of another fae?"

When I wore Raven's pelt, though he had been a hound when I killed him, I sensed him, like an echo in the back of my mind. It was damn creepy sharing that connection with him. I much preferred the bunny's residual thoughts on the flavor profile of dandelions versus ryegrass to Raven's seething hatred of his brother—and of me—but final thoughts seemed burned the deepest into any skin.

Seconds passed before he answered. "Skins are tools. You don't hate a knife for slicing open a throat. You don't refuse to use magic even when it might cost a life. Skins are like that too. You see them as the remains of the previous owner, but they aren't. They're nothing but flesh and fur, nothing but a means of doing our jobs. The memories... Those serve a purpose too. They never let us forget the cost of taking a life. Wearing them is meant to be uncomfortable so you remember who you are and never forget to remove it when the job is done, to put that tool away when you're finished."

Another sliver of guilt fell to the side. "I never thought of it like that—like any of that."

Placing the slinky skin on my head, I shoved out the thoughts bogging me down and narrowed my focus to a single goal. *Be the bunny.* All I needed was my concentration to lapse inside the tunnel. I would explode to Thierry-size while crawling through a tube six inches wide underground.

That would pretty much suck, and would be hell for Mac to explain to my mother.

Our daughter exploded in a tunnel in Faerie, but here's her spleen...

Forget him ever hearing the *L* word from her. She would be hurling *F* and *U* instead.

The heavy scent of damp earth seeped into me and sparked a tiny flame of panic. An hour ago, I had asked Mac if we were there yet. His tail hadn't even twitched. Hop-crawling through utter darkness, I bumped into him as he stopped to gnaw a root that had grown through the tunnel since its last use.

"My nose is cramping," I whined.

The reflexive wiggling reflected my state of agitation—like wearing a mood ring on my face.

"I see light ahead." Mac panted through a narrowing of the walls. "We're almost there."

Paws flying, I hustled through the tight spot and gasped when brilliant sunlight blasted me in the face. I shuffled forward, and the ground vanished beneath me. Tumbling tail over teakettle, I landed on a soft spot with a sharp *oomph*. Blinded, I tested it with my paw. *Oops*. The grunt hadn't been mine after all. "Sorry."

Mac slid out from under me while I blinked away the last of the darkness.

"Are you all right?" He sounded winded.

My furry cheeks heated. I wasn't *that* heavy.

"Fine," I grumbled. "Where are we?"

"Near the kitchen." Mac hopped several feet toward an arched doorway. "Stay close."

I fumbled my first hop-step. "We're not shifting back?"

"We're less likely to be noticed this way." I heard a smile in his voice. He reached the threshold and peered around the corner, scanning the hall left to right. "We also retain the element of surprise."

Flattening my ears against my head, I sank deeper into the pelt, hoping its muscle memory would let me keep up with Mac, who moved as if born to his skin.

Unlike the crystalline rooms surrounded by flowing water and filled with sunlight I remembered from my first visit to the Halls, this area had solid white walls with blue-and-white-checkered floors. The ceiling was translucent. Sunlight glinted off the polished surface, making me squint as I slipped on soft paws.

Ahead of me, Mac tensed as low voices echoed down the hall.

"Prince Tiberius should be made aware of the situation," a feminine voice cautioned.

"Aves are the Morrigan's creatures, Unseelie," a man scoffed. "They are no threat to us."

The click-clack of heels and steady cadence of soft-soled boots brought the pair closer.

Nose wiggling a hundred miles per hour, I shuffled close to Mac, ready to spring where he led.

The woman sighed. "You don't find it odd how they're skulking in the grove?"

He snorted. "Not when the Morrigan is rallying to become the next ruler of Faerie."

"She killed her own son for the throne," the woman mused.

"Rook was a half-blood," the man countered. "No better than the half-blood pup the consuls had chosen as *queen*." He managed to make my once-future title sound like *pond scum*. "There has never been a Faerie queen, and the old gods willing, there never will be. Let alone that feral Unseelie cur."

"Prince Tiberius would be wise to take the Morrigan in hand sooner rather than later," she responded.

"Aye, there is that." He blew out a long breath. "The longer he waits, the harder it will be."

Their shared concerns faded, along with the sound of their shoes, and I slumped against Mac.

"That was close," I whispered.

But he wasn't listening. His eyes were narrowed in the direction they had gone, and a quiet fury had taken root in his expression. I bumped my hip against his once—then again when he ignored me.

"They have no right to speak of you that way." The words slipped out, hard and cold.

"Faerie is one big competition. You're either Seelie or Unseelie, and that's that." I thought about it. "The only overlap is the half-bloods. Both sides seem to revile them equally. Instead of increasing the mixed population, you'd think fae would learn to keep their bits tucked into their britches, huh?"

Mac faced me, ears upright and round eyes serious. "You are my daughter, not a half-blood or a cur." His fuzzy rabbit lip twitched. "*My* child." He retracted his nails and lowered his head. "My father was right. War will come to our land and our folk. It is the fruit of hatred, and they have eaten of it."

"Mac..."

"I grow tired, Thierry. I can no longer prevent this. It is done. Faerie must bleed to be cleansed." His ears swiveled toward me. "The reign of the Black Dog has ended." He shook his head. "Saying it out loud... I shouldn't feel relieved." His emerald eyes, so like mine, pierced me. "I ought to feel—"

"You've been fighting this a long time. You aren't giving up. You're giving Faerie the chance to choose what's right for herself, even if she bloodies her nose in the process. You can still play a role in shaping the new political landscape, but maybe not by working within the High Court." I wrinkled my nose. "Don't take on so much by yourself. If you crave true peace and true freedom, don't force them."

He butted my shoulder with his head. "Should a child be wiser than their father?"

"Ask your dad sometime." I winked. "He's the one who explained it to me."

The Huntsman struck me as wise for a guy covered in mud with sticks in his beard.

Mac chuckled, scooted forward and let me catch my balance, then began hopping down the hall. He padded to a stop when the floor under our paws turned crystal clear. Water rushed beneath us in a dizzying swirl of colors and sound. Mac skirted the glasslike floor, leaping over a single six-inch tile to land on an opaque square in another bland hallway. Flexing my whiskers, I bunched up and leapt.

Lucky rabbit's feet don't fail me now.

I made the jump, botched the landing and skidded nose-first into the opposite wall. "Oww."

A paw landed on my shoulder. "Thierry?"

"Nailed it." Never mind the glittery carrots drifting in and out of my vision.

Nudging me with his shoulder, he got all four of my feet under me. Once I shook the veggies from my eyes, we set off again. Mac scouted ahead, leaving me to coordinate my legs well enough to keep up with him. With a wiggle of his tail, Mac leapt into a low, arched entryway and glanced back at me.

Rich and delicious scents rolled over me, and my stomach rumbled. "The kitchen?"

He nodded and lifted his head, inhaling in fast rabbit-nose twitches, ears swiveling. "This way."

We had covered the distance of four tiles when I heard a humming sound and froze.

My whiskers flexed. "Mac?"

A slapping noise grew louder then stopped abruptly. "What is that sssmell?"

Padding quietly, Mac eased under a low shelf built into a butcher block table on heavy casters. I followed, settling against his side so we both faced out and could see the person entering the room.

The scents of hot sand and scales hit my nose, and it stopped twitching altogether.

"Sssomeone has been in my kitchen." The fae hissed, "Thisss isss not to be borne."

Low as we were, I saw the cook's feet first. Veined and flat, they reminded me of scuba fins and smacked like flip-flops against the tile when he walked. The cuff of rolled-up white pants started at his ankles, and peering up at him, I took in the traditional chef-style top and the knobby green arms sticking out of the sleeves. He flicked his forked tongue between his lips, tasting us on the air, and my borrowed fur stood on end.

Bony knuckles covered in red spots dug into his narrow hips as the cook glared around the room through his round blue eyes. Like a birthday streamer blown too hard, his tongue whipped between his lips.

Hunched as he walked past, I startled when a drawer slammed over our heads. Dull thumping on metal rang out. Stirring the pots simmering on the stove? He grunted as he hefted a thick log onto the fire. It burned in a four-by-six-foot oval chamber built into the wall five feet above the floor with a tiled backsplash. Flames rose and magic siphoned the heat into the oven and stovetop without raising the temperature in the room. Mac used the same convection spell in his den.

A loud slurp and then a murmured, "The sssoup will do."

No one else was here except us bunnies. Lizard Lips enjoyed hearing himself talk…a lot.

Feet flapping on tile, he left in a snit, muttering about speaking with someone, which meant we had to speed this up before more company arrived. Giving Lizard Lips time to get out of range, Mac cocked his head, rotating his ears. A thump of his rear leg was all the warning I had before he bolted.

Clumsy as ever, I followed. He squeezed through a narrow gap left where someone had propped open a door leading outside. Into a garden maybe? Yep. After wriggling through, I popped out into a room with walls of glass overlooking the fields Mac and I had crossed to get here. Sun beamed down onto us through the transparent ceiling. My paws sank into rich, damp soil mounded in neat rows and spiked with growing things. This was every gardener's dream greenhouse. Even I was jealous of it.

Though it might have been the lush carrot tops sticking up that made me drool...

Man, I had to get out of this skin.

A thump of sound brought my head around in time to see Mac leap over a row of cabbages. Ears pricked, he stopped on the far side of the room, in front of the glass wall. I joined him without any major disasters, and that was when the design in the glass registered. Vines rose from the dirt floor to the ceiling, twining to create an archway. Etched with frosted morning glories, it made my heart beat faster. My gut clenched. This was it? This was Summer's tether? Integrated into the wall? *Oh crap.*

I had yet to sever a tether without the structure attached to it crumbling.

I loosed a slow whistle. "Is this as bad as I think it is?"

Furry shoulders lifting, Mac shrugged. "The etching was done prior to my anchoring the tether."

"Yeah, but an anchor pre-existing its tether didn't save the bridge...or the arbor...or the—"

"We have no choice."

"You're right." A shiver rippled under the skin. "Let's do this before Lizard Lips gets back."

"Lizard Lips..." Mac shook his head.

A pulse of magic swept over him, and I backpedaled as Mac—the person—burst from his pelt. I calmed my racing heart and thought Thierry thoughts until the subtle spell transformed me as well. A touch of Mac's fingers to my forehead made me wince. I reached up and felt the goose egg swelling.

"Don't worry about it." I swatted at his hands. "It will be healed up by the time we get home."

Home. The word lumped in my throat. Mac's den was nice, but it wasn't where I belonged.

Runes aglow, Mac extended his left hand. Jaw tight and lips numb, I clasped his with my injured one and stifled the scream rising up my throat when he tore open my wound. A silent tear warmed a damp trail down my cheek. I wiped it dry and set to work with shaking fingers, ready to be finished.

Leaving me to do the heavy lifting, Mac played gardener, examining each row of plantings until spotting a cluster of greenish-blue leaves. Long stems wreathed in tiny silver-colored flowers shot up from the center of the clump to tower above the plant's base. Mac knelt by it and started trimming.

Sure. Why not? These days Rook was cooking for us, and Mac was what—harvesting garnish?

My second sight hummed in my head when the magic surrounding us revealed itself to me. I let my eyes go unfocused and located the threshold of the tether before dripping a line of blood across it that I bent and smeared to cover every inch. Making a fist to slow the blood flow, I recited the Word unique to this tether, its coordinates, and braced for the fallout. Three rapid heartbeats later, I peeked through eyes I didn't remember squinching. Glass crackled and veins spiderwebbed up the wall.

Mac slapped our hands together, flashing new skin over my cut and making my vision blur.

A tinkling sound brought my attention to the widest crack. "Um, is it supposed to do that?"

Water pushed through the seams, pooling in the dirt at our feet.

"We're underground." His eyes tightened. "I didn't realize the river extended this far."

A millennia ago, when he anchored the tether, it might not have. Wait. We were underground?

Pause and hit rewind.

"This is all glamour?" I stammered. Some of it sure, I figured that, but all of it? Whoa. I grabbed him by the elbow. "We should go."

He fell back a step before yanking his púca skin from his air pocket. I still had mine clutched in my uninjured hand. Plopping the pelt onto my head, I tugged it in place one-handed to avoid staining the fur with my blood. A twist of magic caught me, swirling me down, down, down until chill water covered the tops of my paws and soaked my fur. Like a chocolate wrapper crinkling, glass crackled and water ran in rivulets through the garden. Backing away, I tripped over a fuzzy muskmelon vine.

"What isss that sssound?"

Belly exposed, I wriggled onto all fours as Lizard Lips charged into the fracturing greenhouse.

Mac leapt the cabbage, darted between the cook's legs, and shouted, "Run."

Lizard Lips stumbled over the muskmelons, arms pinwheeling, and his gaze shot from me up to the ruined wall. Round eyes bulging, he hissed at Mac, "Nasssty little púca, what have you done?"

LL vanished into the kitchen. I was hot on his flippers, and Mac was already ahead of me.

Damp paws sliding, I scrabbled across the floor. I yelped as an icy draft swept up my back and glanced over my shoulder. A cleaver spun on a chipped tile, and I was smearing a bloody trail.

What the...? *My tail is gone.* He cut off my freaking tail. Snarling low in my throat, I pivoted, putting myself right in his path. Fur lifted down my spine. Head angled low, a growl rumbled out of me. A body part was missing. *Gone.* Freaking monkeys. Who knew what I might have lost once I shifted?

The cook drew back his arm, and metal glinted. Mac's shoulder hit mine and sent us skittering.

"You're prey, Thierry," he snapped. "Act like it."

"Thierry," LL echoed. "That isss familiar."

Cursing under his breath, Mac headbutted me to get me moving.

Turned out all I needed to figure out how to coordinate my bunny limbs was a crazed lizard man wielding cleavers flip-flopping after me. He belted out a keening cry that brought more fae running.

"Kill the púcasss," he lisped. "They dessstroyed the tether."

Voices rose, and shouts rang out. Feet hammered the floor, rumbling tile under my paw pads.

I ran for all I was worth, retracing our steps, wishing I hadn't left blood behind that they could use as a focusing object for any nasty spells they wanted to design just for me. But at least my tail stub had stopped bleeding. The floor behind me was clean. It meant when Mac cut a sharp corner, I left no evidence behind. After my run-in with the never blade, I'll admit I was a tad nervous it might affect other areas of my healing abilities. This reprieve wouldn't buy much time—not with a lizard's sense of taste/smell—but it gave us the precious seconds needed to locate the púca tunnel we had used to breach the Halls.

Clambering inside the opening, I slumped against the moist earth and peered into the welcoming darkness.

"That was close," Mac said, already wriggling through the bottlenecked tunnel.

Flexing my stump, I ducked my head and squirmed to safety. "Too close."

Any closer to my rump, and LL would have been serving rabbit stew tonight.

CHAPTER TWELVE

My right butt cheek smarted when I plopped down in my chair in Mac's living room. The chilly cushion was under me, and my girly bits were numb. Thanks to the lizard man, I now knew that skin physiology translated almost exactly from pelt to person. As in, I lost my tail as a bunny. So I lost an ungodly notch of butt cheek as Thierry. The wound hadn't bled since leaving Summer, and the thick scab was about ready to flake off. I had no intentions of picking at it and risking an unfortunate scar.

Shaw would laugh his ass off when I told him.

A ribbon of doubt sliced through me that I might never get the chance to hear him tease me, and I sobered.

I would get him back. *Soon*. He was running out of time. Days were melting away.

Rook sat across from me in Mac's usual chair. He leaned forward, elbows braced on his kneecaps, watching me fidget with a pensive expression on his face. I glared at him, and he spoke, his voice whisper-soft, pitched low so Mac wouldn't hear us.

"Who did this to you?"

I started at the question, and then I snorted. "Like you care."

Fishing for information on where we had been and what we had done was more likely.

With a growl, he shoved back in his chair. "I can't help you if you don't trust me."

"Then you can't help, because I don't trust you."

"You need me to get your incubus back," he said smugly.

"It would be easier if you cooperated, but Mac and I can find our own way in if we have to."

"Tick, tock." He crossed his arms over his chest. "You'll run out of time being stubborn."

My eyes clamped shut, and I focused on breathing. In and out. Nice and slow. Strangling Rook, while oh so satisfying, wouldn't rescue Shaw any faster. Though being a widow versus a divorcée…

Shaking my head, I opened my eyes and grinned as Mac ambled into the room, papers in hand.

I scooted onto the edge of my seat. "Did you find what you were looking for?"

"I did." He passed me the topmost sheaf. "It's as I said, you require a majority vote."

Paper in hand, I skimmed it and groaned. "Oh joy."

The Seelie consul had seemed like the best bet, but shattering the tether had nixed that. If the Seelie had any doubt who was at fault, LL had heard Mac call me by name. No wiggling out of that blame. It left me one option—the Unseelie consul. He liked me marginally better than the Unseelie magistrate back home, which was like saying you would rather suffer a fork through your left eye instead of the right. No longer his princess, I doubted Daibhidh would be willing to work with me without some leverage.

"A majority vote…?" Rook echoed, eyes narrowing on the paper.

Seeing no reason not to tell him at this point, I smiled. "The honeymoon's over, darlin'."

"An annulment?" He shot to his feet. "You aren't serious."

"You lost the throne." I amended, "*We* lost it. There's no reason for us to be married anymore."

He grabbed my hand. "Except that I—"

"Don't even try it, feather duster," I snarled. "You never cared about me. I was a commodity, and my value has expired. If you have a single decent bone in your entire body, you will help me end this."

"You are here to fight my mother for the crown." He adjusted his grip and snatched the paper. "If you are successful, things can be as they were. You and I can mold Faerie. Together."

"No." I stood and faced him. "I'm here because this is the right thing to do, because if Mac and I can't stop your mother, then no one else stands a chance. People will die. Humans. Fae. Half-bloods. The realms will both be destroyed. I hate to break it to you, but your mom is a few feathers shy of a boa."

He bent closer, eyes cold. "She will kill your incubus if you try."

"I'm all out of tries." I jerked my chin higher. "I will succeed. Bet on it. Shaw is my future. Not this. Not her. Not you. *Him.* If she hurts him, I will put her in a box in the ground if it's the last thing I do." I flung out an arm. "Scratch that. I'll douse the box with gasoline, set it on fire and then scatter the ashes."

Rook shifted his weight onto his heels. "You really do love him."

Knowing it hurt him, even if just his pride, I told the truth. "Yes, I do."

Love for Shaw was heat in my bones, branded knowledge that when I was with him, I was whole.

"It's true then," he whispered. "You mated with him."

It was on the tip of my tongue to ask where he got his information, but Rook kept feathery spies scattered throughout the mortal realm. The fact he knew about Shaw and my reconciliation shouldn't surprise me. But it should have dawned on him before now that love was the magnetic force drawing us together time and time again. Then again, Rook might not understand what romantic love meant. Or any love for that matter. Had he truly set himself on this path out of love for his sister? Or had her disappearance merely been a perfect excuse to take action? I wasn't sure, my butt hurt, and I was too tired to argue if he puffed up his chest and took the indignation route. I had zero time for arguments.

"Shaw mated me, actually, last year, before he was reassigned," I corrected him. "He just didn't bother sharing the happy news with me until after you kidnapped me, almost got me killed and—oh yeah—married me against my will." I jabbed a finger in Rook's chest. "He was prepared to die rather than admit what he had done would bind me to him for the rest of my life. *That* is selfless. *That* is love. Stupid and misguided love, but he is a man, so I forgave him."

Rook blanched. "His claim predated mine?"

My gaze slid to Mac then back to him. "Pretty sure that's what I just said."

Tightness in his shoulders drew Rook straighter. "Then I owe him restitution."

A flutter of hope winged through me. "Does that mean we aren't married?"

"No." His lips twitched. "It means I owe him payment for the use of his...*mate*."

Blazing heat scalded my cheeks, and my jaw dropped. *"What did you say?"*

Mac drifted between us, bringing a cool breeze with him. "Calm down, Thierry."

Pissed as I was, I could have spat nails. Calm down. *Calm down?* "Bite me, Mac."

Over his shoulder, Rook settled a pleased smile on his face.

"He is baiting you." Mac forced me to hold his gaze. "You are better than this."

A roll of Rook's eyes said he disagreed.

Pivoting on his heel, Mac faced him, and Rook's smugness vanished in a pungent whiff of fear. I breathed deeply, protesting when Mac sidestepped into my line of sight. "Imply my daughter is a whore again, and I will prevent you from siring hatchlings indefinitely."

Shock immobilized me. No two ways about it, Mac was changing. Maybe I was a bad influence on him. Or maybe knowing his time as one-third of Faerie's High Court triad was coming to an end had freed him up to do and say what he wanted versus what he ought to. The stone-cold moral code woven throughout the legend of the Black Dog was unraveling, and I enjoyed glimpsing his flaws.

Temper barely leashed, Mac filled the role of a dad protecting his daughter from her bad-boy ex to perfection.

The impulse to hug him rose and fell in me. Opening up to him now would be a huge mistake.

His life was in Faerie, and once I had Shaw, I never wanted to see this side of the realms again.

Ready to diffuse the situation, I nudged Mac. "How do we get in touch with Daibhidh?"

Voice low and respectful, Rook feigned contrition. "He won't side with you on principle."

"Considering I just demolished an entire wing in the Halls of Summer," I parried, "I'm guessing Liosliath wouldn't spit on me if I was on fire. I need this handled before I—" I snapped my jaw shut.

"Our marriage..." Rook's eyes rounded. "Mother can use our bond to nullify your magic."

"Please." I snorted. "This can't be the first time it's occurred to you."

Mottled red splattered his cheeks. Even the tips of his ears glowed.

Crap. "You never connected the dots?"

"There's a chance she can't—" he hedged.

"I will not risk Thierry." Mac glowered. "Your union will be dissolved. Today. Right now."

He snagged me by the arm and started dragging me toward the Hall of Many Doors.

"Wait." Rook lurched after us. "I can help."

Mac hesitated, causing my eyebrows to rise, and Rook wet his lips.

"I researched the High Court's references on annulments and divorces after Thierry left for the mortal realm." He cut me an unapologetic glance. "I wanted to be prepared in case she found a loophole on the other side."

Mac changed position, lowering his shoulders. "I'm listening."

"The only way the High Court can annul a marriage without a full hearing—majority or not—is if both parties agree to the separation and if both are willing to swear while holding a truth charm that the marriage was never consummated." His words tumbled out faster and faster. "Only then can a simple vote dissolve a union." He stepped closer. "You need me. Let me go with you. I can help. Thierry?"

"You aren't worried about word of you helping me getting back to your mother?"

Old anger flashed behind his eyes. "She tried to kill me."

A comment about the world's smallest violin rose to my lips, but I kept my mouth shut. "Mac?"

"There are ways around it," he grumbled, "but his cooperation would count in your favor."

"Then it's settled." Rook beamed. "I'll go with you."

I put a hand to his chest. "Why are you in such a rush to be helpful all of a sudden?"

"Your incubus is starving to death," he said flatly. "Whatever you two have been doing is done. Otherwise, you wouldn't be rushing to find Daibhidh. No. This is the final step. You want to be free of any possibility the Morrigan can twist your magic through our union, and I want to be there when you kill her." The skin around his eyes tightened. "I want to know it's over. I want to see it myself."

I weighed my options. His sincerity when speaking of his hatred for the Morrigan rang true. The thing was, I didn't know if it stemmed from the loss of his sister, as he claimed, or something else. It was dangerous bringing Rook with us to the Unseelie consul. He might be tricking me—again—into doing what seemed harmless and beneficial then ended up hurting me to further his goals.

For whatever reason, I hadn't told him about his sister yet. Not that Branwen was alive, though I bet he knew that thanks to their matching charms, and not that I had found her or that I could contact her.

Something told me less was more when it came to how much information I gave Rook.

"Deal," I said before Mac changed his mind. "Grab what you need. We won't be coming back."

Let Rook think his reminder about Shaw had swayed me. Battles required cannon fodder, and as far as I was concerned, by pleading to join our mission, Rook had just volunteered for the position.

Ready. Aim. Bye-bye birdie.

Escorting Rook into the Hall of Many Doors and through a tether answered a few questions. Yes, others could enter the Hall if Mac or I opened the exterior door first. And yes, they could ride a tether as long as one of us opened the interior door, activating the tether, and shoved them through it.

I meant to ask Mac earlier out of curiosity and forgot. *Time.* There wasn't enough of it, not nearly enough, and I couldn't afford to spend precious minutes on questions that didn't matter with Shaw's hunger rising.

Goose bumps lifted on my arms when a chill breeze greeted us on the other side of the tether. A few leaves whirled around my right ankle, swept off the floor in Autumn. Ice crunched under my left foot, and frigid winds howled in that ear. A barren wasteland sculpted by ice stretched past infinity.

"Mac." I wet my lips, and ice sheened them. "This is Winter."

Okay, so it was the border, but standing here was asking for trouble.

Rook's lips parted, eyes wild, and I began to believe him about his mother wanting to kill him.

Mac raised a hand. "This is the farthest Daibhidh is willing to travel."

I jabbed Rook in the shoulder. "I thought you said consuls could project their likeness anywhere."

"They can." He sidestepped me. "I don't understand."

"Daibhidh is meeting us here." A cunning glint lit Mac's eyes as he removed a roll of parchment from his air pocket and tapped his temple with it. "Voices and projections can't sign paperwork, and a verbal agreement isn't as binding as blood. I want all traces of your bond to my daughter erased. It will cost me more this way, but I don't see a choice. The Morrigan is too powerful to take chances."

Except trusting Daibhidh meant taking a chance too when I suspected one or both of the consuls had orchestrated my running in the hunt in an attempt to lure out Mac. Not to mention the matter of a traitor among the magistrates back home. Out in the open, Mac, even as powerful as he was, was in danger in this new fae landscape, so eager to break the shackles he had lovingly applied to Faerie and her people in an effort to foster peace and understanding in the realm.

He was still powerful, but I had made him vulnerable, and his legendary neutrality was eroding.

"Okay." I toyed with the end of my braid to keep my hands busy. "When do you summon him?"

"I already have." Mac's gaze skated over the icy landscape. "He should arrive in a moment."

A pinpoint of black caught my eye in Winter, and I backed into Rook. His heavy breaths hit my nape, and I elbowed him aside until I stood shoulder-to-shoulder with Mac. Inhaling did no good. It was too cold, scents locked too close to the ground or stolen by the wind. Great. We were head-blind.

I squinted through the flurries. "Tell me that's Daibhidh."

Four more dots joined the first one.

"I knew it was a mistake to come here," a dry voice rattled behind us.

Startled, I spun around, left hand thrust out and palm glowing.

Faint green light illuminated a walking mound of black rags that hung in artfully tattered lengths like feathers. A gaunt face stared out at me, eyes black and merciless, lips blue and glazed with sleet.

"Easy." Mac clutched my wrist and lowered my hand. "It's Daibhidh."

"That's Consul to her." He sniffed, eyes widening on Rook. "I thought you were dead."

"Not yet," he muttered sourly.

"Stand out here any longer, and you will be." The consul shook his robes. "Follow me."

I spared one last glance behind us. A soft *chirrup* carried to me. "Aves?"

"What else would they be?" Daibhidh glared at me. "Stop wasting my time and move."

The shuffling figure hustled into Autumn on spry legs, and we three jogged to keep up with him.

"He's fast," I panted.

"One has to be if one wishes to avoid being caught," Daibhidh replied without a hint of strain.

His hearing is top-notch too.

As a stitch tightened my side, the consul glided to a halt beside a collection of boulders covered in damp moss. He strode up to the nearest, placed his palm on top of it and vaulted onto the next one.

He turned back, taking in our awe with a wicked grin. "Well, are you coming?"

Mac mimicked him exactly, but Rook closed his hand over my elbow and held me back.

"Does this look familiar to you?" he whispered.

A memory clicked into place. "No way."

Rook and I had tried to escape the hunt by climbing these very rocks. We got nowhere thanks to a nasty bit of glamour that made it seem as if we were moving when we had been stuck in an illusion while standing still—in easy reach of the hounds—the whole time. Daibhidh's rock had almost killed us. Now I wondered if that wasn't by design.

"I don't like this." His grip eased. "The consuls never show themselves."

As much as I agreed with him, I trusted Mac to get us out of this in one piece.

"We don't have much choice." I broke free of him. "Keep your eyes open, okay?"

His lips compressed, but he nodded and gave me room to make the first jump. By the time I reached Mac and Daibhidh, they were standing in the mouth of a cavern. My skin crawled as I picked my way to them. The spell messed with my vision and caused me to stumble where magical feedback interfered with my sight. Sparkles cascaded over Mac's shoulder, and I stifled a shudder.

I did not like this. Not at all.

Once Rook caught up, we entered the cave ahead, and Daibhidh sealed the glamour behind us.

I went to Mac's side and waited. "Will the Aves be a problem?"

"They are welcome to try the walls of my home if they wish." Daibhidh's robes swirled, tattered edges slapping my legs as he spun and headed deeper in the dark. "All tire of the climb eventually."

Rook and I shared a glance tinged with remembered frustration.

As much as I wanted to credit him with saving my life and cut the guy some slack, knowing him, he counted on it and was playing me like always. Warped as he was, kindness only confused him.

Speaking of confusing, I was stumped. Daibhidh's cavern left me scratching my head.

Past the rocky entrance, down a short and murky hall, the space opened into an enormous living room with a glass wall straight ahead. The décor was black-on-black-on-red, typical Unseelie tastes. The floor-to-ceiling windows, though, were an unexpected relief. At least until I remembered what I had discovered about Summer earlier, that their light and crystal was nothing but glamour and deceit.

"Take a seat." Daibhidh's hands flew over a series of hooks running down the front of his coat, and he shrugged out of his tattered fabric.

Mac gestured toward a chaise butted against the wall, and I sat. He dropped down beside me. He jerked his chin toward a chair several feet away, and Rook ambled there and took his place. With all of us seated, Daibhidh towered over us. Judging by his preening, he was enjoying presiding over our impromptu gathering.

"You requested a meeting," he began. "The noble Black Dog asks, and I humbly provide."

I kept my eyes from rolling. It was a near thing.

"You know why we are here." Mac relaxed against the wall as if Daibhidh's theatrics tired him. As long as they had known one another, perhaps they did. "Thierry would like her marriage to Rook annulled. We require a third vote, and yours is the one we desire. As the Unseelie Consul, you understand why we felt it proper to petition you instead of, say, Liosliath." A bland smile complemented his posture. "The Morrigan holds the throne, but she is not the rightful queen. My daughter is. If Thierry reclaims her crown, you would be wise to curry her favor."

Denial hammered at my lips, but I pinched them shut. I didn't want the blasted crown now that I was rid of it, but Mac had said *if*, not *when*. Mac was baiting him, and Daibhidh appeared willing to nibble.

Brows sloped in a scowl, Daibhidh glared at Rook. "What of him?"

"I want better for my daughter." Mac brushed my cheek with his fingertips. "Rook is not worthy."

"Agreed." Bobbing his head, the consul paced. "Two half-bloods do not a full blood make."

My lips parted on a snarl, but Mac tapped my chin hard, and my teeth clinked together.

"She must be freed from her…mistake…before proper suitors may begin courting her."

Rook stared at the ground, brow puckered. Playing along or deep in thought? I wasn't sure.

Daibhidh slid to a graceful halt. "Do you have someone in mind?"

"Yes," Mac said with conviction. "I do."

Knowing he meant Shaw gave me strength to play meek and mild. For now.

Fingers tapping his pants, Daibhidh mused, "Ultram, perhaps?"

A shrug from Mac neither confirmed nor denied the match to the sidhe noble who would be named the Unseelie prince upon my coronation.

"Oh, I like this. I like this very much." The consul's smile darkened, and he laughed. "The Black Dog caught in a lie."

Mac didn't as much as blink.

Daibhidh's amusement tapered. "Your daughter should be so fortunate as to land Ultram. He is the future of Unseelie House."

Mac still refused to rise to the bait.

"I know why you want the marriage annulled. The true reason. Not these—" Daibhidh made a fist and shook it, "—lies you bring to me. You want to level the field so that your daughter has a chance to survive the Morrigan." Spittle flew from his lips when he shouted at me. "I am not a fool. I know she has your mate. You are a mistake in birth and an error in the high court's judgment. You are unfit to rule."

A growl rumbled up the back of Mac's throat, and the consul paled but stood his ground.

"Watch yourself," Mac murmured, light pooling in his lap where his hands folded.

"You ask much." Daibhidh swallowed. "I will give you my vote, but I want something in return. I want you to promise me that if Thierry bests the Morrigan, that you will escort me into the mortal realm and grant me citizenship." He wet his lips. "The tethers are broken. All but two. I want passage before you finish the job." His gaze flickered to the ceiling. "The Morrigan can't cross realms to come for me if the tethers die."

This explained how we rated not only an in-the-flesh consultation, but a visit to his home. The woods crawled with Aves spies, and the Morrigan would have kittens if they reported Daibhidh had sided with us.

"No," I snarled. "The whole reason we're severing the tethers is to protect the mortal realm."

The consul's tapping hand stilled. "I will swear a binding oath to do no harm to mortals."

I glanced at Mac. "What does that mean?"

"If he gives you his Name—" Mac began.

"I will not give her my Name," Daibhidh blustered. "That is not what I agreed."

"I'm a conclave marshal." I pushed to my feet. "I will not break our laws to let you skate."

A hiss passed the consul's lips. "Not even if it costs you your life?"

I spread my hands.

The hiss turned to laughter. "Not even if it costs your mate his?"

"Shaw made me the marshal I am." I anchored my hands on my hips. "He would never forgive me if I compromised myself for him. It's a fast slide after the first step, and I won't be manipulated."

"Fine." The gaunt man fussed with his cuffs. "I will give you my Name to hold, Thierry."

Unease whispered over my skin. A Name was a high price for passage to the mortal realm, but I had demolished all but two tethers, and Winter's was next on my to-do list. Not that the Morrigan would let him use the tether—assuming he could without an assist from Mac. That left Autumn, which was our ticket out, and he must know that. Plus its wards would fry anyone who tried activating it without us.

Maybe it was a fair trade after all. What good was a Name if it next appeared on your tombstone?

I dipped my chin. "I want your signature on Mac's paper first."

Rook scoffed at the proceedings.

"I assume you have something to add?" Daibhidh's eyebrows climbed. "Well?"

Rook lifted his head, defiance glowing in his midnight eyes. "Thierry is my—"

"Branwen is alive," I blurted.

Between one heartbeat and the next, his righteous fury snuffed. "I—I never told you her name."

Digging in my pocket, I tugged out the conch-shell charm she had given me to call her with news of her brother's fate, and offered it to him. "She's waiting for my call. Play nice, and I'll let you do the honors."

His fingers shook when they brushed mine, lifting the delicate shell off my palm as though it were made from spun sugar and the sweat on his hands would melt it. He closed his fist over it gently.

"I release Thierry from our marriage." His voice grated. "It was initiated without her consent."

Shock that he accepted my word so easily struck me mute.

Eyeing the shell, Daibhidh stuck out his hand. Rook clutched his fist to his chest, shoulders tight and gaze dangerous, but Daibhidh only offered him a charm. "You know what I must ask you."

Rook held the charm on his open palm and enunciated clearly, "Our marriage was never consummated."

He passed it to me, and I did the same. Daibhidh nodded and took the charm from me. Mac removed the contract he had shown me earlier from an air pocket and slapped it into the consul's hand.

The consul, not to be outdone, removed a pair of surprisingly modern, wire-rimmed glasses from his own air pocket and perched them on his long nose before unrolling the scroll and reading it.

"This seems to be in order." He pocketed the glasses. "Does anyone else have anything to add?"

My head turned, seeking out Rook, but his knuckles were white and his mouth was shut.

Good boy. He was learning.

I clapped my hands together. "I think we're good here."

"Indeed." Daibhidh strode to a black lacquer desk and sat with a flourish.

While he prepped his quill and ink, I locked gazes with Mac, who gifted me with a slight grin.

We were okay. This was actually working. We would be ready to take Winter within the hour.

A dull thump overhead brought my gaze to the ceiling, from which plaster dusted into my hair.

Brandishing his quill with efficient strokes, the consul kept his head tucked until after he signed and sealed the scroll. He shot to his feet and slapped the roll hard across Mac's palm before turning.

"Come with me." Daibhidh circled my upper arm and dragged me. "I won't risk them hearing."

"Call if you need me," Mac said simply as he settled in to skim the document.

With his faith in me shining through, I straightened and jerked away from the consul. "Will do."

Daibhidh shoved me into a massive library and slammed the door behind us.

I spun a slow circle. "Where are all the books?"

Custom shelves lined the walls, carved with grape leaves and clusters, but not a book in sight.

"Packed," he grumped. "You can hardly expect me to leave them here, can you?"

I shrugged. "Were you that sure I would show, or are you that desperate to leave?"

"Both." He dusted an empty shelf with his fingers. "I feared you would turn to Liosliath. He was the logical choice." A genuine smile lit his face. "Then I heard you destroyed

Summer's tether—and half the Halls too. That meant I was the only choice you had left, and I finalized my preparations."

Another thud sifted dust into the air between us. I cocked my head to listen. "What is that?"

"Trolls I'm sure. They tend to act as the Morrigan's watchdogs." A grin formed. "No offense."

I returned it with a toothy smile. "None taken."

Eyes narrowed, the consul swept closer. "I will speak my Name once, and only once. If you fail to hear or understand it, the fault is yours, not mine, and you will be held to our bargain regardless."

"That sounds fair." Sarcasm dripped from my voice.

Unfazed, the consul leaned close, his chapped lips brushing the shell of my ear as he whispered. A burst of power fizzled through my ear canal and sparked through my mind as the Name was recorded.

The pucker of his lips told me he felt it register too.

A muted scream lifted the hairs on the back of my neck, and my gaze shot to the ceiling.

"We need to move." I darted past him and made a beeline straight for Mac.

His head was tilted back, gaze on the sifting dust. "Trolls."

"So I heard." I checked to make sure the consul had followed. "Now what?"

"The Morrigan is making her move." Mac tucked away my annulment. "It's time to face her."

I expelled a breath. "Why now? She hasn't bothered us this whole time."

Rook gained his feet. "You haven't tiptoed across the border to Winter yet either, have you?"

I scowled at him. "No."

"The Aves must have seen us leave with Daibhidh," Mac said.

"Yeah." I dusted off my shoulder. "I guess."

This didn't feel right. The Aves had watched us for days. Besides our first encounter with them, they hadn't tried to hurt us or stop us. They had watched and waited. So why throw trolls at us now?

I rubbed my face, wishing Shaw were here. Mac was great, but Shaw thought like me. He got it. I missed that, him being two steps ahead until I tripped him up with an angle he hadn't considered. As much as working with my father had taught me, I missed the way Shaw and I meshed on every level.

Nerves jangling, I turned to Daibhidh. "How do we get out?"

"There's an exit—"

An explosion knocked me onto my knees. Smoke billowed into the room, and I coughed against my shoulder to keep from sucking it down. Eyes tearing up from the magical discharge, I spotted three shadows.

A sharp inhale from one of the bulky figures. "Smells like feathers, it does."

"The Morrigan said to eat it," a deep voice rumbled, "and I will."

"It was I's spell," a third troll snarled, "and I get the first bite."

The air cleared, and Mac shifted to stand between me and the trolls. Palm bright, he shoved me toward Rook and turned to face our enemies.

"We aren't leaving you behind." I gripped his arm in one hand and Rook's in the other. *Move.*

Daibhidh darted ahead, and I lurched after him, dragging the guys behind me.

Ready or not, here we come.

CHAPTER THIRTEEN

The consul's escape route twisted us around and spat us out into merciless Winter. Thank God I had worn the spelled leather. The biting slap of frigid air stung my cheeks as I stepped from the protective stone tunnel. My lungs ached to breathe, and my eyes watered until a thin sheen of frost spiked my eyelashes. Behind us frustrated curses rose, and when I turned, black smoke blanketed Autumn.

"We had better get moving before the trolls locate the tunnel." Daibhidh gathered his feather-inspired coat around him. "We will reach the Halls of Winter before sundown if we hurry."

I put the question to my father. "Mac?"

Shaw was at Rook's residence. The Morrigan and the tether were at the Halls.

"If we fail to subdue her…" Mac's gaze lowered.

Then Shaw died either way.

A shake of my head rattled thoughts I didn't want settled yet, and I threw out an arm, indicating Daibhidh should lead. "After you, Consul."

Mac fell in behind him. Rook walked past me, and I let him go. All I needed was to miss something because I was looking over my shoulder every step of the way.

Our trek across Winter was aided by an odd trick of familiar magic. The more you dreaded reaching your destination in Faerie, the longer your journey took. The more eager you were, the faster it went. How it made adjustments for people traveling together… I had no idea. But I was eager enough for us all.

Not that I had a watch—or my cellphone—to check, but my internal clock was guessing the trip lasted two hours. That was it. That was all the space we got to mentally prepare, and it felt too fast.

To pin a name to it, I felt herded, rushed toward something I ought to circle before approaching.

No time.

Our ragtag quartet was all in.

A shudder rippled through Rook's shoulders, and his steps hesitated. "Here we are again."

Knowing he was addressing me, I stepped beside him and suppressed my own shiver. The Halls of Winter rose bleak and ominous from the frozen ground. Blocks of ice taller than me built the walls. Spindly turrets rose in three of its four corners, and a snow-dusted platform hung suspended from cables over a quarter of the exposed interior courtyard. Frowning, I thought the cables must be important somehow.

I craned my neck to glimpse the icy peak, but heavy clouds obscured the upper level. Guards strolled along the high walls, and each held suspension cables in hand. That seemed important too.

Rubbing my forehead, I dropped my hand when I caught Rook's eye. "Do you feel strange?"

A slight curl lifted his lips. "Is something the matter?"

"I feel like I've forgotten something. Like it's right there—on the tip of my tongue—but I can't find the words." I smoothed the gooseflesh from my arms. "I have the worst case of déjà vu."

"Thierry?" Mac, who stood several feet behind Daibhidh, twisted to face me.

I shot him two thumbs up. "I'm good."

He nodded and fell into step with the consul, and I nudged Rook back into motion.

They crested the hill first, and when they did, the ground shook beneath my feet. Jogging the last several yards, I had to swallow a smile at the sight of the only ogre I had ever seen. He towered over us, taller than anyone or thing I had seen in Winter. Snow dusted his gray-green hide, and his beady black eyes landed on me. A jagged smile cut across his face, and he chuckled, the booming sound rolling like thunder.

His voice rang out, and this time Mac answered him in words that held no meaning to me.

Scratching his chin, the ogre studied our gathering, then lifted his shoulders and knelt with a thud. I caught my balance before he toppled me, and that amused him too. He was in a jolly mood, and my gut knotted at how eager he was to help us. Shouldn't he be protecting the Halls?

Head up and shoulders back, I crossed to Mac. "Why is he so happy?"

"He heard you came to challenge the Morrigan." Mac kept his eyes on the ogre. "He says he will help us if you set him free after she is dead."

I swung my head toward him. "Why the faith in me?"

"You beat the odds once." Mac gestured toward the giant. "You won the hunt, and he respects you for it."

When the ogre extended his thickly muscled arm and flattened his curled fingers for me to climb aboard, I knelt in the crushed ice before him and touched the pad of his finger, which was wider than my entire hand. I called out to Mac, "Tell him he has my word. He will be free before the sun sets."

Or I would die trying.

Mac lifted his voice, and the ogre's lips parted, eyes widening as he understood what I had said. A long minute passed before he rumbled a response, and Mac came to my side and helped me to my feet.

"He says may all the old gods light your path, and though he is bound to this stretch of land and can't help except to carry us up the hill, that he will guard the fortress and keep out reinforcements."

Being the seat of Unseelie power in Faerie, I was betting the walls were packed to bursting with all the reinforcements the Morrigan would need to smear me across the cobbled pavers. But I smiled at the ogre and his stark hope that I might somehow survive this and that he might finally get to go home.

I prayed all of us were so lucky.

He made a grunt of sound, and we stepped into his palm. Daibhidh followed, sneering as usual, and Rook leapt as the ogre began lifting his hand. Apparently, he had no love for the Morrigan or her children. Who could blame him? Except for the novelty factor, or as a punishment, I couldn't guess why she would want to keep an ogre magically chained here.

That same prickling sensation crept over my brain as we rose higher, like I almost remembered something important, but it vanished, and I couldn't call it back. *What have I forgotten?*

Watching the scenery blur as he brought us to his chest height, I viewed the rut around the Halls with fresh eyes. The rise where we had stood and the fortress were of a similar elevation. The trench around the Halls, which looked steeper than last time, was a track the ogre walked, his steps digging it deeper and deeper over time. This was all he had, and my heart hurt to see him doomed to this fate.

"Steady." Mac put his arm around my waist before Rook got the chance.

The ogre's drumbeat steps pounded the ground, carrying us closer to the frozen fortress, but my gaze kept tagging those thick, black cables. Something about them was important. Why couldn't I...?

Oh. My. God.

Knees weak, I sank into the ogre's palm, gaped up at the sky and *remembered.*

"Dragons," I croaked.

Sleek lizards glided over our heads, metallic scales catching the light. Their heads were massive, their jewel-toned eyes faceted like gemstones. They flew in matching pairs. One set for each primary color. Enormous wings, filmy and delicate, supported bodies the size of school buses. A frilly spine made their tails flutter like streamers, and their massive heads sluiced through air currents.

Behind me Rook chuckled, and even Mac laughed as he sat beside me to steady me.

Head tilted back, he let his gaze soften. "They're beautiful, aren't they?"

"I can't believe I forgot." I shook my head. "I didn't think I could."

My first encounter with them came rushing back now that I was within the parameters of the forgetful spell cast over the dragons to protect the knowledge of their existence from those who might harm them.

Or free them...

Without warning, the ogre's hand began its final descent, and I tottered, falling onto my butt. His knuckles smacked the dirt with a thump that jarred my teeth. Mac hooked his arm under mine and hefted me onto my feet. *My kingdom for a Dramamine*. We leapt onto the icy pavers leading up to the main gate. Daibhidh and Rook hit the stones with synchronized thuds, jogging away from the ogre when he lifted his hands to dust them together. Folding his meaty arms over his massive chest, he indicated the enormous set of double doors with a jerk of his chin. I raised a hand in thanks and squinted ahead.

The way was clear. No alarms sounded. Guards on the walls continued ignoring us.

Not good.

"This is too easy," I mumbled within Mac's hearing.

"She's had time to plan," he agreed. "This will all play out as she imagined it."

Time? Try life*times*. Centuries of planning was about to rise up and smack us in the face.

The dragons earned one last glance before I tore my gaze from them.

Rook stepped beside me, swinging his arm out in a formal bow. "After you."

"Thanks," I groused.

And they say chivalry is dead.

"Rook, I can't believe I'm saying this, but stick close. Daibhidh, you stay with Mac." I smiled at Mac as realization dawned and his expression turned black and fierce. "You get to watch the show."

Green light burst from Mac's pores in a furious rush. "I am *not* staying behind."

"Yes, you are." I squared off against him. "You're the one she wants. I'm the one she'll settle for. I won't give her both of us."

His hands clenched at his sides. "The Morrigan wants—"

"Nope. Not happening." I went to him and stiffly embraced him. His arms rose to lock me against his chest. "She only needs one of us. Hang back. Please. I need you safe. You have to get Shaw home if…" My throat worked. "She won't kill me outright." *Probably.* "She needs me alive to bleed for her." I breathed in the scent of tobacco and parchment off his skin. "I can do this. *We* can."

"I am your father." Jaw tight, he kissed my hair. "It is my duty to protect you."

"Protect me by staying put," I begged. "As long as you're safe, I won't have to worry—about either of you."

His voice broke. "I would fight her for you."

Tears blurred my vision. "I know."

But if he picked this fight, she might end him permanently.

Breaking his hold, I stepped back and straightened my shoulders. The fortress loomed ahead, and a manic giggle caught in my throat as my boot heels crunched through ice on frozen pavers angled in a crosshatch pattern.

I tensed when Rook touched my shoulder and sang softly, *"Follow the ice brick road."*

Who did that make me? The tin man? The scarecrow? The lion? Ruby slipper girl? Her dog?

Keep it together, Thierry. Don't freak out now.

A pair of guards with dark eyes and black hair met us at the door wearing bland expressions. I scanned their faces, wary that Daire or Odhran might put in an appearance, but they were unfamiliar. Neither paid me any mind as they stepped aside and allowed us entrance.

The Morrigan was this confident she had me beat? We hadn't even started.

Anger warmed my belly, and I welcomed the burn. Mad worked. Pissed worked better. Anything beat the twitching in my fingers, the quiver in my thigh muscles. *No.* I would not run away from this.

I used to think fleeing Faerie into the mortal realm would save me, that I could duck my head and pretend I hadn't made promises to these people. Because of me, Faerie had been left without her ruler, and the worst possible candidate had seized control in that moment of weakness. I owed them freedom from the Morrigan, a chance to make their own decisions…without Mac. It was time for me to woman up.

"Are you ready for this?" Rook's smooth voice didn't falter.

"Are you?" I shot back.

"I'm tired of being afraid." His voice rasped, hand rising to touch a pocket on his sleeve. "I want to return with you, find my sister and…" He rolled his shoulders. "I don't know what comes next."

Prepared for his request to cross realms, I nodded. "There will be limitations placed on you."

He chuckled softly. "There have been all my life."

Ignoring the guards, I tugged on the thick iron ring used for pulling the door open and cracked it wide enough for us to slide through. Inside, the Halls remained unchanged. Arched doors. Black accents. Death as art. Flames licked charred logs in wide-mouthed hearths in each room we passed, thawing the mantles above them and melting the carved fireplaces. Puddles of water seeped over the polished ice floor, and no one seemed to care. Why they didn't use elementals or spells to prevent dripping was beyond me.

We walked until the main hall ended and we stood before a familiar set of doors. I raised my hand but hesitated.

"Thierry, dear, do come in," a throaty voice called. "I've been expecting you."

That's what I was afraid of.

OLD DOG, NEW TRICKS 147

CHAPTER FOURTEEN

The Morrigan lounged on a white chaise in the center of the massive room. Furs the color of the first snow in winter covered the floor, and her bare feet dug into the strands. Her upswept hair was as black as pitch, her eyes wide and colder than the edge of the universe. Despite the lavish setting, she opted for a simple ivory pantsuit with the jacket unbuttoned, similar to the black one she favored when cleaning up bodies for marshals in the mortal realm. The rest of the room was empty and bare.

Her beauty tugged something low in my gut that made me shift uncomfortably from foot to foot. This was where Rook got his killer looks. Her ageless beauty made them siblings instead of a mother and her grown son. When she crossed to greet us with a broad smile painted on her red lips, her eyes were level with mine. Dismissing Rook with a brief scowl, she clasped my hand, pumping my arm with all the enthusiasm of a politician lining up an unregistered voter on Election Day.

Not the greeting I expected. Somehow this one was worse.

She was playing human. Her speech pattern, her appearance, all fake. Stolen from observations made while in the mortal realm.

Looping her arm through mine, the Morrigan spun me back toward the door and lugged me into the hall. "I assume Macsen told you where to find the tether?" Her laughter tinkled like rain chimes. "Well, no more sneaking around for you. I will take you there myself. This way saves us both time."

"Mother," Rook said quietly. "Release her."

She pretended not to hear, her eagerness making me queasy as she kept me stumbling along.

Rook caught my opposite arm. *"Mother."*

"I warned you." Her sigh blew carrion breath against my cheek. "Goodbye, son."

She flicked a delicate wrist, and crimson motes left her fingertips, flinging Rook headfirst into the opposite wall, the one that was a football field's length away from us. He hit with a sickening crunch of bone and slid to the floor. The tang of Rook's blood hit the air, and I breathed in his fear and pain.

"What have you done?" I dug in my heels. "He's your *son*."

"Never mind him." She tugged on my arm. "We have pressing matters to attend to."

Numbness tingled over my skin. She had attempted to kill her last remaining son without a hint of remorse. She was a monster. No. She was death personified. The final gasping breaths of life didn't scare her. The blackness, the terror, it was simply a part of her identity. Too bad the rest of us weren't so lucky.

"Honestly, Thierry." She ushered me forward. "You didn't even like him."

"I—" I had liked him. Once. I just hadn't loved him.

"See there?" She patted my cheek. "You should be thanking me, really."

I take it back. All the times I wished I was a widow—I take them all back.

"You are too human for your own good." She tsked. "Come on. The tether is this way."

"Why are we...?" I shut my eyes. It didn't help. I still saw Rook's crumpled body painted on the backs of my eyelids. The Morrigan didn't seem to notice, that or she didn't care. "Why take me to the tether?"

"Why, so you can cut it, silly. It is the last one, after all." She sounded far too reasonable. "Well, except for Autumn, of course, but we'll have another use for that one soon enough, now won't we?"

Struggling got me nowhere with her iron strength. "You *want* me to sever Winter's tether?"

"Dear child, if I didn't want the tethers cut, I would never have allowed you to make it this far."

Stunned, I let her drag me. "You want Faerie cut off from the mortal realm?"

Cherry lips curved. "It solves so many problems, don't you think?"

Yes, it did. For us. Not for her. "I don't get it."

"I want what you want. Faerie cut off from the mortal realm. *Permanently*. Just think, with your blood at my disposal—" she squeezed me in a one-armed hug as we walked, "—I can finally make it happen. I can reinforce the threshold from the mortal realm, and no one will be able to cross." Mouth pursing, she shrugged. "Except for your father, of course, but Macsen ought to be dead by now."

"What do you mean?" I yanked my arm out of her grip with a force that stunned both of us. "What have you done?"

"I had to kill him." She justified her crazy. "I only needed one of you. I chose *you*. Aren't you lucky?"

Black seeped into the edges of my vision. "You're wrong. Mac is fine."

"No. He *was* fine. When you left him." She pursed her lips. "Daibhidh eliminated Macsen after you came inside. Witnessing such matters is traumatic to half-bloods. Your psyches are so…fragile."

"Daibhidh?" My mouth ran dry. "That's not possible."

He wouldn't dare. I had his Name. Magic spun through my brain when I thought of it. I reached out tendrils of awareness, brushing against nothing. Either the Name wasn't his, or he had fled too far for me to summon him with it.

Doubt swirled through my fingertips, making them burn as magic pulsed in my runes. The consul was on our side. He wanted out. Didn't he? Mac would know if we had been lied to, wouldn't he? Even if Daibhidh had turned on him, Mac could take care of himself, right? He was the freaking Black Dog of Faerie. One frumpy consul couldn't put Mac down. He couldn't die. It was impossible.

A calming breath sifted through me as reason trickled in past the frantic burst of panic.

Mac couldn't die. Not for real. Not in any permanent way. It *was* impossible. He had been killed dozens of times, and he rose after each. Even if Daibhidh succeeded, Mac's death wasn't permanent.

It couldn't be.

I wouldn't let it be.

"Who else would I mean? Honestly, Thierry, it's like you're not even trying."

The Morrigan was the voice of reason yanking me back from the edge of hysteria.

"I don't believe you." Fear coated the back of my throat. "You're lying."

"See?" She threw up her hands. "This is exactly what I mean."

Ten minutes max. I had been inside for ten minutes, and already our plan was shot to hell.

Sniffling at the insult, she fastened one of the buttons on her jacket. "Would you like to see proof?"

My head bobbled on my neck. "Take me to him." I had to see this for myself.

"First, I must insist you sever Winter's tether." She flashed a grin. "Then, sure, why not?"

Heat sizzled in my palm. "I want to see my father *now*."

"I was afraid you'd be difficult, but I was hoping you might surprise me. Oh well." She tapped a fingernail against the center of my forehead. "You can come back when you're willing to play nice."

My eyes rolled up into my head. Blackness descended, and I fell.

"There she is," the Morrigan cooed. "How are you feeling?"

My mouth tasted like rotten fruit and old blood. I had bitten my tongue. "Where is Mac?"

"Not this again." Her buoyant mood shattered. "He is *dead*."

Blinking away the haze covering my vision, I sat up and took stock of my surroundings. I was in the same hall where I'd collapsed. How long had I been out? Minutes? Hours? I shoved onto my feet.

Her shoulders tensed in expectation of a strike. I didn't give her the satisfaction of attacking. For one thing, it wouldn't do any good. She had knocked me unconscious with a touch. I shivered to think of what she was capable of when she set her mind to it. For another, my nap had done a fantastic job of clearing away the cobwebs. Mac was okay, even if he wasn't. Rook... I couldn't help him. He had known the risks and still chosen to swagger into the room next to me and put her threat to the test. It wouldn't help the guilt, wouldn't stop the nightmares—nothing did—but I knew what I had to do now.

This mission had cost us all too much to fail. I was going to see it through, and then I was going to pick up the broken pieces and pray that I could put Mac and Rook back together again once this was all over.

I dusted my hands and ran a palm over my hair to smooth it down. "Where is the tether?"

Her eyes widened. "Well, well, I should have knocked you unconscious sooner."

My lips bent in a brittle smile with jagged edges. "The tether?"

Hers warmed with genuine amusement as she strode past me. "Right this way."

The whole way there, she never once glanced back. I was trapped, and she knew it. So far below her concern, she had turned her back on me without hesitation. It was an insult, and my pride stung.

"Here we are." The Morrigan spun on her heel and stopped at the mouth of a new hall identical to all the others we had traipsed through.

I raised my second sight, and sure enough, the ambient glow of magic suffused a blue-green net. The mesh tube appeared anchored to a particularly ornate row of ice blocks inlaid into the floor. I let my vision go unfocused as hazy numbers floated in a slowly drifting string. I lifted my hand, and a pang hit me. Mac had done the spell to bleed me. It required finesse I lacked, but I had committed the Words to memory and had seen him do it so often I knew I could replicate the process. Even though I really, really didn't want to, I had no choice.

The tethers had to go. It put us one step closer to penning the Morrigan in this realm and protecting mine.

The fact that she wanted it too was troubling, but I would burn that bridge when I got there.

Murmuring the Word, I braced for the spell as it ripped through my skin. *Freaking monkeys, that hurt.* Woozy from the shock of pain, I wobbled toward the tether's shimmering threshold and sank to my knees in the center of the hall. Hand dripping, I leaned forward, and a tarnished silver disc slipped from my armor to hang loose around my neck. The amulet. Crap on toast. I had forgotten all about it.

Rook was unconscious, I hoped. Mac was...I didn't know. All I knew for sure was the Morrigan wanted my blood, which meant staying here was a Very Bad Idea.

Pushing out a tight breath, I smeared the threshold with my blood while the Morrigan kept watch with interest. Clutching the amulet, I soaked it in crimson to tune it to my aura. Under my breath, I spoke the Word to cut the tether in the same breath as I thought, *Take me to Mac* and lunged forward into the warped reality of the tether.

A bloodcurdling scream lifted behind me, and taloned fingertips dug into my shoulder. Magic swirled, sucking me down, disintegrating me as it struggled to fulfill its purpose and my will. My fingers and hands were misted nothings. The tether was collapsing with me inside it. Fear shivered through my insubstantial limbs. Twisting my head, I sank my teeth deep into the top of her hand until rancid blood coated my mouth and her shrieks muted to nothing as I vanished.

With a hard shove, the tether spat me out onto snow-covered ground. I backpedaled as a hand shot toward me. Magic pooled in my left hand, lighting my runes and making the ice glisten.

"Stop."

The power in the word choked the magic out of me. "H-Huntsman?"

Green light spilled over the brawny man's skin and glinted off metal beads woven into his bird's nest of a beard. He stood bare-chested and furious against the cold. Ice trimmed the cuffs of his leather pants, and snow dusted the tops of his boots.

Leaves rustled and twigs fell from his hair when he shoved a wide palm at me. This time I accepted it, let him yank me onto my feet before I shouldered past him. "Where is he?"

The Huntsman caught my arm, but not before a drift of crimson snow drew my attention, and not before my gaze swept over Mac's lifeless body, soaking in the gaping slice across his throat with dread carving my soul hollow.

"*No.*" My heart shattered for a man I barely knew but loved all the same.

"Look away, child." He angled himself between me and what remained of my father. "Don't see what you can't unsee." He pulled me against his chest and wrapped his burly arms around me. "Spare yourself the ache when there's no need for two hearts to break."

Hot tracks burned down my cheeks as I accepted his bear of a hug.

"I am destined to forever arrive too late." He clamped my shoulders after a moment and nudged me back a step. "Macsen's death summoned me, as it always does. I will carry my son to his resting place, and I will ward his remains. I will gather all those who would see him whole again, and we shall weep over his grave." He touched my cheek, collecting my tears. "He will rise on the seventh day, love. I swear to you."

Throat tight, I nodded. "Thank you."

"He is my child, as you are his." His gaze lifted. "What I do is my duty as his father."

They had talked. Of course they had spoken. Mac was his son in a magic-twisted, blood-but-not-blood kind of way. The Huntsman had known what Mac and I were doing, known Mac had accepted his death as a possible outcome, and he must have warned his father to claim his remains as quickly as possible.

An ear-shattering *caw* rent the air with its fury, and my breath hitched. With the amulet clasped tight in my palm, I reached for the magic of the portal behind me and found null space.

"It worked," I said, scarcely daring to believe it. "I severed the tether."

"Good girl." The Huntsman patted my head. "Though you are bleeding a trail."

Grimacing, I made a fist, knowing it wouldn't help. Sucking in a breath, I blew out the Word on a fast exhale, grinding my teeth while my skin repaired itself for the moment. "You should leave."

"The Morrigan is on the warpath, eh?" He grinned with pride. "Aye. I'll leave you to your fun."

Fun? Not the word I would have used. Horrendous death? Utter annihilation maybe?

"Wait." I kept my gaze low, too afraid I might see what remained of Mac. "Where's Daibhidh?"

"Dead," he growled. "When I arrived, the ogre, Tierney, had captured the bastard after he slayed Macsen. Tierney spelled the consul stiff as a nail and hammered Daibhidh feet-first into the ground."

"Oh." I swallowed the bile washing up the back of my throat.

Well, that solved the problem of what to do with him once we got back to the mortal realm. That also explained why he hadn't come when I attempted to summon him. He was dead. His Name held no power over him any longer. As far as I was concerned, he had chosen his end.

Bouncing on the balls of my feet, I shot him one last question. "What about Tierney?"

Severing the tether might have slowed the Morrigan down, but she was winging this way.

Huntsman squinted into the sun. "He's securing you transportation."

"Transportation?" I went still. "What does that mean?"

A throaty roar bellowed behind us, and I cringed.

"Oh, God." My palms went slick. "He's not serious, is he?"

The ogre plucked one cable among many, taking the dragon attached to it with him. A fierce blue beast with shimmering scales writhed in the air, fighting his grip on the bridle. He reminded me of a kid clutching a balloon in his fist. *Sheesh.* Childhood trauma, much? I had to let the balloon thing go. Ha. Let it go...because it's a balloon. *Crap.* I was losing my ever-loving mind. There were worse things in life—including the fact an *ogre* expected me to ride a freaking *dragon* out of here to safety.

Ground shaking as he walked, the ogre lumbered to us. He rumbled to the Huntsman then knelt softly and offered me the frayed cord. His eyebrows rose, and he offered again, frowning when I didn't accept it.

"He says he trusts you to come back for him," the Huntsman said thoughtfully.

My knees were knocking as the dragon landed, its serpentine head swinging toward me. Forked tongue flicking between scaled lips, he tasted me. The dragon huffed, blowing smoke from its flared nostrils. Of course he chose the fire-breather in the bunch. Gah. *Please don't barbeque me.*

A screeching caw jerked my eyes toward the fortress and the black shape emerging from within.

"You best get on with it." The Huntsman cracked his knuckles. "I can hold her off for a while."

His fingers stabbed the air, and he hauled a hulking ax that dripped eerie green light from an air pocket.

I wiped my damp palms on my pants. "How am I supposed to drive that thing?"

"You'll manage." His laughter rolled. "He's well broken in."

Whatever that meant.

The dozen yards I walked to the dragon were the longest of my life. It was massive, gorgeous, a nightmare brought to life, and it was my ticket out. With the tethers dismantled, it was either ride the lizard or roll over and give the Morrigan my belly. I liked my entrails where they were just fine, thanks.

"Good dragon." My hand shook when I reached for the cord and jangled the bridle. "Nice dragon."

I almost wet my pants when the ogre pinched my backpack between his thick thumb and finger, lifted me dangling into the air and dropped me onto the dragon's back between its sapphire wing joints.

Another squawk rose. I glanced over my shoulder as the Huntsman charged the Morrigan, ax swinging in cutting arcs. I hoped he knew what he was doing.

Tierney nudged the dragon until it climbed into his palm then he straightened to his full height. He eyeballed me while I held on for dear life. Testing the wind by licking a finger, he held us up in the breeze and then *he threw the dragon like a paper airplane*.

I screamed, and I screamed, and I screamed until nothing came out anymore.

Jerky grumbles rose from the dragon's core. I think he was laughing at me.

"Go ahead and laugh," I grumbled. "Not all of us have wings, buddy."

Note to self: Acquire skin with big honking wings.

What could I do? What was left? Shaw was trapped at Rook's house, and now I had no Rook to get me in the back door. I would have to face Bháin. Great. At least I knew for sure I could close the final tether on my way out of Faerie. One less thing, right? All I had to do was make it that far. Face cold, I narrowed my focus to my remaining goals. *Get Shaw. Go Home.* Branwen wouldn't thank me, but I couldn't risk going back for Rook. I wouldn't survive butting heads with their mother again. I was far from safe yet. I mean, sure. I had a dragon. But I had no idea how to steer him…or land him.

Vibrations shook me, starting between my legs, working through my core to rattle my teeth. The horse-size head of my mount swung toward me, and his lip quivered at what he saw over his shoulder. I was scared to look. I didn't want to know. My imagination was filling in the blanks just fine.

"You saved my bacon, Blue." I patted the warm flesh of his shoulder. "It's much appreciated."

A fleshy pink crest flashed up the length of his neck. Wait— was that a blush?

Palms damp, I clung to him. "Can you understand me?"

The steady bob of his head made my heart pound.

"Can you speak?"

He shook his head and lowered his crest with a resounding *snick*.

Hot damn. I could work with this. Maybe the ogre wasn't nuts after all.

A shadow spilled over me, blotting out the sun, and I gulped. Blue faltered, his great wings losing their rhythm. Tilting my head back, I cringed away from the Morrigan's talons. I melted against Blue's spine and buried my face against my forearm.

What did this mean for the Huntsman? For Mac? If the Huntsman had to choose between getting his son to safety or giving his granddaughter a head start, I was glad he had chosen to protect my father.

The dragon shied away from the Morrigan, but she rode his draft, her razor claws raking the length of one wing. He roared and twisted, his tattered wing flapping, ripped from her assault. She was going to take him down to get to me. I had to get off this ride, had to set him free.

Peering over his rippling shoulder, I soaked in the red and gold carpet blurring underneath us as we sped over Autumn. Blue's defensive maneuvers had nudged us clear into the next season. Miles in the distance, I spotted the green-spiked tip of Mac's tree, and my shoulders relaxed. The ground was heavily warded. I would be as safe there as I was now, and Blue would be even safer on his own.

"Take us there." I pointed into the wind. "The tallest tree. *Go.*"

A sinuous bob that rippled down his body was better than a nod for telegraphing his understanding. Seconds. It took an instant for Blue to slice through the air toward the den once given direction. Snorting, he flicked his whiplike tail and tagged the Morrigan's wing with a *crack* of sound.

She thrashed while spiraling toward the ground, but Rook had once mended a broken wing by shifting, which meant we had minutes to build our lead. Wrapping my arms around the base of Blue's neck, I clenched my thighs and tried not to fall to my death as he started his descent. Even before we reached the redwood, I saw the problem.

Blue landing in the clearing going this speed was as likely as me pirouetting on the head of a pin.

The fastest way in was straight down. The Morrigan had taught me that. There was one way off this ride, and it sucked. I had done this once before with Rook as a buffer. All I had to do was let go.

And then pray I wasn't impaled by a limb on the way to the ground.

"I really don't want to do this," I groaned. "Okay, fella, change of plans. Slow down as much as you can and get as low as you can. I will slide under you and drop into the trees when you get close."

He snorted like I had offered to bungee jump into the Grand Canyon using a hairband as a cord.

Heat flushing my cheeks, I demanded, "Do you have a better idea?"

One of Blue's limber front claws reached behind him, snagging my ankle and yanking me off his back. A scream rose up my throat. I clamped my hands over my mouth, digging my nails into my cheeks to keep it contained. Hanging upside down sent blood rushing into my head until my temples throbbed in time with my racing heart. My gut twisted into knots until the scream wasn't all I was having trouble holding down. I was going to be sick if he didn't get me right-side up soon.

Claw tightening on my ankle, Blue spread his wings wide, catching the air and jerking us backward. The landscape above my head slowed from a blur to distinguishable landmarks. Ones I would really hate to barf on at this altitude. With a sharp dip, Blue dropped into the canopy of trees. Limbs slapped my face, tore out my hair and lashed my neck. Another gust of wind blasted from his wings, and Blue hovered over Mac's tree. He rumbled at me, what I couldn't understand, and then...he let go.

CHAPTER FIFTEEN

The ground rose to meet me at an alarming rate, and I squished my eyes shut so I didn't have to see it coming. My shoulder glanced off a limb, and stars exploded behind my eyelids. Sprigs swatted me across the face, leaves slapping me as I fell. One branch struck me in the gut, and a year's worth of oxygen exploded from my lungs. That one, though, saved my life. As I clung to it, gasping for air, I first thanked God I seemed to have the same amount of holes as I was born with, and then I inched toward the trunk. Gripping the next branch down, I stretched for a foothold and swung myself lower.

The sooner my feet hit dirt, the better. There was no asking Mac if his wards extended up here or if they were embedded in the earth. I shimmied lower, breaking fingernails off in the bark. Splinters slid underneath the skin of my palms while I raced against the Morrigan. Gritting my teeth, I leapt the last six feet to the carpet of leaves below, tucked into a ball and rolled to cushion the impact. My form dissolved, and I flopped onto my back on the cushion of crinkly leaves to suck in a few *grateful to be alive* breaths.

A black shadow glided over me, cooling my skin where the sun had warmed me.

I flipped onto my side and shoved my feet under me. Ten feet stretched between the entrance to Mac's den and me. I rolled *that* far? Overhead, the Morrigan's anger reverberated through the trees. I sucked in air and ran. My fingertips brushed fuzzy bark as a wriggling mass smelling of damp feathers thumped into my shoulders. My head shot forward when a wing glanced off it, and my forehead met tree trunk with a dull thud. *Yowch*. Reaching behind me, I pulled out fistfuls of feathers until I caught one of her leathery legs and yanked her hard to one side before she pecked my nape more than once.

Larger than a horse, she had shrunk to fit into the clearing or I would have been bird food by now. Head spinning, I hated admitting she still wasn't trying to kill me. She couldn't yet. She needed my blood. Putting myself this close to the final tether was not the best decision I had ever made. She would peck at me until I collapsed or—even worse—she would regroup and drag Shaw into this. As much as it pained me, I knew what I had to do. I had to sever the final tether before she bullied her way through it. Mac was still responsible for setting the threshold into Faerie. Surely he could thin a section or set a new tether to get Shaw and me home? If not, he was about to make my room a permanent addition.

Not expecting my change of direction, the Morrigan rustled her feathers and cocked her head to see what I'd do next. *So long, safety*. I turned and bolted into the forest. More familiar with Faerie than I ever had been, it was simple to tune out the ever-present white noise and focus on the hum of the final tether.

I hit the tree line before the Morrigan blurred into action, shrinking yet again to match my speed. Jerking my head forward, I stopped watching her transformation and started looking where I was heading. Smashing into a tree—*again*—was not the way to save the mortal realm, Shaw or me.

My calves burned and lungs blazed as I pushed harder, faster. Weaving through tree trunks with low-hanging limbs slowed her down. It slowed me down, too, but I recovered faster.

The size of a real crow now, she pumped her wings in my periphery, her body shrinking to give her more speed. Cutting toward me, she flew right over my head and sank her talons in my hair, scraping my scalp and making my eyes water. I swung my arms over my head, not caring if my fists never made contact. It kept her off me, and that was enough. *Just a little farther...*

At last the final tether came into view. A perfect circle set into the ground, it was paved with stones in concentric rows to create a miniature amphitheater with three levels of seating, each ring dipping lower into the earth than the first.

Pulling up my magical sight hurt with my head throbbing, but I did it. I got all the information required to sever the tether then tucked my arms to my sides and ran. Agony stole my breath when I murmured the Word to reopen my wound. Immediately, warm liquid trickled through my fingers. I clenched my fist tighter and pushed harder. My nostrils were raw from sucking down the chilly Autumn air, and it felt like someone had taken an icepick and jabbed it into my side.

The Morrigan's cries grew frantic. She caught up, talons ripping hair and beak tearing skin. One frustrated grab left me clutching the small crow in hand. I flung her hard against a passing tree and watched her tumble to the ground, wings spread across the leaves and orange legs twitching.

Out of time, I slid into the amphitheater and began smearing blood across the threshold.

"No."

The sound of her graveled human voice startled me, and I forced my shaking hands to smooth faster. Her voice worked just fine when magically projected from her crow form. That she had opted to shift before confronting me told me the running was over.

One of us wasn't leaving here alive.

"I can't let you cross realms." Sitting back on my calves, I wet my lips and spoke the Word, the coordinates for this tether. Behind me, a fierce scream rose. I sat still until the snap of disconnection told me the tether was truly severed.

"There must be another way," she snarled. "You wouldn't have trapped yourself here."

"I thought you wanted me to sever the tethers," I taunted. "Well, you got your wish."

Her fingers speared through her hair. "You don't understand."

"I understand you killed my father." I stood and dusted off my knees. "You left me no choice."

"He will rise." At my glare, she amended, "Don't play coy. You knew this."

Her petulant tone left me cold. Had she killed Mac only as a matter of convenience? Did it matter? In the mortal realm, death was permanent. Humanity was fragile. Mortals didn't get second chances.

"What about Rook?" I challenged.

"My son is my concern." Her lips flattened. "He has survived worse and come out stronger."

Okay, so maybe she hadn't snuffed either out of existence, but murder was murder, and it was damn inconvenient. You couldn't go around killing people because you figured they would recover later.

Swaying from blood loss and exertion, I planted my feet to keep me standing. "Daibhidh?"

Her shoulders rose and fell. "He shouldn't have discounted the ogre."

A flicker of pissedoffedness ignited in me at what the consul had done. *Liar. Murderer.* He bought his death when he sided with the Morrigan. Now he had paid for his loyalties. His slate was wiped clean.

"You have ruined everything." Calm stole over her. "Centuries of planning… Gone. *Poof.*"

I folded my arms over my chest. "I don't get it. I figured you wanted the threshold erased."

"Erased? No. Try reinforced." She threw back her head and barked with laughter. "You thought I would share my Utopia with the dregs of Faerie? The mortal realm is flush with prey and ripe with potential. I would never have given away such riches so cheaply. It has been my hunting ground—mine alone—for more centuries than the length of most fae memories." She smoothed the hairs away from her face. "I grew tired of my leash. I wanted a clean break. I wanted to cut my ties to this realm."

Understanding made me grateful I had chosen severing the tether over saving myself.

"You orchestrated all of this." I should have suspected her sooner. "King Moran's death—everything."

Her lips curved into the sly kind of smile house cats wore after canaries went missing. She let the accusation stand, let me read what I wanted into her expression. Her silence answered loudly for me.

"Mac witnessed it." He confided that much to me himself. "That's when he went into hiding. To cover your tracks, you and Daibhidh blamed his absence on him tracking down the killer, which is exactly what everyone would expect him to do." It felt right, so I kept going. "Except you needed his blood. So when Mac vanished, you enlisted Rook. You sent him to fetch me, figuring it was win/win. Mac would either come out of hiding and turn himself in to save me once word got around I was here, or I would counteract his magic and you wouldn't need him anymore. You could bleed me dry instead."

"You're being dramatic again." She rolled her eyes with a snort. "You bled all over Faerie under Macsen's supervision and seem perfectly healthy to me. What difference does it make who pulls your strings?"

Rather than answer her, I fed her another line of thought.

"I bet you were surprised when Rook married me to steal the throne out from under you."

"I was," she admitted. "It required a level of cunning I never suspected he possessed."

"And you rewarded that cunning by attempting to murder him as soon as I left Faerie."

"If I wanted him dead, he would be dead. True dead. He proved himself a valuable asset." She shrugged. "I was willing to let him live, as long as he kept his distance. I could have used an emissary in Faerie."

"What about Daibhidh?" He was the logical choice. "What did he want from you?"

"The same as he no doubt asked of you." She smirked. "He wanted to graze in fresh pastures."

Uncertain what type of fae that made him, and equally sure I didn't want to know, I didn't ask.

"You plunged Faerie into chaos—into the war they'd been craving—so no one would notice the tethers had been cut until it was too late. By the time the houses finished fighting, the fae would have been sealed in this realm." I rubbed my forehead.

"You planned on bringing Macsen along so he could renew the threshold on the other side, trapping the old fae here and limiting your competition."

"If he hadn't gone to ground," she assured me, "I never would have brought you into this."

I scoffed, knowing better. "Yes, you would have. One way or the other. You can't control Mac."

Unruffled, the Morrigan inclined her head. "Perhaps you're right. It would have been so simple. I had no idea until you became a marshal that he even had a daughter. Oh, I wondered what his ties were to the mortal realm, but I didn't know. No one did. Then the king died, and I knew Macsen would run to you."

I battled against the grief I had caused him. Mac had known the Morrigan would target me when he vanished. He had been in Wink, masquerading as Diode, watching over me and waiting, since King Moran died.

"Moran didn't die," I reminded her. He had help. "You killed him."

"His death was a small price." She waved her hand. "Think of it. *Me.* Living where and how I choose. No more being yanked back across realms after completing a summons. No more waiting for the dinner bell to ring. I could have fed without compunction. I would have been...free."

"*Free?* Why should I care about your dreams of freedom?" My voice lowered to a growl. "What about all the death-touched fae you kept imprisoned in the caves? *What about me?* Daire and Odhran delivered me to Balamohan on your orders."

"That was the one right thing they did," she sneered.

Her vehemence surprised me. "What do you mean?"

"They took the charmed portals I gifted them and vanished. They haven't returned to Faerie."

I laughed in her face. "Betrayers through and through then."

"I see nothing amusing in the matter, and when they are discovered, their insolence will be punished."

"You don't get it, do you? Is it really so amazing that your followers aren't loyal? That they would ditch your special brand of crazy the first chance they got? It's more shocking to me that any stick around at all." I marveled at her gall.

"Balamohan feasted on your daughter, and you allowed it to happen. If you would do that to your own child, then what wouldn't you do to anyone else?"

"Branwen made her decision." The Morrigan's face blanked. "She chose her selkie over me."

I sucked on my teeth. "With a mother like you, I can't imagine why."

Maybe the rift between mother and daughter had nothing to do with Branwen choosing her lover over her family and everything to do with her ability to leave Faerie for the mortal realm without repercussions. She could have lived a good life with Dónal if her mother hadn't sent Balamohan to acquire her for his death fae menagerie.

Now the jailed fae made more sense. The Morrigan had tasked fae like Balamohan and others to gather her a food source large enough she could survive in the mortal realm without being noticed. The mass murder of humans would paint a mark between her shoulders. Fae weren't anxious to come out of the closet to humanity, and they wouldn't thank her for exposing them. Unless she turned on her own kind first...

A spate of fresh kills would expose her location to the conclave before she cemented her base of power, but the methodical abduction of fae over centuries? Well, that was harder to trace. She had cultivated the means to sustain herself for as long as the savory bits of death shaved off her victims satisfied the twisted cravings she harbored.

Memories raised gooseflesh down my arms and made my stomach clench.

Balamohan had fed on me, used his sticky-slimy tongue with serrated teeth on the end to cut out a plug of my skin and drink deeply of me. Death clung to fae like me. I was a portent, after all. What he did went beyond collecting the debris of my nature. He delved into the part of me marked by age, by past sickness and injury, by the natural passing of time, and he devoured the dark spots that I had earned from living these nineteen years. Balamohan could have kept me alive—and undying—forever.

"You are a single lash in the eye of eternity." The Morrigan's bleak gaze unfocused. "You can't understand what it's like to feed on death while living in a realm of immortals. You can't know how the gnawing hunger of forever feels in your gut while you wait for the next summons, the next meal. Strife and war are just as filling as death, and I have been denied those too, by your father's policies. His dream of peace became my unending famine. I am a *goddess*." Rage simmered in her tone. "The realms should tremble before me. The fae should fear me and my teeth the way they once did. Half-bloods and cowards secure behind their conclave badges should not have the power to control me. *Not* me." Her body shook with barely leashed fury. "I am tired of starving. I am ready to feast."

"I'm sorry." I understood the burden of hunger. More than she would ever know. "I can't let you enslave others to save yourself. People shouldn't have to suffer for you to live. This ends here, now."

"You want to end me?" A vicious snarl curled her lips. "I can't die. *I am death*."

She slid a serrated blade the length of my forearm from an air pocket, and my stomach knotted.

My voice trembled. "Killing me solves nothing."

"No, it doesn't." Her knuckles whitened on the handle. "But it will make me feel better."

She lunged, slicing the air inches from my throat before instinct kicked in and I dodged her aim. Power flooded my runes, lighting me up, igniting the hunger low in my gut that resonated with hers.

"Your magic can't hurt me." She danced out of range. "Did Rook teach you nothing?"

The light show wasn't a threat. It was the magical equivalent of my stomach rumbling.

I reached for the knife strapped to my thigh and came up empty. *Are you kidding me?* I had used it for practice when Mac taught me how to make my own air pocket and forgotten to remove it. Who does that? Me apparently. I wasn't nearly as proficient as the Morrigan at snagging items out of thin air. In the time it took me to focus and reopen the blasted pocket, she could poke me three new holes.

"Is that it?" She cocked her head. "You have no defense?"

The best answer I could manage was gaping at her like a suffocating carp. *Classy.*

"This will be easier than I thought." Faster than she finished her sentence, she sprang at me.

Hands sifting through the air in front of me, I latched on to my pocket and spread my fingers. The Morrigan's aim was true, but her form was sloppy, and I whirled to one side, using the flat of my forearm to deflect the blow while fumbling with my pocket. She continued the motion, spinning left, her shoulders brushing against mine as she whirled behind me. Instinct brought my head around as a whisper of air parting sang in my ear. Her blade shot forward, nicking my throat. My eyes closed on a prayer and popped open when she braced a hand on my shoulder and began jerking her arm backward.

"Release me," she hissed near my ear.

"You're the one wrapped around— Oh." I dared turn my head. "That was unexpected."

Her blade had rung the hole made by my hands, and just as my hand had entered Mac's pocket that night in his kitchen, mine was nursing her fingers. Fear clenched my grip around her wrist, and I tightened the mouth of the bubble, trapping her hand and her blade inside the pocket.

I yelped when her teeth sank into my ear, and slung my arm hard into her gut. She bent forward, and I threw all my weight behind slamming my elbow into her spine. She dropped facedown with a grunt, but I hit the dirt with her. My tailbone screamed in agony, but I still gripped her wrist through my pocket. Delayed reaction to the sheer depth of the crap I was in dumped buckets of icy adrenaline over me. The shock to my system left me jittery...and inspired.

I firmed my grasp on the mouth of the pocket and leaned backward, drawing my hands up past her elbow, and the fragile-seeming bubble expanded, coating her in a wash of invisibility. I lost my grip when her battle cry startled me. Her other fist hit my spine, and I grunted, arching my back. Holding the pocket with one hand, I sank my elbow into the base of her neck once, twice, until she slumped to the ground. Sheer panic sent me into hyperdrive. I pushed to my knees and straddled her hips, bringing her arm with me. I had to flop across her back to reach her other arm, but I managed to thread it through the widening mouth of the pocket too. I had her locked inside the bubble up to the elbow when she flung her head back and hit me in the jaw with the crown of her skull.

Fireworks exploded in my mouth.

Blinded for a moment by pain, I struggled to hold on to her, knowing this was my one shot. She wriggled under me, managing to flip her body over by the time my vision returned. Hatred boiled in her black eyes as she stared up at me, and her narrow chest heaved. She bucked her hips, but I held her wrists.

"You think that pathetic bit of child's magic can hold me?" The Morrigan thrashed her head and wedged her heels into the damp ground. "No common spell can contain a goddess. It is *impossible*."

Death-touched fae were impervious to other death magics. Other benign spells? Not so much.

Too bad I only knew a handful by heart. At the moment, the air pocket was the best I had.

"It doesn't have to last." I shot forward when her knees hit my throbbing tailbone. *Ouch.* "It just has to keep you out of my hair long enough to handle business. Then I couldn't care less what you do."

A knowing smile crept over her face. "You mean fetching your incubus."

I hesitated, and that was all the opening she needed.

"I gave him to Bháin." She was all smiles. "I thought a plaything might soften him toward me."

My brow furrowed. "Shaw can't…"

My thoughts spun toward the complex glamours Bháin was capable of fabricating. If he wanted Shaw to believe he was me, then Shaw stood an ice cube's chance in hell of resisting him. Oh God. I would kill Bháin if he used Shaw that way.

Her brittle laughter shattered my panic.

"Shaw is mine." Sliding down her body, I used my weight to flatten her knees to the ground and keep her still. Spreading my hands, I blocked out the vile, detailed fantasies she spewed at me and let my focus narrow to widening the mouth of the bubble. Sweat poured down my temples as I cleared the crown of her head. Her pupils disappeared, leaving black voids of terror.

Magic shimmered between my thighs. Skin and cloth turned to feathers. Mass shrank until the legs vanished under my butt and her waist shriveled. Her face elongated into the weathered, orange beak.

Heart pounding, I fought her transformation. Once she turned into a crow, she could expand her body until it was the size of an elephant. I had ridden her that way, watched her gulp down a hound while in that form, and I did not want to be her next meal.

With an ear-ringing *caw*, her body morphed into that of a crow. One oily wing wriggled free. My pulse sprinted, hands tightening on the wing still inside the bubble. Her squawk of frustration set my nerves jangling. Her voice rang deeper. Her pinching beak snapped closer. I couldn't hold on much longer.

Risking it all, I released her wing, and the writhing, cat-sized crow hit the ground. She landed on twiggy feet and hopped. Her wings snapped out to her sides, and I clapped my hands over her head.

"*Buille*," I shouted, and magic gathered between my fingers. I spread my hands a foot apart and fell forward on top of the Morrigan. She beat at the walls of the pocket, but the barriers of her invisible prison held. Scooping my hands underneath her—which earned me a peck hard enough to rip tender skin from my palm—I sealed the pocket and rocked back onto my knees. Panting, I gasped, "*Eitilt.*"

The bubble, now stretching about two feet in circumference around the giant bird, rose from the ground and bobbled on the breeze inches from my nose. The Morrigan's beak opened, but the pocket muted her screams. A tingling sensation on my nape pushed me to stand, and I breathed, "*Imíonn.*"

Between blinks, the Morrigan vanished, but the uneasy feeling persisted.

Act casual. Not like you've got a death goddess and current ruler of Faerie trapped in a bubble.

Thank God for the annulment. At least Daibhidh got that much right. After pulling this stunt, I did not want my ex-mother-in-law tapping into my power through any lingering familial bond to burst her prison before I was long gone and she had no way of retaliating.

If that made me a chicken, well, *cluck, cluck.*

Unhurried steps brought me closer to the safety of Mac's den. I exhaled when I spotted the tree, then cursed when a flock of Aves landed between it and me. Clearly, they wanted their master back.

Too bad I had no intention of setting this little bird free. Not now. Not ever if I could help it.

"Move aside," I ordered them, exhaustion thick in my voice.

"Move aside," the nearest one said, head tilting.

"Move," the next said.

"Aside," a third parroted.

From there a wave of nonsense broke across the flock, and they all did that freaky head-twisting thing that makes birds look like their necks have been wrung. I stifled a shudder and took a step. A rustle of feathers made me cringe as the largest bird—a female?—did the same. Aggression or more mimicry? I wasn't sure. I took another step. She did the same. So did the two Aves closest to her. No way to know, but I was betting those were her mates. Maybe those three were the head tweety birds?

No attack. No aggression. What gives?

I braced my feet apart. "What do you want?"

"What do *you* want?" the centermost one queried.

Tired laughter shook my frame. "A hot shower, some food and a safe place to sleep?"

Fat chance of me getting even one out of the three anytime soon.

A scrawny bird shoved its way forward, bowing to the female and keeping its head tucked when the males began hissing at him. Inching nearer to me, the tiny Aves studied the scuffed tops of my boots.

"Want Morrigan," he said on a soft hiss of breath.

My gaze pegged the slight male. "You can't have her."

The small bird bobbed his head. "Want Morrigan gone."

"What?" I cocked my head. Crap. Now they had me doing it.

"Dog Girl rule Faerie." He hopped in place. "Dog Girl rule Aves?"

"Um, no." I backed up a step like they held a crown aimed at my head. "I'm going to pass on the whole ruling-Faerie thing." A collective hiss spread through the flock. "That means I won't be ruling the Aves either." I gestured toward the tree. "Do you mind? I would like to get inside for a minute."

Turning to the others, the male beside me whistled and clicked a string of information to his kin. I was about to ask what that was all about when the lot of them launched into the sky, lighting on the lowest tree limbs. Even the smaller male, my apparent interpreter, had flown up there to watch me.

It was damn creepy.

Before droppings rained from the sky, I strode toward the door and held it open long enough for my pocket to drift inside. I closed it with a *thud* and let my back hit the solid wood. On wobbly knees, I caught my breath. The spider-web-sticky sensation of having an additional air pocket made me want to swipe my hands down my arms. Now that I had captured the Morrigan, what should I do with her?

I thumped my head against the door behind me, and when I lifted it, I saw my answer.

The Hall of Many Doors.

Perfect.

CHAPTER SIXTEEN

The trouble with any brilliant idea is planning its execution.

Pacing the Hall of Many Doors, I felt both my pockets jostling the air behind me. One held my skins, and I needed those. The other held the Morrigan, and I wanted to deposit her in here beneath the pixie lights for Mac to deal with after he shook off his most recent death. He and I were the only ones able to operate the doors. No one else could get into the hall or use any of the doors either.

Not that those led anywhere anymore. They opened on solid walls of compacted dirt.

The one door that still worked led to Mac's study. I passed through it, bubbles in tow, and sat on the edge of his desk, glancing around, wondering if I would ever see this place again. Or worse, if I would see it every day for the rest of my life. A pang arrowed through my chest. Home was so far away.

Shifting my hips, I knocked over a small inkwell that spread black ichor across his desk. I leapt to my feet, snatching papers out of the black liquid's path and setting baubles on the floor. I spotted an old shirt of mine, one Mac must have brought back with him, and used it to mop up the mess I'd made.

Crisis averted, I dropped into his chair with a fistful of papers and started shuffling them. One of the cleaner pieces caught my eye. It was a note—sort of—addressed to me. My name was written in a neat script. Below that a series of numbers—coordinates?—were listed. Underneath those it I read, "*Tethers may be established from one point to another so long as fresh blood ties the ends together.*"

Taking care not to smear more ink on the writing, I folded the paper and tucked it into my backpack for later. An idea was itching the back of my mind, but I couldn't stop now to devote brainpower to the pondering of logistics. I had to stash the Morrigan, and then I had to go after Shaw. That ought to be fun.

Bháin was hard to read. He had shown Mom kindness. But had he chosen to do so, or had he been following Rook's orders?

Like so many other things, I just didn't know for sure.

I never thought I would actually wish Rook was around. I had so many questions.

Word of the Morrigan's capture would spread quickly. Even if the Aves kept their beaks closed, the trees and rocks had eyes and ears in Faerie, and it was too dangerous to assume the flock was the only witness to our altercation. That meant I had to get moving. Fast. Before word reached Bháin.

Fifteen minutes and twice as many failed attempts to extricate myself later, I slapped the door to the Hall of Many Doors shut behind me. Straining my senses, I winced at the discordant sensation of having one of my air pockets trapped. The slight pull on my essence reminded me of shutting the door on a lock of hair and having them yanked out as you walked away.

It hurt, yeah, but I could deal.

Turning a slow circle in the living room, I decided I had all I needed for the final leg of the trip.

Outside, chirps and whistles rained down on me from where the Aves kept their perches. Great.

I tugged the elastic band from my hair and ran my fingers through it, twisting it up into a sloppy bun that kept the stragglers from my eyes. Determined to see this through, I set out for Rook's home.

Faerie's nifty travel magic made the journey back to Winter a quick one. The problem was I had no idea how to reach Rook's house, and without him or Mac to lead me, my campaign spluttered out.

Hours lost in the blizzard conditions of Winter turned me around, twisted my perception and left me standing in a barren field. White stretched as far as the eye could see. The extreme cold began to punch through the heat spell on my armor, and I shivered. My breath frosted in the air.

A single black feather caught on a drift and swirled around my ankles.

My heart leapt into my throat.

"Rook?"

A dull thud and a blur of dark feathers hit the snow. Shaking off the flakes, the Aves translator, who I decided to call Pie, as in *four and twenty baked in a*, blinked up at me with his beady black eyes.

I blinked right back. "Where did you come from?"

"I followed." He puffed out his chest. "*We* followed."

Well shoot. I thought they had ditched me on the edge of Autumn.

He bobbed his head. "Walk circle?"

Heat prickled in my wind-chapped cheeks. "I'm lost."

His feathers rustled. "I can direct."

Hope warmed my chest. "Do you know where Rook lives?"

Pie hopped in place to keep his feet from sinking in the snowbank. "Ice house."

"Yes, the ice house."

"This way." He took to the air and vanished sixty seconds later.

"Slow down," I yelled. "I can barely see my own nose in this weather."

Okay, so visibility was closer to six feet in any direction, but I felt claustrophobic trapped in my circle of whited-out sameness. A wispy voice startled me, and I sucked down an icy breath while scanning for its origin.

"Too late, too late," it whispered. "You came too late, too late to save him."

I froze in place, cold panic seeping into my bones. "Who said that?"

"Master likes you, likes you." Trilling giggles. "He likes you, likes you enough to spare you."

A shimmer of white light zinged past me.

The master? Surely the voice didn't mean…

"Wait." I stumbled after it. "Who are you?"

A squawk jerked my gaze skyward. When I glanced back down, the light had vanished.

"You follow." Pie hovered over the frigid ground. "This way."

I lurched ahead, wading through drifts. Some came to my ankles, others to my chest. Pie kept in view, his erratic flight a smudge against the flawless white perfection of the snow-laden Winter sky.

Try as I might, I didn't hear the singsong voice again.

I couldn't decide if that was a good thing or a bad one.

Around the time my eyelashes stuck together and I slipped on a spot of ice I hadn't seen, a light swung into my line of sight. Sort of. I couldn't see much. The orb of golden light was real, wasn't it?

"I heard you had arrived." The silky voice slid through me. "We've been expecting you."

Firm hands grasped my upper arms and hauled me to my feet.

"Bháin." My lips were so numb, his name came out as mushy as baby food. "I came for—"

"Your incubus." He chuckled at my ear. "Even if the master had not informed me who he was, I would have known him by the turn of his thoughts. His hunger… It is as stark and endless as Winter. You are all that keeps him sane, and he is far from it at the moment. You may have waited too long."

"I didn't have much of a choice," I snapped.

Save the mortal realm from a deranged goddess bent on devouring it or rescue Shaw.

Oh God. Maybe he was right. Maybe I made the wrong choice. Maybe I should have…

"Love is complicated, is it not?" he mused. "The worth of such love—how can it be measured?"

"Was the Morrigan telling the truth?" I swallowed hard. "Did she give Shaw to you?"

"Yes." A thoughtful pause lapsed. "It was a most unexpected boon."

Jerking from his grip, I let simmering magic fill my palm. "Take me to him."

"First—" he ignored my threat and grabbed me again, "— the master wishes to speak with you."

"R-Rook?" I stammered. "He's here?"

He's alive?

"You are not the only half-blood to inherit a burdensome gift from a fae parent."

Befuddled as I was, I caved to the inevitable and allowed Bháin to drag me inside Rook's home. This was much less *you shall not pass* and more *come inside, but you can never leave* than I had expected.

Ushered over the threshold by Bháin's tight grip, I sighed as warmth hit my face. A dozen steps later, he clamped his hands on my shoulders and spun me around. He pushed down until my knees gave, and I dropped into a chair.

He snapped his fingers, and the room grew several degrees hotter.

"The elemental?" I reached up and examined my frigid cheeks. "I remember from last time."

"It is indeed." He tapped the crook of his finger beneath my chin to tilt my head back. "This might burn. Hold still."

His ice-cold finger traced the chilly lines of my eyelashes where they had frozen on my cheeks. I hissed at the burn, his touch like fire in the depth of its frigidity. The pressure vanished, and I blinked.

Bháin dusted powdered frost from his fingertips, which were stuck to his skin like iron shavings to a magnet.

I traced the chilled imprints of his fingers on my cheek and shivered. "I appreciate the assist."

He bowed slightly. "I will go fetch the master."

"Is Shaw all right?" I grasped his wrist then yanked my hand back when his icy flesh stung me. "Tell me that much." I held my hand out to the elemental, a roaring flame standing on cartoonish feet next to me, and let it thaw my fingers. "You were very kind to my mother. I remember how well you treated her."

His sigh circulated a nippy breeze. "He is as well as can be expected."

My gut cramped with sympathetic pain. "His hunger."

"He is starving." He turned to leave then hesitated. "I will try to prevent him from killing you."

Throat tightening, I bobbed my head.

Shaw was alive. That was all that mattered. Rook was here. Did he know about his mother yet? I doubted it. If Bháin or the Aves sentries had tipped him off, then Rook would have greeted me at the door with a gleam in his eyes and a scheme on his lips. *Good.* I could use that then.

"I wondered how far down on your list the incubus fell."

The calculation in Rook's voice snapped my head up.

"I understand that Faerie is now cut off from the mortal realm." He glided into the room and sat in a chair near the hearth of the spacious seating area where Bháin had situated me. "Where does that leave you?" Bitter laughter spilled over his lips as he held up the shell. "Or me for that matter?"

I slid to the edge of my seat. "Do you want to live in the mortal realm?"

"Not particularly. I don't belong there any more than I do here." He shrugged. "I would have—for her. Tell me... Is she well?"

"She was recovering the last time I saw her."

Red splotches mottled his pale gray cheeks. "Explain."

Knowing this for the game it was, I filled in the blanks of Branwen's life. I told him how the Morrigan sent Balamohan to kidnap his sister from her selkie husband. How she had remained entombed until the day Shaw rescued me, hoping to ingratiate Shaw to him. I informed him of Dónal's passing and Branwen's grief, how she had begged me to save her brother. I ended it with the shell she had given me, so that whatever his fate, she could know it with certainty.

"After all this time, thanks to your efforts, she was within my reach," Rook murmured into the silence. "And yet, thanks to your efforts, she has never been farther away." He stared at the conch shell. "Am I such an affront to the gods that their joy stems from my pain? Is being Earth-born that foul? Is my blood tainted so that the loving embrace of the one person who has ever cared for me is forever denied me? All this...my life...all for nothing."

I shifted on my seat, trying to appear attentive when I wanted to jump up and search the place.

Rook's dreary sentiment rang eerily similar to his mother's, and that had me nibbling my lip.

"I came for Shaw," I said, when he remained quiet.

"I know."

He snapped his fingers, and the fire elemental scampered back to its blackened hearthside perch.

I gripped the arms of my chair. "I sense a *but* coming."

"I had goals, Thierry, a plan. I labored to get into Mother's good graces, did unspeakable things to earn her trust, all so I could mount an effort to rescue my sister and those like us." He leaned back in his seat. "Then fate presented me with a perfect opportunity to realize those dreams. You fell into my lap, the best gift I had ever been given." His head tilted back, eyes closed. "I wed you. I fought to have you named queen. I even argued in favor of your sabbatical, which I see now was my mistake."

My nails pierced the leather upholstery. "Everything you did was to further your own agenda."

"Yes."

"You lied to me, almost got me killed, *married* me without my consent, foisted the wellbeing of an entire realm on me, and you expect what from me—pity? You want me to be grateful that you, in all your selfish scheming, experienced a prick of remorse and let me go home?" I snorted. "When we both know the real reason you lobbied for it was so I would name you prince regent and let you steer the realm while I was gone. You weren't doing me any favors or a kindness. You did it for *yourself.*"

"Yes."

"Is that all you have to say?"

His black eyes opened on me, deep and dark and fathomless, cold and eternal and lost. Lips bent in a mockery of a smile, he got to the broken heart of it. "You cost me everything, Thierry."

This made the second time someone had accused me of that today.

"You can't expect me to be sorry for doing what it took to survive." I slid my hands into my lap, linking my fingers to cover the subtle glow of magic that could not save me but might distract him. "I did no less than you would have done in my shoes. Stop playing games. It's over. Let me have him."

"No." He picked at the collar of his white shirt, which was darkened with dried blood from his recent near-death experience. "Your whole life you've wanted someone to love who knew the worst of you and forgave you for it. I had that, though not romantically, and I lost it." He crossed his ankles. "It's fitting that you will too."

I launched myself out of the chair at his throat. Ice-cold arms encircled me. Arctic breath panted across my throat. Bháin restrained me while his master raked thoughtful eyes over me and chuckled.

"Bháin," I pleaded. "The Morrigan gifted him to you. Can't you—?"

"I am a slave, lady." Chill words beat against me. "I own only what the master says is mine."

I screwed my eyes shut tight. "She wanted me to come to you."

"I think so, yes." Rook's chair creaked. "She wanted you to grovel at my feet and beg me for the life of the man you chose over me." Footsteps thumped softly. "If you had loved him less, you could have been mine." Warm fingers traced the curve of my cheek. "We could have been good together."

Eyes snapping open, I glared at him. "I never wanted you."

"You kissed me. Kisses are seeds of potential sown in the hopes love will blossom."

A blush crept up the back of my neck. "I thought I was going to die."

His hands balled at his sides, but he made no move against me.

"You say you want to make a difference. You want to be an advocate and save other half-bloods from the fate you and your sister faced—so do it." I struggled against Bháin. "Stop whining. Stop pouting. Stop acting like a spoiled little boy. Act like a man if you want to be treated like one. *Get off your feathery ass and do something about it.*"

Rook's eyes shot wide, and his mouth dropped open, but I wasn't done yet.

"Daibhidh is dead. The Unseelie will need a new voice in the High Court. Why not yours?"

His head jerked toward Bháin. "Is this true?"

"I heard gossip and dismissed it as impossible." He shifted behind me. "How can it be true?"

A smirk twisting my lips, I bared my teeth. "He had a disagreement with an ogre."

"That's not possible." Rook rubbed a finger between his eyes. "Mother would have…"

"About that—" Sweetness and concern dripped from my voice. "Heard from her lately?"

Gray cheeks paled to stark white. "What have you done?"

A ribbon of fear sifted through me, panic I might have pushed Rook too far, but this still wasn't far enough. He didn't believe me. Not yet. He wanted to. Oh, how he wanted to. I had no proof, but I had an idea that might save my bacon…if Bháin ordered his snowflake-y minions to do some recon.

I bumped my chin higher. "I propose a trade."

Rook backed away from me until his knees hit his chair and he sank into it. "The terms?"

"You give me Shaw and a blood promise that this is over. That whatever imagined debt we have is paid in full." I wet my lips. "In exchange, I will return your mother to you. She's immobilized at the moment. I would prefer she stay that way until after Shaw and I are safely back home, but after that you're free to release her—or not. That's your business. She's your mother after all."

Rubbing his hands over his face, he spoke through his fingers. "Bháin, I need confirmation."

The hands restraining me eased, and the sparkle of a snowflake fused with magic danced across the still air to hover over my head. Bháin commanded it with a flick of his fingers, and it flew away.

"Can you call him off?" I yanked my arm. "I'm getting frostbite over here."

Rook gestured toward the chair I had occupied. "Let her sit."

Sit I did, and then we waited.

CHAPTER SEVENTEEN

I'm not sure how long I sat there with Rook, Bháin standing behind my chair in the event I leapt for his master's throat a second time. Long enough I worked up a head of steam. Knowing Shaw was here, hidden, set my teeth on edge. Aware of his suffering, Rook and Bháin let me sit and stew instead of taking me to him, letting me feed him and try to bring him back from the brink.

A glimmer of magic drew me up straighter in my seat. The snowflake drifted to Bháin, twirling, singing in the same childlike voice I'd heard on my trek here. I wished the thing would spill it already.

"Thierry speaks the truth," Bháin announced. "Elena confirms that flurries stationed at the Halls of Winter saw the ogre drive Consul Daibhidh into the ground with his fist like a spike after he killed the Black Dog." Curiosity lit his eyes. "Both sets of remains were claimed by the Huntsman."

Rook sneered at his servant. "They knew this and failed to report it?"

Amusement tipped the corners of Bháin's mouth. "Apparently, Thierry rode a dragon to escape your mother. The flurries followed them to the edge of Winter but then got distracted by racing the beast."

Seeing how I recalled the other dragons' existence with perfect clarity, I was betting Blue voided the spell when he left the castle.

Rolling his eyes, Rook scanned the ceiling for patience or answers. Maybe both. "What else?"

"Aves have surrounded this place." He let the snowflake dance trilling on his fingertip. "I noted them earlier when I went to fetch Thierry. They are hardly subtle. I assumed they still tracked her as the Morrigan had commanded, but it seems they are here to defend their new Crow." He glanced at Rook. "Communication with them is beyond even Elena's abilities, but the flock would not be under Thierry's control if the Morrigan were not...indisposed. That Thierry sits here and your mother does not is more testament that what she says is the truth." His gaze lingered on me. "I believe she is honest."

High praise from a fae. Too bad I was about to smash that feel-good vibe we had going.

I cleared my throat. "Bháin, ah, is Elena your snowflake?"

I swore his snowdrift-white cheeks flushed. "She is a *flurry*."

My mouth opened, ready with a follow-up.

"Flurries are sentient." Rook rose to his feet. "They're kept as pets by those who command them."

The sour twist of Bháin's mouth told me he disagreed with the designation, but he didn't correct his master. From what I had seen, the two rarely agreed. On anything. Their animosity worked in my favor, so I kept my mouth shut too. I had no clue why Bháin sometimes helped me, except maybe to spite his master, but I hoped he would again. Rook was bending to the possibility of freedom—even if it was temporary—from his mother. I was tempting him with power too. Both played in my favor.

"Shaw doesn't have much time." I clapped my hands together. "Let's kick off negotiations."

A long moment passed where fear nipped at me like hounds on my trail, but then it passed.

Rook folded his arms over his chest. "First tell me how you plan to return home."

"I can create a new tether." Maybe. I hoped I could. Inspiration struck, and I added, "I would be willing to create the threshold in your home if you like." I schooled my features to keep them blank. "If you control access to the only working tether in Faerie, the High Court must recognize you. They will panic when they realize the two realms are cut off from one another. You could step in and save the day." I noticed the gleam in Bháin's eyes and added, "Though the same travel restrictions would apply."

Bháin smirked at me, but I wasn't convinced he hadn't been prompting me in the first place.

I wished I understood his stake in all this.

"There are those who would stand beside you if you but asked them, Master," Bháin said cryptically.

"Even so," Rook acknowledged, eyes bright, "it might not be enough to sway millennia of prejudice."

"The tether is plenty, and we both know it." I snorted. "You'll have to fight to keep possession of it, but you're used to that, right? The consul position is yours for the taking. Consider it my gift to you. This way you get everything you wanted—power, influence and...a means of seeing Branwen again. Though, no offense, I'm going to have to ask you to stay on your side of the divide."

His fingers stroked his shirtfront. "You would bring her to me?"

"Sure. Why not?" I rolled my shoulders. "I'll be visiting my dad anyway."

My *dad?*

Where did *that* come from?

"All right," he agreed. "That sounds fair."

"Good." *Finally.* "We're settled."

"Not so fast." He raised his hand. "I—"

"No," I said firmly. "Take it or leave it."

Rook eased to his feet and crossed to the glowing fireplace, giving me his back as he braced his palms on the mantle. After a moment, the tension washed from his shoulders, and he dipped his head.

"This is why you chose him over me," he said, voice almost lost to the crackling fire. "I force you to do as I wish, when Shaw does as you want for the simple fact it pleases you."

"You have a decent heart in there—somewhere—down deep." I had glimpsed flashes of it. "You were never in a competition with Shaw. You've got to let that go. You were the glimmer of *best-case scenario* when my life was going to hell in a handbasket. We might have worked out in the end. I don't know. It's a future neither of us will ever see, and that's just it. Shaw is my tomorrow. He was my yesterday, and he is my today." I rose slowly so as not to startle Bháin into subduing me. "I've wanted him for so long, I don't remember a time I ever wanted anyone else. I see a future with him. I've planned it out in my head a million times and in a million different ways. It's not an easy love, but he is all I want."

Without facing me, Rook raised his voice. "Take her to the incubus."

"Thank—" I bit off the phrase before ending it.

Rook waved away my words, and I turned to go.

"Bháin?" Rook's voice carried over my shoulder. "Don't let him kill her."

Bháin walked ahead of me at a sedate pace while I bounced on the balls of my feet behind him. There was no mystical fated-mate bond guiding my feet forward, no sixth sense of awareness tingling in proximity to Shaw. Did he register my nearness? Incubi senses were razor sharp where feeding was involved, and he had gone days without energy from me.

Walking the hall, I felt like a piping-hot carton of his favorite takeout delivering myself.

Bháin paused in front of a door and turned. "I wanted to warn you what you might see."

"I've seen him wild before." He had been starving, crazed when he found me in the caves.

"It's not that." His gaze lowered to the doorknob. "The illusion—I picked it from his memory."

I shifted on my feet. "Okay."

"It's your apartment."

It took me longer to decide why that might be a bad thing. "All right."

The fingers of one of his hands caressed the doorframe. "The one where you and the incubus first..."

"I— Oh." I thought about that. "Okay."

So not my current digs, but the quarters I'd shared with Mai at the conclave during the academy. I stayed on several more days after she dropped out and moved back home with her parents, and yeah. *Memories.* Shaw and I created lots of them on those twin beds with the squeaky springs and crinkly, plastic-covered mattresses.

Knowing Bháin had seen that, experienced it, tarnished some of those nights for me.

"I used glamour," he said even softer. "I pretended to be you."

My throat tightened, fear racing up my spine. "And?"

"He saw through it. Eventually." His hand fell to his side. "He might not trust you until it's too late."

Heart sore, I leaned my shoulder against the wall. "Why are you telling me this?"

"He was mine." His fist clenched. "She gave him to me."

"He's a person." A warning growl deepened my voice. "No one owns him."

"I am owned." His gaze flashed to me. "Am I any less a person?"

"*No.*" I straightened. "I don't agree with you being owned, either."

"I knew I would not be allowed to keep him." He murmured, "I wanted to know how it felt."

"How what felt?" The possibilities were endless.

"The difference in how you love him." Bháin's brows slanted, and his lips thinned. "I saw you through your mother's thoughts. Her love for you is part of every decision she makes." He shrugged. "I have heard it's like that with mothers. I wondered if it was the same for the incubus. If thoughts of you consumed him. They do. But the quality is…different. Darker, hungrier, possessive. I decided it must be the difference in loving that which you birthed and that which you aspire to create life with."

"Um." The anger I expected fell away and left me confused. "You don't know what love is?"

"I can create the illusion, and it is flawless. Fae wonder at my skill." Pride warmed his tone. "I am very good at what I do. Emotions, the meanings behind them… I lack the capacity to understand subtle nuance in the degrees of affection, therefore my constructs lack realistic depth."

I crossed my arms over my chest. "What do you do with the emotions and images you acquire?"

"I create what the sidhe call sensation exhibits, where they go to experience that which they are incapable of perceiving." At my puzzled expression, he glanced aside. "Fae are not human, and if I were to be honest, I believe that is the discordant thread that causes fae parents to loathe their own half-blood children when they evidence a spark of humanity that makes them *more*. They carry fae magic in their bones and human empathy in their hearts. It is one thing to gaze fondly upon a partner whose differences bring you pleasure, but it is another to bear a child who can see and hear and feel outside of your reach. It births a bitter envy."

"Rook never said how you feed." I stifled a shiver. "You're sustained by emotion?"

Making him more similar to Shaw and me than I thought possible.

Bháin chuckled under his breath. "The comparison is close enough that I will let it stand."

Learning this about him brought up all sorts of uncomfortable suspicions.

Be careful who you give your trust.

Rook had warned me about Bháin the day I met him. For once, I should have listened to him.

"Your mother was a font of emotion, full of textures and layered meanings. I enjoyed my time with her." When my teeth began grinding, he raised a hand. "I did not force myself upon her. I touched her in no intimate or physical way. I simply walked her thoughts to glean better understanding. It also allowed me to ensure her stay was as comfortable as possible."

"I've said before that I appreciate the pains you took to make her 'stay' pleasant." I chewed the inside of my cheek while sifting through possible replies and giving up on finding a response that wouldn't ruin our peaceful chat. "That's all I can handle on the topic right now, okay?"

"I wanted you to understand that what I did for your mother—for the incubus—I did for myself. I fed from them, learned from them. Though neither is worse for it, those were not benevolent acts."

Head pounding, I wished Bháin would stop talking before I resorted to the height of immaturity and plugged my ears with my fingers. Granting him permission to dig around in my mom's head had been hard enough, but discovering how he used what he learned from her and Shaw, that he shared it with fae who had no business knowing my loved ones' minds or hearts, was a violation I had trouble forgiving.

"I get that," I growled. "Let's drop it."

"I find I am having trouble letting it go," he admitted. "I am experiencing..." his pale eyebrows slanted downward, "...I believe it is called guilt? I feel I owe you for what I have taken from them."

The admission sounded like he had spent too much time in the heads of people who loved me to outright hurt me. But was he feeling those emotions? Like a residual echo? Or was the knowledge of what Mom or Shaw might feel in his place causing him to—perhaps unconsciously—fabricate them?

I had no idea, but man did it make my head hurt thinking about the possibilities.

"You don't owe me anything," I said. "You want to make amends? Do that with them."

"That's just it." He offered me his hand. "I can't. Your mother is no longer in this realm, nor do I expect to ever see her again, and your incubus is either unwilling or he is unable to feed from me to sustain himself. So I offer myself, my energies, to you instead. Take from me as an apology to him."

Rubbing the heel of my palm into my eye, I cursed. Accepting his offer was a done deal as soon as he made it, and I hated that, but the bottom line was I was out of juice. I hadn't fed or sipped on anyone in days. I had no spare energy, and I would need every last drop to establish a new tether.

The burn in my belly ignited, and I grasped his hand. "I accept your apology."

Interest crossed Bháin's face when my runes lit, and I took the first slow pull of his magic.

"It doesn't hurt as I expected," he said, studying our illuminated grip. "Do you need more?"

I studied him right back. "Do you *want* to get hurt?"

The only thing keeping that look of wonder fixed on his face was the fact Mac had worked with me for weeks on nibbling energy instead of allowing my magic to sink its teeth in and tear out hunks of power for me to devour. Hunger for me wasn't constant like it was for Shaw, not as demanding or crippling, but it was ever-present, waiting for those internal scales to tip inside my head and a switch to flip me into hunting mode. Knowing Bháin had preyed upon those I loved most was about to do it.

And like anyone who has ever been on a strict diet, one taste left me wanting more.

"Will it hurt?" He sounded far too curious for my comfort.

Since he asked, I told him the truth. "It could kill you."

"I doubt that." He tightened his grip. "Try it if you like."

"I'm not into attempted murder," I said flatly.

"Take as much as you like," he offered. "I draw from Winter herself."

"Are you serious?" That might explain his high endurance. Maybe I wasn't as skilled in sipping as I let myself believe. "If you're plugged into another power supply, I can speed up the process."

His lips curved. "Take all you require."

Permission granted, I cranked up the pull. Bháin felt it. He swayed on his feet before flinging his free hand out to brace against the wall. He stabilized just as fast, grinning down at me like I had proved some point to him, and then I was drawing Winter straight through him. It shivered up my arm from my hand and spread ice through my chest, freezing my lungs and making it hard for me to breathe. I drew on him until my skin tingled and sparks dripped from my fingertips, until I was full to bursting and fresh runes joined the old ones, searing themselves into my skin until they covered my arm up to the shoulder.

"I'm done." I jerked free of his grasp, our fingers almost frozen together. "That's enough."

"If you're sure...?" His eyebrows rose. "All right." He gripped the knob. "I will wait here until I am certain you are safe with him." He cracked the door a fraction and then peered inside. "Call if you need help restraining him. Don't be fooled by the act. He is rationing his remaining strength."

I wedged the toe of my boot in the gap before he closed it. "I'll take it from here."

Bháin released his hold, and I got my first glimpse of Shaw.

He sat on the floor with his back pressed against the wall. His knees were bent, his forearms stacked on top of them. He wore jeans with socks and a new white T-shirt. He was clean, so he must have been allowed to wash off the blood and change at some point.

His head was tipped back against the ice-block wall, and his eyes were closed. A tremor ran through him, and before my eyes his fingernails lengthened to wicked claws. Tanned skin paled until pronounced veins crisscrossed his exposed skin. His eyes, when they cracked open, had gone chalk white and empty. The full curve of his lips stretched wide, exposing his elongating teeth.

Lifting his head, Shaw stared through the door right at me, and then he charged.

CHAPTER EIGHTEEN

I darted into the room to give Bháin time to twist the lock, and vertigo swamped me as his glamour took root in my senses. Color blossomed in my mind. Scents poured into me, familiar but faded. The stomp of cadets running with a drill sergeant outside the window carried to my ears. It was like I had fallen back in time, into my old room. Complete with twin beds, a ratty desk and a broken task chair.

The tendrils of disorientation parted two seconds after Shaw slammed into me.

My spine popped on impact with the wall, and a pained breath shot past my lips.

"I missed you too," I panted.

His wide palm circled my throat. "I warned you not to come back."

Fingers clawing at him, I gasped. "It's me."

"I didn't believe you the first three times, and I don't believe you now." He applied pressure, and I saw bursts of bright light on the periphery of my vision. "Stop being a coward. Shift. Show me your face so I know whose head I'm ripping off." He leaned closer, nostrils flaring. "You even smell like her. Is that some new trick? Is that why you haven't been back? You're trying to fool me with this?"

"Can't. Breathe." My fingers weakened. "Let. Go."

Curling his lip, he thumped my head against the wall. "This time get the hell out and stay out."

When he spun on his heel, I bent double, sucking in precious air. Once I caught my breath, I ran straight for him and leapt onto his back, wrapping my legs around his waist and hooking my left arm around his throat. Chokehold complete, I rode that bad boy all the way down.

My kneecaps cracked on ice-carved tiles, but I had Shaw's attention.

"Listen to me. I get Bháin was screwing with your head, but it's really me."

Shaw's palms smacked the floor, and his body rose like he was doing a push-up, leaving me astride him like a jock on a pony. I tightened my grip, but he shoved upright and staggered against a wall, slamming me into it. My teeth clacked, my grip loosened, and the room started spinning.

"I can—" I shook my head, "—prove it to you."

Weak as a newborn pup, I slid to the floor in a lump when he spun around to face me.

"Go on then." His wild eyes shone. "Prove it."

I extended my left hand. "I know you're hungry."

His lip quivered at my offering. "I am bonded."

"You're also an idiot," I slurred, staggering to my feet and leaning on the wall for support.

Clear across the room, the door cracked a fraction, and Bháin stuck his head inside.

"Are you all right?" He glanced between us. "I heard thumping."

"Just my head against the wall." I touched the base of my skull and winced. "Nothing critical."

"Hear her out, Incubus," Bháin said coldly. "If you kill your mate, where will you be?"

The door closed, and Shaw's expression shut down with it. He paced across the room, staring at me, measuring me against some figment in his mind. Hope warred with doubt and exhaustion. In his eyes, hunger gleamed. Need peered out at me, desperate, hurt, recognizing me as that which sated it.

Thanks, Dad. His moderation tactics had worked. Shaw was…not in control…but not frothing at the mouth either. Suspended between starvation and salvation, he walked a razor-thin line. His life was mine to save. What I did next determined his fate.

"Take my hand," I coaxed.

"I won't feed from you." He turned his back on me. "I can't."

Expecting his answer, I sighed, took a running leap and tackled him. He grunted when he hit the floor, and so did I. *My poor knees.* I hissed out the Word marshals used for restraining difficult suspects. This one lacked a generic off switch that another marshal—say, Shaw—could flip. Either I removed the binding or it didn't come off without magical intervention.

With Shaw's arms locked behind his back, I scooted down until I sat on his knees, pinning him. He thrashed when he realized he was caught, tried to un-invoke the restraints and failed. As tempted as I was to smack him, I gripped his hand, sliding my runes over his warm skin, and pushed energy into him.

Magic tingled through our grip, and his shoulders jerked, bones popping as he struggled to free himself. I caressed his back, his thighs, murmuring assurances to him as I force-fed him. Bit by bit the tension drained from his body, and he relaxed against the floor.

Cheek pressed to the illusion of linoleum, he let his eyes close and his breathing steady. At some point, the biting grip he meant to break the fragile bones in my fingers eased, and his muscles flowed into fluid lines from tight knots.

Shaw croaked my name, voice hoarse and strained by exhaustion.

"I'm here." I stroked his cheek. "You're safe."

I murmured the Word to unravel his restraints and slid onto the floor next to him. He turned on his side, and I eased forward until he could rest his head in my lap. Fingers raking through his hair, I kept our link strong and steady, passing the glowing vitality I had gleaned through Bháin into Shaw.

Around us, the illusion flickered. The door opened behind me, and the glamour snuffed out completely.

Bháin stepped into my periphery. "How is he?"

"I've almost got him topped off." I smiled when a snore escaped him. "He's going to sleep for a while now." How long I wasn't sure since this was the first time filling his tank hadn't emptied mine in the process. "Do you have a spare bed he can use? I don't want him to wake up in here alone and think—"

"I understand." Bháin studied the picture we made. "I will have him brought to a guestroom."

Shaw and I were a little bruised, a little bloodied, but a whole lot satisfied.

We had this feeding thing beat. I could feel it. And that meant...

I bit the inside of my cheek. The man was unconscious. Sex ought to be the last thing on my mind.

I couldn't even play innocent and blame his lure. All that tumbling on the floor had made my breaths come harder, and not from exertion. Maybe it was the simple act of touching him, knowing he was safe and mine and wanting to celebrate us surviving our mission. Or maybe straddling him while he was restrained, sweaty and mad, growling and totally at my mercy wasn't my brightest idea ever.

I leaned over and pressed my lips to his temple, feeling to my bones the absolute truth of what I had told Rook. This dangerously sexy man was my future. I had been foolish to ever think otherwise.

A throat cleared, and I glanced up to find Bháin standing in the doorway.

He gestured to someone behind him. "Are you ready?"

"I didn't realize Rook had more staff tucked away in the walls." I eased Shaw's head onto the floor. Poor baby was out cold. "Who's going to bring Shaw to his room? How are they going to lift him—?" I started when the help arrived. "Um, Bháin, what are they doing here?"

Pie stood in the hallway. A taller Aves ruffled its feathers behind him.

"They sought assurances their Crow was unharmed." He poked Pie's shoulder. "Do you not trust them?"

Wide black eyes sought mine. At my hesitation, Pie's gaze slid to the floor.

Crap. I think I hurt his feelings.

"I don't mind as long as you supervise," I hedged. "I assume Rook is waiting for me?"

Bháin nodded. "He would prefer you to begin work on the tether as soon as possible."

Knees protesting as I stood, I skirted Bháin and headed for the Aves. Shoulders hunched, Pie shed feathers in a panicked flex of wings when I brushed him in passing. I shot him an encouraging look I don't know if he saw and then went to find Rook and discover if Mac was as clever as he thought he was.

Given how spectacular the locations of the original tethers had been, I anticipated nothing less grand from Rook. So when I found him cleaning rusted bits of ancient armor out of a hall closet, I didn't expect him to turn and grin.

He gestured toward the mostly empty shelves. "What do you think?"

I set my hands on my hips. "That Bháin deserves a raise for having to clean up the mess you're making?"

Rook kicked aside a charred helmet. "He is well compensated for his work."

I toed the hunk of metal when it spun too close. "Tell me something I don't know."

Bháin had it made with Rook serving him piping-hot emotion skimmed off his kidnapees. Their experiences and memories, their sheer variety, was a banquet of potential energy for a fae like him. As quick as Rook was to snatch up innocents and stash them at his home, in the room I suspected he had designated for Bháin's particular use, his home was a freaking buffet. Human, incubi, elementals...

I nudged a rusted gorget with my toe. "What's with the spring cleaning?"

"This is the location I have chosen for the tether," he said smugly.

"Do tell." Not what I anticipated, but it made good sense. "At least Bháin won't have to worry about cleaning this mess again."

"No, he won't." A smug expression wreathed his face. "I plan on freeing Bháin."

My mouth forgot how to work for a minute. "*What?*"

"I don't need his particular skills anymore." He rescued a battered shield from his closet and let me admire it before he flung it skittering down the hall. "I acquired him for one purpose, and thanks to your promise to escort Branwen to me, that purpose is being fulfilled without his aid." He ducked into the closet and tossed out more junk. "His kind is temperamental and exhausting to maintain. I'm relieved I will soon be rid of him."

All I had done was give Rook the potential to secure political power by anchoring a new tether. That didn't jibe with Bháin's particular talents. It wasn't fulfilling an emotional need, except feeding his ambition. Unless he didn't mean the actual tether, but who he expected to step through it one day.

Oh man. It all clicked with a nauseating *snick* in my head.

Bháin had been indulging Rook with glamour-enhanced role-playing…as Branwen.

It explained the room, Bháin's drive for perfection of a talent he might use to create exhibits, but I bet only one fae was ever invited to experience them. This explained a lot, like Bháin's all-you-can-eat pass and Rook's animosity toward him.

They had been playing house.

Not in a creepy way. Well, okay, it was a little creepy, but Bháin had given Rook the illusion of what he craved the most—love and acceptance and…his sister.

Rook must have read the realization on my face because his flushed scarlet.

I cleared my throat and found somewhere less awkward to look. "What will happen to him?"

A shrug dismissed the problem. "He will return to his people."

"I cannot return." Bháin's voice startled me. "I cannot leave my master's service and survive."

Meaning no one else would feed him or no one else could?

I glanced between them before glaring at Rook. "Is that true?"

Rook mashed his lips together and glared at Bháin.

Proof positive.

"Already thinking like a politician, I see." I let my head fall back on my neck. "You're covering your tracks. Unseelie House thinks you're weak because of your mixed blood. Now you're lobbying for the consul position, and you're afraid your peers will uncover Bháin's role in your household and expose your weakness for what it is." It boggled the mind. "You would really let him die after all he's done for you?"

A smirk twisted Bháin's expression. "This is how the sidhe have always treated us. I expected it would happen one day. It is the nature of our talent that we are feared by those who desire us the most."

I groaned and forced myself to interact with Rook without throttling him. "Has it occurred to you that you're treating him the same way full-blooded fae treat you?" When that failed to elicit a response, I tossed out another idea. "Why not use him? He can slide into people's heads, Rook. I mean, he can't read minds, but harvesting memories is almost the same thing. He's loyal to you. Use him in other ways."

Bháin tilted his head. "Why do you care what becomes of me?"

Once I might have confided it was because Shaw and I shared a similar link, that his dependence on me to survive made me sympathetic to Bháin's situation, but the thought of failing Shaw terrified me beyond my ability to speak of it except to him, and Bháin already knew too many of our secrets.

"You two have some kind of symbiotic relationship happening that I don't fully understand, and if I'm honest, I don't want to." I held up my hands to stall Rook's protests and kept on addressing Bháin. "Rook knew what he was taking on when he brought you into his home, and that makes your health and wellbeing his responsibility. As your master, he damn well better honor his end of the bargain."

I forced my teeth to unclench as I awaited a response.

Gesturing toward Bháin to finish clearing out the closet, Rook crossed the debris-strewn hallway to me. He dusted his hands and exhaled through his mouth. "What other ways do you have in mind?"

"Be the opposite of Daibhidh. Mingle with the Unseelie. Host lavish dinners here in your home. Allow Bháin to serve your guests. Let him lift information you can use to better conditions in Faerie. I'm guessing few are aware you've retained Bháin except for your mother. Slap some glamour on him to hide his distinctive coloration, and let him earn his keep in another way, in a more lucrative way."

Gaze distant, Rook murmured, "Aren't you afraid I'll abuse the power given to me?"

"I expect you will bend rules and use your questionable morals to get the results you want." The truth was that fae he managed to deceive would likely respect him more for his cunning, much as his mother had. "You're not the upfront or honest type, no, but you love your sister, and when I bring her here, you'll want her to see what you've made of yourself and to be proud of you. You'll want to show her that her faith in you was not misplaced." I played the highest card I had left. "Or, you follow in the Morrigan's footsteps, and when Branwen sees how corrupt you've become, she will never forgive herself for leaving you. She will spend the rest of her days carrying the burden of guilt for not choosing family over Dónal. Make no mistake, I've met Branwen, and she will be ashamed of you."

Brow creased, he shoved his hands into his pockets. "If I wore a belt, that would have landed below it."

I shrugged. "You've done worse to prove your point."

"I can't deny that." Indecision rippled across his face. "All right. I will use Bháin as you suggest. For the time being." His demeanor shifted when Bháin overheard and straightened to stare at us. "He can remain." He aimed his next words at Bháin. "Should he betray me or if his usefulness diminishes..."

"I will not," Bháin snarled, "and it will not. My skills surpass all but those of my dame."

Discard him and leave him to die, and Bháin kept his cool. But insult his honor or his talent, and he became High Lord Hissy Fit. Priorities much? I mean, you can't very well art when you're dead.

Sidestepping the mess and arguing males, I inspected the closet. "You're sure this is where you want it?"

"The old tethers' locations were common knowledge." Rook turned his back on Bháin's scowl, ending the argument. "They were unassuming at first, meant to blend in and go unnoticed. Over time they became adorned as the status symbols they were, and it made them obvious." He walked to me and patted the doorframe. "I prefer this. Modest and tucked out of sight."

Given the unrest in Faerie, it made sense to keep it hidden. "Fine by me."

I knelt in front of the threshold and dusted the area clean. Hunching forward, I placed the paper I took from Mac's office on the floor and smoothed it flat. I read it one last time before bracing myself for pain. I spoke the Word to open my wound and gasped at the sting. Blood stained my skin while it flowed through my fingers to pool on the tile. Figuring that setting an anchor must be similar to how I severed them, I smeared blood across the threshold from left to right, from doorframe to doorframe.

The pendant around my neck was warm in my palm when I gripped it tight in my crimson fist. I let my second sight rise while pushing magic into the charm Mac had given me. I chanted the Word, the coordinates Mac had jotted down, and I pictured where the shifting blue-mesh tunnel should end.

Power churned through my core and spun through my runes into my fingertips. Blood ignited in a blue wash of cool flames that licked up the sides of the door and caused Rook to curse behind me. Air swirled, catching tendrils of my hair and blowing them into my eyes. A faint suction began, and I leaned forward, testing the limits of the threshold. My ears popped, and the whirling vortex took me.

CHAPTER NINETEEN

I landed hard. My left hip took the brunt of it, but impact popped my wrists when I flung out my hands to stop my head from bouncing off the floor. Vision wavering, I saw why. Rough cement slab bumped under my palms. I listed—no, the room did. The floor tapered to a steel drain in the center. The walls were concrete blocks. Bars filled the narrow window. The stink of ripe blood hit my nose.

It worked. It actually worked. I was in the mortal realm, almost back where I started.

"Come to see me again?" a familiar voice taunted. "Didn't get enough last time?"

I lurched to my feet and backed against a wall for support. "Nice to see you again too, Red."

"I remember the taste of you like it was yesterday." His fingers inched toward his temples where rivulets of blood leaked from the soaked rag on his head, but he paused, as if denying himself a treat.

"That's not creepy at all," I said dryly. "Call the guards."

"Why would I do that?" He gave up and smudged crimson over his cheekbones.

"Look, I don't have a whole lot of time here." I sighed. "If you could—"

He charged me, sprung into the air and landed a kick to my solar plexus. Hunching over, he slid his slick fingers through my hair and brought my face down to his knee. I jerked my head to the side, but pain ignited in my jaw. The edge of my teeth cut my cheek, and a copper tang filled my mouth.

Red's lusty growl of approval when I spat blood on the floor sent an answering rumble pumping through my chest. I was sore, cranky, hungry and wearing dirty leather. I wanted a long, hot shower, to dump this outfit down the trash chute, and to crash on my own bed with Shaw beside me tonight.

Clamping my left hand around Red's wrist, I made a connection. He tried to pull back, but I held tight and sent magic blasting up his arm. Feeding Shaw had depleted me, and the desire to drink Red down burned in my gut. Those internal scales tipped, and I sank magical teeth deeper into his aura. Devouring chunks of his energy sated the gnawing pit in my belly, but not the moral compass I had inherited from Mac, the one whirling as I fought my instincts over what was the right thing here.

Deep breath.

Red had been captured. He was serving his time. He was not a threat.

To kill him now was to murder him in cold blood.

I was not that person.

Tightening the leash on my magic, I slowed my intake until he collapsed on the floor. I checked his pulse. Steady. Vitals were good. He was fine. Knocked out and no longer my problem. Stepping over a twitching arm, I reached the door to his cell and hammered on the thick metal with my fists while shouting for the guards.

"What's all the—? Where is prisoner number zero-one-five?" The guard's eyes slitted where he peered through the Plexiglas square at me. "Ma'am, remain calm. I'm going to open the door..."

I tuned him out before losing all faith in faekind. Did he really think I accidentally stumbled into the big, bad redcap's cell on accident? Heck no. You didn't stumble anywhere inside of a maximum security prison. He was right to question me. I would put the screws to me too. Plus Red was unresponsive...

"Look," I said, an hour and a pot of coffee later, "I need to speak with Officer Littlejohn. He can vouch for me." I wish I had my phone to check the time. "How much longer is this going to take?"

"Officer Littlejohn is a NocT officer, ma'am. He works third shift. He ought to clock in any minute." The officer who had "rescued" me slouched in a metal folding chair angled toward me. A scarred metal table that had seen better days separated us. Bolted to the floor of the formal interrogation room, it didn't budge an inch no matter how hard I kicked the nearest leg in frustration. "Want me to top off your coffee?"

My mouth opened in a biting retort when the door flung open and smacked the wall.

The officer across from me jumped to his feet, and his hand went to a holstered stun baton.

"What the hell you doing, Fitz?" Littlejohn's low voice soothed my frazzled nerves. "You know who this is? You damn sure better be glad her daddy's not here to see this." His gaze sliced over to me. "I apologize for the wait."

I strained my neck staring up at him. "Hope I'm not putting you out."

Fitz stomped out the door, and Littlejohn dropped into the vacant chair. "Last I heard, we were cut off from Faerie. Yet here you are." He rested his beefy forearms on the table. "You punch a new hole, yeah?"

"Yeah."

He rubbed the shadow bristling his chin. "How'd you manage that?"

"My dad—" there was that word again, "—left me instructions that were open to interpretation."

Using a redcap to hold a sample of my blood for the spell? Brilliant if you asked me.

"That foot of yours is tapping a mile a minute." He took my hand and stilled it. "These are clacking like you're typing up a report on the table. Let's get down to it. Just tell me what you need."

Easing my hand from under his, I shot him a genuine smile. "I knew I liked you for a reason."

After switching to water, I sat with Littlejohn and hammered out details for locking down the tether. The favor I asked put him in a tight spot, but he agreed to sit on the news of its existence for six hours. Long enough for me to conclude my business in Faerie before I made my report to the magistrates.

Entrusting sensitive information to those two made me ill. Once Mac got on his feet, our mole hunt would begin. Until then I had to honor the chain of command if I wanted to keep my job, which seemed prudent considering the whole princess thing hadn't panned out.

One much more productive hour later, I strolled into the cell housing the world's only tether to Faerie and smeared more blood across the threshold to anchor it in both realms. Glancing around, I decided the place had a certain ambiance.

Then I laughed all the way back to Winter.

Rook snatched me out of the tether's mouth with sweaty palms and a meaty *grunt-thud-flop*. On second thought, *snatched* might not be the right word for it. More likely he had been standing inside of the closet, trying to figure out how to operate the tether without me, when I pinwheeled into him.

"I hate this." I slumped against the doorframe as the world righted itself. "It sucks every time."

"Thierry?"

I cracked open an eye and found Rook sprawled half in and half out of the closet. "Hmm?"

He elevated himself into a sitting position and dusted his palms. "I assume it worked?"

"Like a charm." I edged out into the hall for some fresh air. "Now if you don't mind, I'm calling our deal done. I want to get out of here before you start campaigning. I do *not* want to get caught in the crossfire this round."

Scrambling to his feet, Rook backed me against the wall, careful not to touch me. "Thierry..."

"*No.*" I put up my hands to keep him an arm's length away. "Whatever you're about to say, no."

"Are you sure I can't convince you to stay?" he purred. "We could rebuild Faerie *together*."

"That's gonna be a *no*. You threatened to let Shaw starve to death in order to punish me less than five hours ago. That's kind of a deal breaker."

He harrumphed like I should have been over that by now.

"You're going to have to do this alone. Stand up to the Unseelie. Help them mend fences with the Seelie and figure out where the hell Faerie goes from here." I shoved him backward. "And make sure none of them discover the tether until there's a new ruler on the throne, okay? A sane one. No one crosses that tether who isn't cleared by Mac or by me, got it?"

A grin warmed Rook's features. "I will guard it as though it were my own hatchling."

"Um, yeah. Okay. You do that." Backing away, I made it two steps before snapping my fingers. "I almost forgot—what about your mother? I left her back at the den inside the Hall of Many Doors."

The smile fled his face. "Is she secure there?"

"I think so." I tapped the toe of my boot on the tiles. "I trapped her inside an air pocket."

His jaw came unhinged, and choking sounds spluttered out of him.

"What?" I folded my arms over my chest. "She was trying to *kill* me."

"Only you," he said, shaking his head. "Nothing you do should surprise me."

Bristling, I snapped, "I'm sure she's fine."

"Maybe it's for the best." His gaze went distant. "She soughs dissent wherever she goes, and what we need now is peace." His smirk mocked my shock. "The fae are not nearly as eager to go to war as they think they are. Let riots break out. Let differences be settled and old slights be forgiven at sword tip. After a few months of chaos and bloodlust, they will tire of the dirt and the blood. They have grown soft in the years under your father's tenants. Soon they will lament the days of the Black Dog's rule, and settle into—perhaps not peace—but mutual understanding. At least until they grow bored again."

Not sure I believed him one hundred percent given the Huntsman's assessment, I wasn't about to argue with Rook's rosy new outlook on life. He was seeing his potential, possibly where there had been none, and those were good things. He was a veteran of surviving Faerie. He knew the score. He knew what he was up against, and I wasn't about to burst his bubble while he was feeling optimistic.

As close as I was to getting a hot shower and crawling into my own bed for many blissful hours of uninterrupted sleep, I was ready to pin a *Vote for Rook* badge on and call it a day. But I wanted the details ironed out before I left to prevent unexpected visits from Rook…or from his mother.

A thoughtful silence lapsed. "When do you plan to return?"

"In seven days," I answered without missing a beat.

When Mac rose, I was going to be here to welcome him back.

"Do you think that you might…?" He rubbed his chin. "If you are certain you will return in such a short time, I wondered if you would consider…" He dipped his hand into his pocket and then extended it—palm up—toward me.

The dainty conch-shell charm Branwen asked me to pass along to him sat there.

I saw where this was headed, and I approved. "You want me to ask if she will consider spending the week with you."

"I would understand if she preferred to wait and make our reintroduction a day trip." His stiff posture braced him for a rejection I hoped wouldn't come.

I accepted the shell, knowing how much this possibility meant to him. A small kindness could make or break a man on the edge of becoming something more or less than he was. Branwen stood at a crossroads too. Her newfound freedom sparkled less without her mate by her side. Maybe a week together was what they both needed to begin healing.

"I'll speak with her. If she agrees, I'll make the return trip. If not—" I rubbed my thumb over his token, "—then you'll see us in a week."

"That sounds more than fair." He pinched his chin. "If you don't mind, I will consider the matter of what to do with Mother, and we can discuss it seven days hence."

I shot him two thumbs up. "That works for me."

I had to explain to Mac about the death-goddess balloon I left floating in his hall anyway.

"Oh, hey." I worried my lip between my teeth. "Can you do a favor for me?"

Cunning sparkled in his eyes. "A favor?"

Asking him for help stuck in my craw, but I was on a deadline. "Can you release Tierney for me?"

"The ogre?" His gaze flicked down and then back to me. "This makes us even—for Branwen."

I nodded in agreement, relieved when he didn't ask for more than I had already agreed to do for him.

Calling for Bháin, Rook turned and left. No doubt the boys were settling in to strategize.

Fine by me. I didn't need to be escorted to the door. Or in this case, the tether.

Thanks to Shaw's penchant for snoring, I figured I could find him on my own if I wandered the halls long enough. I knew where the bedroom suites were in general, and where Rook's quarters were in particular. It was enough to give me an idea of where I ought to be searching for Shaw. Sure enough, I turned the corner past the master suite and heard the muffled sounds of sawing logs. Trailing the noise, I stopped before a door and tested the knob. Unlocked. I pushed inside and hesitated when I found the bed empty.

"Shaw?" I nudged open the door. "Are you in here?"

Movement caught my eye as I entered the room, and I spun as he slammed the door behind me.

My hands shot up, and I backed away slowly. "We already had this conversation."

I was still bruised from it.

Rims of white frosted his copper eyes. "I remember."

"Are you feeling okay?" He looked good to me. Better than good. "Are you still—? *Oof.*"

Somehow my back was against the door and Shaw filled my vision. His gaze dropped to my lips. "I hurt you."

"You didn't know." I lifted my hand slowly and touched his cheek. "I'm fine."

His grunt said he wasn't as ready to forgive himself for his actions as I was.

"I can kick you where it counts if you want to even the score," I offered.

He pressed his hips against mine, and I shivered.

"Give me a fifteen-minute pass."

"Fifteen minutes?" I choked on a laugh. "What do you need fifteen minutes for?"

Fingers brushing over the buckles running up my side, tugging straps that secured my armor, he unfastened them one by one and didn't answer. Lines marred his forehead. His white-rimmed eyes savored my bare skin as he uncovered it inch by inch. He traced the new runes with a reverent fingertip before dropping to his knees before me. Leather fell away. Pants were peeled down my legs. My left foot jerked, and that boot vanished. Shaw swore softly when the other refused to budge.

I let my head fall back against the door and watched through my lashes as he undressed me.

"I was afraid." I hadn't meant to say it, hadn't meant to ruin the moment with words.

The bare toes of one foot brushed the faded jeans covering his closest kneecap. He locked my other leg under his arm while he fumbled with the uncooperative closures. My pants hung from that leg, above the stubborn boot, and the icy door was breaking chills over me.

Or maybe it was the contrast of the cold door and the hot glint in his eyes as they raked over me.

His warm palm cupped my exposed calf. "I wasn't."

"You aren't allowed to trust me that much," I scolded. "*I* don't trust me that much."

"I love you." His hand smoothed up the back of my thigh. "Trust comes with the package."

A flush rose in my cheeks that softened his expression.

Boot forgotten, he placed my foot on the floor and stood. His fingertips moved light as butterfly wings over my stomach, and I quivered at his touch. While his thumb circled a hipbone, I found the hem of his shirt and eased my hands underneath, sliding them over his hard stomach, letting my nails bump over the firm ridges of muscle clenching tighter as my hand dipped toward the button of his jeans.

I flipped my thumb then grabbed the metal tab below it. The sound of a zipper lowering blocked out the pounding of my heart. A shudder racked Shaw, and the earthy citrus scent of his lure rose in the air, burning my nose where I breathed him in, sizzling in my lungs when they filled with the warm, heady fragrance of his arousal.

I worked a hand inside his pants, my fingers closed around him, and he gasped. I met his molten copper eyes, glad it was him. Our hungers were part of us, but God I loved the sincerity in his dark eyes, loved seeing that the man desired me as much as his hunger craved me, loved knowing he wanted me. I loved him, period.

He leaned in until his forehead rested on my shoulder, and planted his palms on the door behind me. His chest pumped, and his skin smelled so damn good I licked off beads of sweat forming there.

I moaned at the taste of him. "Should we be doing this in my ex-husband's spare bedroom?"

"Tell me no," he grated between clenched teeth. "I can wait. *This* can wait."

But in that moment, holding him in my arms, breathing in the scent of his skin, I couldn't.

I gripped Shaw's shoulder, hopped forward and hooked my free leg around his hip. "Now."

"That's not what I said—"

I rolled my hips and guided him inside me.

He groaned my name in broken syllables.

"You always did talk too much." I fastened my mouth over his.

His hands molded over my butt, held me still against the frozen door as he drove into me over and over, urgency making us both tremble. Familiar tingles started in my core and spread through my limbs. I gasped as the prickles exploded in a burst of heat that arched my back. My fingernails sank into his shoulders to hold him closer, raking down his back to leave red trails in his slick skin as I came undone around him. Shaw threw back his head and shouted his release.

Nuzzling the base of my throat, he began chuckling in a purely masculine way that oozed satisfaction. The man was pleased with himself. I mean, he ought to be. My thighs still quivered. But this was grab-a-Sharpie-and-print-*I-won*-in-block-letters-on-his-forehead kind of proud.

I fisted his hair and yanked his head back so I could see his face. "You did this on purpose."

A satisfied smile curved his swollen lips. "I don't know what you're talking about."

My pants-encased leg shook under the strain of supporting me, but Shaw was slow to release the thigh hitched over his hip.

"Sex." I wiggled to get loose, but somehow he managed to get closer. "Here. Now."

His dimple winked at me. "It must be that reaffirmation-of-life thing I've heard so much about."

"Uh-huh." I popped his bare butt. "And here I thought only dogs marked their territory."

He looked dead at me and said, "Woof."

CHAPTER TWENTY

Seven days after Shaw and I left Faerie behind us, we found ourselves right back. Mac rose like clockwork, and I made sure the first thing he saw was Mom's face. Never in all my life would I have imagined she would volunteer to travel into Faerie. And yet, here we all were. One big happy family.

The *L* word Mom had so much trouble saying? She hadn't stopped since Mac's eyes opened.

Clearing my throat, I brought his attention from her lips onto me and wiggled my fingers. "Hi."

Mom scooted to the end of the cot where he rested, and Mac opened his arms.

"Come here." The skin around his eyes crinkled as I shuffled toward him. "Any day now."

Secretly pleased, I grumbled under my voice and sat stiffly next to him. This time there was no hesitation in his embrace. He wrapped his arms around me and squeezed until my eyes bulged. I shut them before silly tears spilled down my cheeks and returned the favor, holding on to him like I was afraid he might leave me—leave *us*—again.

"I'm glad you're back," I mumbled into his shirt.

"I'm glad you're all right," he mumbled back.

Pulling back, I wiped under my eyes. "That was too close."

"It was necessary." He shifted closer. "What news from the mortal realm?"

"Well…" I drew out the word, "…it's quiet at the moment. The magistrates called another meeting. I testified to our side of events, though they still want to speak with you. After that they dispersed to their regions." A smile quirked my lips. "I got a promotion—or maybe a demotion considering this time last week I was the future queen of Faerie."

He glanced between Shaw and me. "Oh?"

"She's been appointed liaison between realms. She'll be representing the mortal realm." Shaw grinned. "That leaves you as senior liaison with a home base in Faerie."

"And Shaw has been appointed the official liaison babysitter," I grumped. "Apparently there's concern for my safety once news of the new tether breaks. Everyone and their momma will want to know where it is, and I'm not telling until we've plugged our leaks. For now, we're both off the streets and stuck behind desks."

Mac winced in sympathy. "This *promotion* is in light of my…separation…from the High Court?"

I nodded. "Faerie still needs you, and the conclave wants to maintain a close working relationship with you now that you're a free agent."

"Be that as it may…" his gaze sought out Mom and then slid back to me, "…I have other priorities now."

She scooted closer to me, wrapped an arm around my waist and rested her chin on my shoulder. Mac took my hand and hers and squeezed them both. We sat there like that, almost like a real family, until the hand-rubbing next to me took on an uncomfortable urgency and the air between my parents began crackling like wild faefire whooshing through a forest after a drought.

I tried sticking it out long enough to ask Mac about getting my hand healed—it bled worse each day spent under the charm—but I conceded defeat once the kissing started. Shaw and I bolted for the exit from Mac's underground tomb after their reunion noises shifted to a whole different kind of happy.

Shudder.

"Well, girl, are you satisfied?" a loud voice rang out overhead. "Is he well enough for you?"

Squinting up the long flight of stairs ahead of me, I gave the Huntsman a wave. "I am, yeah."

The warmth of Shaw's hand at my lower back nudged me up the stairs and into the sunlight.

"I can heal that if you like, or you can wait for your father," the Huntsman offered. "Your choice."

I must have been rubbing the cut. Again. "Can you?"

Mac had made it seem like a difficult fix. Wouldn't he have simply said, *My father can do it*?

"Oh, aye." He stroked his muddied beard. "Long as I have the right herb, it's easily done."

I groaned and fell back against Shaw. "Tell me you're not sending me on some epic quest."

The Huntsman flicked a leaf from his braids and eyed me speculatively. "The kitchen's there."

My gaze traveled the length of his arm to a small circle of stones arranged around a roaring fire. The more I noticed about the layout and the supplies, the more it resembled an outdoor kitchen.

"You have everything you need?" Shaw sounded as doubtful as I felt.

"Your father picked agrimony for you from the Halls of Summer." He set off toward the pit. "It must be hung to dry out in the sunlight. Given the situation, he felt it best I handle the preparations."

That explained the plants Mac had shoved into his pants while I was working my mojo on the tether.

"I had forgotten about that," I admitted, not having understood their significance.

Trailing after the Huntsman, I dropped down on the wooden stool he indicated with a jerk of his chin while he put a kettle on to boil over the fire. He crossed to a set of open shelves and grabbed bandages and a stone basin. He swung open a tree trunk like a cupboard and removed a clear jar filled with silver flowers.

The Huntsman grunted. "I understand you are to thank for our new consul."

Deciding he didn't sound angry, I owned up to it. "I might have encouraged him, yes."

"His ideas are modern," the Huntsman groused. "I don't care for them."

"Faerie wanted change." I grinned. "They got it."

Besides that, *modern* was generous when it came to Rook and his sentiments.

"So it seems." He sighed. "The High Court is meeting again."

My thoughts shot to Mac. "You mean Liosliath and Rook?"

His nod shook more leaves fluttering from his hair. "It seems the foundation for the new era was laid while your father slept." He shrugged. "Perhaps that is for the best. He has other concerns now."

"Mom," I said.

"And you," he replied.

Warmth spread through my chest. "Do you think he'll come back with us?"

"Faerie isn't ready to let him go yet." He smiled as my shoulders drooped. "Perhaps a compromise could be struck?"

Six months spent in the fae realm and six months in the mortal realm?

The possibility of such a compromise blew my mind.

"Don't think too hard about it," Shaw said softly. "They'll figure it out."

When his hand landed on my shoulder and squeezed, I twined my fingers with his.

"There have been rumors of another half-blood queen rising." The Huntsman eyed us curiously. "I heard it said she is Unseelie but that she has Seelie alliances, that she herself was once wed to a selkie chieftain."

Turning my face into my shoulder, I masked my shock by kissing Shaw's knuckles.

Branwen?

Queen?

"That's, ah, interesting." I tried for smooth, but my tongue kept getting tangled. "Really?"

He nodded. "The High Court is considering the benefits of such a union."

I had to ask, "Is that what you meant by modern?"

"Putting a half-blood on the throne is an ambitious undertaking, but you set a precedent. Though you never wore the crown, you were given the blessing to ascend." He rose to fetch the whistling kettle. "If you ask me, and no one has, the cooperation of both Seelie and Unseelie House has been bought with the whispers of a half-blood army."

I blinked. "A half-blood— What?"

Not two hours ago I left Branwen with fair warning she had to decide if she was coming home with me or staying with Rook, and neither had mentioned these developments to me.

"Seems half-bloods are taking notice of one of their own being named as consul and are wanting to serve Rook to further his cause." The Huntsman filled the stone basin with steaming water. "Some say he rallied them. Others say they rallied themselves. Me? I think he didn't lift one feathery digit. I don't think he had to."

"Will this make the fighting worse?" I wondered.

"Aye, it will." The Huntsman shook a liberal amount of flowers into the water. "Don't frown so hard, girl. This is a good thing. Now the houses have a common enemy. Their fighting won't last half as long when there's a direction to aim all that fury. Besides, rumors aren't yet fact. Remember that."

After what Branwen had endured at her mother and Balamohan's hands, I didn't want to see her get hurt again. God, I hoped Rook wasn't sweet-talking his sister into one of his half-baked schemes.

I worried my top lip between my teeth. "What if the queen and the army are more than gossip?"

Shaw's fingers tapped mine. "Worst-case scenario, Rook and Branwen use the tether and seek asylum in our realm."

I tipped my head back. "You wouldn't have a problem with that?"

His lips smashed into a bloodless line. "No."

"*Liar.*" I screwed my thumb into his side. "It would drive you nuts."

Shaw grabbed at my hand, and I twisted aside, tumbling off the stool and landing on the ground. He covered me, his weight pressing me into the loamy earth, and my breath caught for reasons that had nothing to do with the fall knocking the breath out of me and everything to do with the punch of citrus tingling through my nose while Shaw restrained me. Good as it felt under him, I didn't struggle.

"I was going to suggest you hold her still." The Huntsman towered over me. "This works too."

I wiggled as he knelt by my head. "Wait—why are we holding me still?"

"So you don't run."

He spoke the Word to rip the skin from my palm.

Blinding pain ricocheted through me, engulfing my hand, and I dug my heels into the soft dirt so I wouldn't scream. Warmth encased my throbbing palm. Jagged spikes of agony shot from the edges of the never-blade wound. Hissing and shaking like a coiled rattler, I waited out the worst pain.

Shaw expertly adjusted his hold on my wrists, pinning them over my head while the Huntsman's poultice made my fingers twitch and curl and burn like he had set fire to them. I actually twisted so I could make certain I hadn't fallen into the freaking fire pit. No such luck. That I could have escaped.

This...not so much.

Slowly bleeding to death would suck worse than what I was enduring now. Right? *Right?*

An eternity of swear words later, I remembered how to breathe. "I can't feel my hand."

Shaw shifted his weight and brought my hand with him as he sat upright. He examined my palm for signs it wasn't done bleeding. Satisfied no leak was impending, he pressed his lips to my lifeline.

His husky voice whispered over my skin. "Can you feel that?"

I swallowed hard. "No."

His mouth traveled down to my wrist. "What about this?"

The skin stung where he had kept me pinned. "It's hard to tell."

His lips moved lower, over my forearm. "This?"

"You two can take it from here," the Huntsman said on a chuckle I barely heard.

Shaw's gaze held mine, never flinching as my grandfather rose in my periphery and left.

"I think I felt that one," I said softly.

Lips curving, he pressed them in an agonizingly slow procession downward, toward the bend of my elbow and lower, to where my arm met my shoulder. He pressed kisses to those places, too, and I felt the burn through the fabric of my top. The warm Autumn day had coaxed me out of the leather armor Shaw insisted I wear when we crossed realms. I kept the pants, but the top was gone. Nothing but a flimsy T-shirt separated his hot mouth from my flushed skin.

His hand found the hem of my top and yanked upward. Fingers spreading over my abdomen, he swept higher until his fingertips brushed the band of my bra. I hissed in a breath and jerked my head to the side to make sure we were alone. Mocking me with his smile, Shaw conceded to my modesty. Or not. His calluses scraped over the tender skin of my navel as he sent his hand seeking lower. I was panting by the time his index finger eased under the waistband of the leather pants I should have ditched earlier. They were skintight and suffocating me.

"Are you feeling any of this?" His teasing finger withdrew. "Or should I stop?"

Screwing up my face in consideration, I wrested control of my arms from him. I worried the thin shirt from his pants and smoothed a hand over the bare skin of his lower back. Wearing my best *butter-wouldn't-melt-in-my-mouth* expression, I sent a pulse of magic rolling from my runes straight into his spine, and he arched above me, copper eyes rolling shut and lips parting as a groan tore from his throat.

When those molten eyes opened and fixated on me, I dug in my heels and scooted higher, but he still straddled me, and he had no intentions of letting little things like our clothes or my family, the lack of walls or the fact there were three purple-shelled garden snails (say that three times fast) with protuberant orange eyes on long blue stems ogling us like the best live pay-per-view event *ever* stop him from taking what he wanted.

Lucky girl that I was, the thing Shaw wanted was...me.

AUTHOR'S NOTE

Dear Readers,

When I wrote *Heir of the Dog* as the first book in the Black Dog Trilogy, I planned Thierry's journey to span those three novels and no more. But then I attended the RT Booklovers Convention, and all that changed. *Heir* won the American Idol Contest, and that brought two agents with fresh ideas into the mix. The next thing I knew, the trilogy had expanded to include one more title – *Dog with a Bone*.

Dog with a Bone is a prequel to the series in the sense that the novella cuts a hole into the ceiling of Thierry's past and gives us a glimpse of those first steps that set the events of the trilogy into motion one year later.

With that in mind, I hope you have fun meeting Thierry as a bright-eyed cadet in *Dog with a Bone* and enjoy watching her mature through *Heir of the Dog, Lie Down with Dogs* and *Old Dog, New Tricks* into a woman who knows when laws should be upheld and when they are meant to be broken.

Best,

Hailey Edwards

HAILEY'S BACKLIST

Araneae Nation

A Heart of Ice #.5
A Hint of Frost #1
A Feast of Souls #2
A Cast of Shadows #2.5
A Time of Dying #3
A Kiss of Venom #3.5
A Breath of Winter #4
A Veil of Secrets #5

Daughters of Askara

Everlong #1
Evermine #2
Eversworn #3

Black Dog

Dog with a Bone #1
Heir of the Dog #2
Lie Down with Dogs #3
Old Dog, New Tricks #4

Wicked Kin

Soul Weaver #1

ABOUT HAILEY EDWARDS

A cupcake enthusiast and funky sock lover possessed of an overactive imagination, Hailey lives in Alabama with her handcuff-carrying hubby, her fluty-tooting daughter and their herd of dachshunds.

Chat with Hailey on Facebook, **https://www.facebook.com/authorhaileyedwards** or Twitter, **https://twitter.com/HaileyEdwards**, or swing by her website **http://haileyedwards.net/**

Sign up for her newsletter to receive updates on new releases, contests and other nifty happenings.

She loves to hear from readers. Drop her a line at **http://haileyedwards.wufoo.com/forms/contact/**

45396767R00139

Made in the USA
Lexington, KY
16 July 2019